Edith Pa novels, and continue ⬚⬚⬚⬚⬚⬚⬚⬚⬚⬚⬚⬚ 5. Under the name o⬚⬚⬚⬚⬚⬚⬚⬚⬚⬚⬚⬚ e praise and recognition for her meticulous re-creations of monastic life in the twelfth century in the Chronicles of Brother Cadfael.

The Lily Hand and Other Stories

Edith Pargeter

HEADLINE

Copyright © 1964 Edith Pargeter

The right of Edith Pargeter to be identified as the Author of
the Work has been asserted by her in accordance with the
Copyright, Designs and Patents Act 1988.

First published in hardback in 1964 by
William Heinemann Ltd

First published in this edition in 1994 by
HEADLINE BOOK PUBLISHING

Reprinted in this edition in 1997 by
HEADLINE BOOK PUBLISHING

10 9 8 7 6 5 4 3 2 1

All rights reserved. No part of this publication may be
reproduced, stored in a retrieval system, or transmitted,
in any form or by any means without the prior written
permission of the publisher, nor be otherwise circulated
in any form of binding or cover other than that in which
it is published and without a similar condition being
imposed on the subsequent purchaser.

All characters in this publication are fictitious
and any resemblance to real persons, living or dead,
is purely coincidental.

ISBN 0 7472 5242 4

Printed and bound in Great Britain by
Cox & Wyman Ltd, Reading, Berks

HEADLINE BOOK PUBLISHING
A division of Hodder Headline PLC
338 Euston Road
London NW1 3BH

Contents

A Grain of Mustard Seed

When I was a little girl in Lahore my father had a friend who was a Muslim. Indeed, he had many, but Mahdar Iqbal was a very special one. He was the shoemaker who used to make our sandals. When we first knew him he was heavily in debt, but my father began to throw business his way, and tell our friends about him, and gradually he was able to pay off his debts, and even to save a little. He had only a poor booth in the doorway of his house, and his dream was to have a shop in the bazaar. By the time of the troubles he had more than fifteen hundred rupees saved up towards it, so he told my father.

In appearance those two were not unlike; both thin, bright, active men, but my father's slenderness was small-boned and frail, and Mahdar Iqbal's was sinewy and tough as his own leather. Two or three times a week I'd see them bent over the chessboard in the cool corner of my father's shop – he was a jeweller, and we were quite well off in those days – putting the whole world right. One thing they had in common was that they both believed it was possible.

1

It was my father who taught me, also, to believe that God was universal and benevolent, and man was perfectible, and by his very origin disposed to good. I adored him, so naturally I took his word for it.

The bad days were already coming upon us then, though I did not realize it. No need to tell you how it was with us in Lahore when partition came and the hate burst out from nowhere and overwhelmed everything. The time came when we dared not go out in the streets at all. Our shop was looted and burned down. Then the house, although they left us a roof, at least, and there we stayed in hiding, and thought now only of getting away, back to India. It was very strange to us to have to get used to the thought that Lahore was no longer India.

My father suffered, perhaps, more than most of our people, because all his ideas about men were being broken in pieces one by one, and kicked into the dust. At first he would not believe that this hatred and unreason could go on, and he would not run before it. But in the end it was plain that we must run or die.

Those of our people who had left in good time had been able to take some of their possessions with them. By the time we set our minds on leaving we had nothing left to take but the clothes we stood in. And by then, too, it seemed that we might not be able to leave at all, upon any conditions. But at last they said that a train would be allowed to leave on a certain day, and we could go with it; but no one was permitted to take away anything of value.

On the morning when the train was to leave we crept out of the shell of our house, and went to the railway station.

The streets were full of Muslims, decent people who had been our neighbours, all screaming threats at us, spitting at us, even throwing stones as we hurried by. It was on my mother we leaned by then; she had never thought as highly of her fellow men as my father had, and therefore she was not so terribly hurt and shattered as he was; she could hate them back, and he could not, and that made her lot so much easier. As for him, he had lost half the little flesh he ever carried, and his face seemed to be struggling with disintegration, as the form had disintegrated from everything he had known and believed in.

They had hardly let us on to the platform when the crowd broke through the barrier and ran after us. And suddenly I saw Mahdar Iqbal's face among them. We had not seen him for weeks; no one dared move about normally, or go near his friends. I saw the flare of hope that brightened the wreckage of my father's face, for one meaningful glance exchanged with Mahdar Iqbal could at least save something for him, the ultimate, necessary thing on which everything else can be built again.

And Mahdar Iqbal elbowed his way through the press, flung himself upon my father, and shook him savagely by the shoulders.

'Dog of a Hindu!' he yelled into his face, 'Let's see what you've got there in your pockets! Let's see what you're stealing from us!'

He plunged his hands into my father's pockets and turned out everything he had there: his handkerchief, his spectacle case, the fragments he had left from a life, all the time raving and reviling him like a madman.

My father stood like a dead creature, and let himself be mishandled. The man who had been his friend pawed over the last of his possessions disgustedly, spat his contempt on the ground, and laughed, bundling the poor bits back again.

'Go, then, and get fat on it! Take your pocketful of garbage home with you!' he shouted. And he took my father by the shoulders and threw him into the train, so roughly that he stumbled and fell.

My mother thrust me in after him, and put herself between me and the rush of people that suddenly welled down the train, beating at the slatted windows and yelling curses at us. The last I ever saw of Mahdar Iqbal, he was standing on the platform with a demon's grin on his face, shaking a fist at us. But we were in the train, we had a corner to crouch in, a wall at our backs.

There were riots before the train moved out, several people were killed, and others badly beaten up. But we were lucky enough – is that the word? – to escape with nothing worse than my father's broken glasses and broken heart.

People died in the train, too, before we reached Amritsar. We were crushed together so that we could scarcely move. And that was terrible, to be welded to my father's side like a piece of his very flesh, and to know that he was not there with me at all, but somewhere a long way off, and quite alone.

'What did you expect?' my mother said to him, sounding angry as she always did when she was most anxious and in the deepest distress. 'Could he fold you in his arms, and

4

wish you a safe journey? He has a wife and children to consider, just as much as you.'

My father sat with his broken glasses sagging on his nose, and stared at nothing.

'I know he could not come to me with his blessing,' he said. 'But could he not be content with holding off from me? Was it necessary to lay hands on me in unkindness? To call me a thief? Was he forced to do me violence?'

'He had to show himself a good Muslim,' said my mother bitterly, 'and good Muslims hate us. It is not enough not to love us. He wanted to show how utterly he had cut us off. Do you think they don't know he used to visit us?'

'He could have put that out of mind better,' said my father, with quiet, hopeless certainty, 'by staying out of sight, not by running to be the first to humiliate me. No, he is gone mad with hate, like all the rest, like all the world.'

And after a while of silence he said, in that soft, distant, haunting voice, 'I would not have claimed him. He need not have come near me. One look of kindness would have been enough. I could have lived on that, simply knowing he was as he had always been, and that men are not all damned. That there will be a time beyond these times.'

My mother, because she was frightened, began to abuse him a little, saying that there surely would be a time beyond, and that there were still good men in the world; but I knew by the sound of her voice that she did not really believe it. If hate could destroy Mahdar Iqbal, it could destroy every man, and there was nowhere any safe place to hide from it.

My father turned his face to the wall. And in a moment I heard him say in a deliberate and cold voice, as though he felt himself forced to formulate the conclusion to which this betrayal had driven him: 'Man is irreclaimable. There is no hope for him. And God does not care.'

I had been listening to every word that he uttered, and I could understand what he meant. But he had taught me so well that I could not believe what he was now telling me.

If God did not care, then why had Lord Vishnu entered the world nine times already to help his people? Why had Christ come to be among men, and suffer as the least and worst of them suffered? Why did the Bodhisattva turn his back on the perfect bliss of Nirvana and return to the world, to show men the way by which they could enter and share enlightenment? Why should God – all the aspects of God in all the world – spend so much time on the reclamation of man, if man was irreclaimable? Who would know it better than he? My heart told me that it could not be true.

It seemed to me that if I really had faith, it ought to be possible to turn this experience inside out, to find in it the fallacy that quite altered its meaning, and would restore my father to life. So I made up a very short and pointed prayer within my mind, and said it to God. There was no time, and I had no resources then, for ceremony.

'Please consider, God,' I said to him reasonably, 'that I am only a little girl, and you can't leave it all to me. I know I'm right, I know the proof is there, but I don't know how to find it. Please take my hand, and lead me to whatever it is I need, or else my father will surely die.'

6

I didn't expect anything to happen at once, and nothing happened. I didn't mind that. I had taken action in declaring myself, and that is always a liberating thing to do. The oppression seemed to lift from me at once, I even felt cooler.

I looked again at my father, and I saw that there were tears streaming down his cheeks among the oily rivulets of sweat. We were so crushed that he could not get his hand to the pocket of his achkan to pull out his handkerchief, but my hand was smaller, and already folded into the hollow of his side, and by wriggling patiently I got my fingers into the opening, and drew out a corner of the handkerchief between them.

And something else came out with it, a tight little roll screwed into a square of tissue. It rolled into my father's lap, and the wrapping parted; we saw the crumpled edges of a number of banknotes slowly uncoiling, and a scrap of white paper in the heart of the roll.

My mother instinctively put out her hand to cover all that money from sight, partly for fear of having it snatched away, partly to hide what seemed almost indecent here, where no one possessed anything.

My father had taken up the scrap of paper in a trembling hand, and was staring from that to the banknotes as though he had been shocked back into life by the certainty that he was going mad.

'But it is impossible! I had no money. I had nothing, I swear. Where did this come from?'

But *I* knew! I pressed my cheek close to his shoulder, and gasped into his ear: 'Don't you see? Don't you understand? Where else could it have come from? Who put his hands into your pockets? Who was it turned out all your belongings, and then pushed everything back in again?'

'Mahdar Iqbal!' he breathed, and stared and stared at the money; but I knew it was not the money that was bringing back feeling and form and meaning into his face.

'Read the note,' said my mother urgently.

It was as he read it through for the first time, silently, that he became in his essence the man he had always been, and a little nearer, surely, to being indestructible. And when he read it the second time, aloud, he was already a little less and a little more than he had always been. A little less by not being able to make amends, a little more by accepting humbly his eternal disability.

'"Forgive me,"' he read, '"but there is no other way of getting this to you. If I spoke with you as a friend both you and I would be torn to pieces. Take in kindness to me what you now need so much more than I. Forgive me, and remember me not as I am to you today, but as I shall be to you always in spirit. I shall never know a better man."'

There were more than fifteen hundred rupees in the roll of notes. Mahdar Iqbal had given us everything he had.

Light-Boy

The boy with the name of a god was standing among the tamarinds at the edge of the clearing when they came, one shoulder hitched easily against a tree, his thin brown thumb just piercing the membrane that covered the first sweet juice-pocket of a palmyra fruit. Before him, beyond the trees, the tumbled sandy rocks were piled, the dark mouth of the cave-temple cool black in their hot redness; and beyond again was the wide waste of beach and the infinite blueness of the sea. Behind him was the narrow road, and on the other side of it the squat houses of the village. All through the day he had one ear cocked for any sound of a car approaching by that road; but this time there had been no car. The two women walked out of the trees below him, close to the temple, on the dusty path from the Mission settlement.

One of them was an Indian woman from Madras, with a green and gold sari, and jasmine flowers in her coiled black hair; but the other was an Englishwoman, tall and fair-haired and slender in a sleeveless cotton dress. True,

she carried no camera, but by the winged sunglasses and
the un-Indian sandals, and the very walk, aloof and a little
self-conscious, the boy recognized a migrant. He put down
his palmyra fruit against the bole of the tree and came
running, eyes and teeth flashing in an eagerness and
purpose that looked all too familiar.

'Oh God!' said Rachel. 'Even here!'

Sudha turned her head, following the blind, hooded stare
of the sunglasses, and saw the boy bearing down upon
them at a headlong run, beaming gleefully. She lifted an
indifferent shoulder. 'Oh, well, we're fair game. Did you
think you'd be immune in Anantanayam?'

'I suppose it was too much to hope for. But after all,
Andrew's a resident. He's been digging and teaching and
doctoring here for four years now. I hoped I might get by
under his shadow, and be tolerated, anyhow – resident by
courtesy.'

'How's he to know you're connected with Andrew? It
doesn't show yet. Now if you'd been staying in his
house . . .'

But that was exactly what Rachel had not wished to do.
It would have committed her too far, and she was not yet
sure how far she wanted to go. Andrew Cobb was a pleasant
enough person, she respected and liked him, but she wasn't
sure of anything beyond that.

They had met at a cocktail party in New Delhi; she
couldn't even remember now how she had come to be
invited to such an improbable function. She had wandered
aghast among the sophisticated chatter of nylon-sari'd
ladies with lacquered western faces and pointed scarlet

nails; slender, languid males in dinner-jackets; expatriate English merchants and officials, thinking of the beggars in Old Delhi, and the labouring poor clir.ging to life by its fringes, aware that these people were insulated from that outer world with disastrous thoroughness by their cars and their servants and their calculated want of imagination.

Andrew Cobb had come as a breath of fresh air, blurting out, as they met in the crowd, exactly what she had been wondering: 'For heaven's sake, what are you doing in this shower?'

A big, energetic, blunt-jawed man of nearly forty, so she had seen him; a good, pig-headed, upright medical missionary, so her Aunt Mildred had afterwards recalled him. A doctor first and a schoolmaster second, who ran an Anglican school and clinic attached to the archaeological site of Anantanayam, far south in Madras State. Within ten minutes, heaving breaths of the spiced evening air into him as if he were stifling, he had seized Rachel by the arm and invited her urgently to get out of there with him. And since, whatever else he might be, he was undoubtedly real, she had gone with him gladly, and sat out the evening in a small restaurant uptown, listening as he talked about the sculptural school of Mahabalipuram, that ebbed to its remotest ripple just where the archaeologists of Anantanayam were digging, and his medical practice, and his colony of precarious converts, of whom he spoke as of unpredictable children. Later she had talked in her turn, telling him about her three-month's visit to her scattered relatives here, and about the tour south which she was planning in March.

And something, too, of the bewilderment, disillusionment, doubt and hope with which India had presented her since the day of her arrival. This he had understood; he had been through the same throes. And did it, later, begin to fall into proportion and make some kind of sense? He still hoped it would, he said ruefully, some day.

And it was then that he had invited her to his remote and minor settlement, looking at her across the table with the first spark of calculation in his eyes. She had observed it, and been experienced enough to recognize it. He was lonely, and she was congenial; and where was the harm in inviting the acquaintance to unfold, and waiting to see what kind of growth it achieved? Their recent experience of the insulated bubble-civilization of wealthy India had shown them how to value each other.

So she had come. From Madras it was not so far. But she had come cautiously, jealous for her freedom and respectful of his. If she had come alone he would have insisted on her staying in his own household, but she had brought her friend Sudha with her, and made her the excuse for taking the travellers' bungalow at the edge of the beach. Nothing but a narrow plantation of young trees between the compound and the sands, deep, wide, honey-pale, with that incredible sea beyond, shading from aquamarine along the rim to the dark cobalt of the deep water. Southward, the Bay of Bengal opened into the Indian Ocean. The waves were too rough for good swimming, but to bathe there was a delight, and the view from the windows of the bungalow was beautiful beyond belief.

Andrew had accepted humbly that his own cramped quarters by the schoolhouse could not possibly compete, and had made no attempt to persuade her to alter her plans. With Sudha presiding over the domestic arrangements he could be easy about the comfort and propriety of her stay. And this neat and convenient distance between them gave him time to think before he did anything irretrievable; his good Scottish blood would appreciate that.

The boy arrived before them gleaming and panting, and halted with bare toes spread in the sand. He was slender and small, his head came no higher than Rachel's shoulder. He might have been eleven or twelve years old, she judged, but it was difficult to put an age to him. He stood straight and easily, embracing them both in a broad, white-toothed smile. No mendicant palm crept out wheedlingly, and no throaty whine fished for small coins. She saw that she had mistaken him. He was not ordinary, he was not a beggar. He had a rope knotted round his waist over the brief khaki shorts and tattered brown shirt, and an old-fashioned glass-sided lantern slung by a loose yard or so of cord from one hip. He held the lamp up before them by the metal ring at the top, and addressed Sudha confidently in Tamil.

'We were both wrong,' said Sudha, contemplating him with a quizzical smile, 'This one works. He wants to show us the shrine.'

'I am Subramanya,' announced the child in English in the voice of honey and gravel to which Rachel had become accustomed, but with a large dignity all his own. 'I am light-boy.'

'It seems it's quite dark inside the temple,' said Sudha. 'He says we wouldn't see anything without his lamp. All right, Subramanya, you lead the way.'

'Are there still priests here? We're allowed inside? Even me?'

'No priests,' said Subramanya, beaming. 'You come with me, I show you the god. You come this way.'

He pattered before them to the rough steps that led up from the first outcrop into the low face of sandstone, and there paused to open his lantern and put a match to the wick. The light was feeble enough, the corners of the glass panels ingrained with smoke from long years of use; but he held it up towards the velvet black of the entrance as if he had been lighting princes to their coronation.

The facade was borne aloft on three rough pillars, with a relief of apsarases in flight over the lintel. A small temple it was, perhaps never used as a temple at all, only as a study in design and carving, like some of those at Mahabalipuram. The deep chamber within was carved out of the living rock. Three paces into it, and the day fell away behind them, and the chill of stone closed on them with the darkness. The boy held his lantern high before them at arm's-length, so that his thin little body might cast no shadow to complicate their footsteps.

Because she had thought him a beggar running to blackmail her for new pice, and felt herself recoil from him in weariness and revulsion, Rachel found herself deeply and penitently aware of him now as a person. Proud, conscientious and self-respecting, a small working man

14

bent on earning his fee, he went before her carefully, step by step; and the deeper he led her into the cave, the brighter and taller grew the flame of his lamp.

'Subramanya!' she said. 'That's a fine name you have.'

The long lashes rolled back from his dark eyes as he looked up at her and smiled brilliantly.

'Do you know who that is – Subramanya?'

'Yes, I know. He's the same as Kartikeya, the son of Siva. The beautiful one,' she said, to distinguish him from Ganesh, who was also the son of Siva.

He laughed aloud with pleasure, and the lantern waved and danced. 'Yes, you are right!' He was delighted with her for knowing. Was it possible that tourists so rarely even took the trouble to read a little before they came here? It had seemed to her an obvious thing to do, and she was ashamed of the glow of achievement his response gave her.

'But this is a shrine of Vishnu, isn't it, not Siva?'

He said: 'Yes, of Vishnu,' but he said it with a vague smile and a lift of expressive shoulders, as if it mattered very little. 'Here, on the walls, see – all the comings of the god. Nine times he came.'

Deep within the rock and lost to the outer light, the chamber in which they stood was yet quite small, and all its centre taken up by a great recumbent mass of stone, on which, for the moment, Subramanya turned his back. First he must show the deep reliefs on the walls, four on either side. He reached a hand to lead Rachel carefully along after him, holding up the light to each panel as he came to it. Thicker, vaguer, coarser carving than the best she had seen, but with the same passionate movement and flow. The dynamic figures and haughty, superhuman faces loomed out upon her in the flickering light, every shadow gouged deep into blackness.

'This is Varaha. You see? He came as a boar, because demons had captured the earth goddess and buried her deep underground, but the Lord Vishnu dug her out with his tusks.'

For every avatar there was a reason, every strange form of divine incarnation had its own logic. He led her through them all, as ardently as if he saw the carvings and told the stories for the first time. Behind her, Sudha rustled her silks against the stone, and the scent of her jasmine flowers revived in the coolness and the dark.

'And the seventh is Rama. And the eighth is Lord Krishna. All Vishnu. All God. And he will come another time.'

He turned at last to the centre of the chamber, and laid his hand with a possessive gesture on the long curve of a great stone thigh. The lantern, held aloft over the reclining figure, showed them Vishnu sleeping. More than lifesize, the vast, graceful body filled the circle of light and jutted out beyond it. Subramanya lit it for them piecemeal beginning at the head. This was a solitary Vishnu, unattended by the heavenly beings she had seen afloat above him at Mahabalipuram, watched over no longer by his consort Lakshmi, stripped even of the cobra-hood canopy and the tall crown. An older Vishnu, perhaps, and a simpler – austere, beautiful and remote. His body was half-naked, thinly-carved draperies covered his loins. The pure, still features of the great face balanced death and sleep. Rachel was aware of a loneliness and a sorrow that reminded her of something closer to her own experience, and for a moment groped in vain for the key to her memory.

The great hewn slab of stone, the stretched body and the monumental hands laid lax and calm drew curtain after curtain for her, and showed her the image she needed. There was no instant of revelation, only the knowledge with her suddenly that these things had always been one. This noble and withdrawn figure could have been a Christian sculpture of the entombment. The face was not less lovely and lonely and sorrowful. The body contained no less surely all the doom of mortality, all the promise of immortality.

'It's strange,' said Rachel aloud, 'he makes me think of my own God.'

'Strange?' said Subramanya, puzzled. She saw the delicate brown face for the first time utterly grave, lit sharply from above as he held the lantern high. 'It is not strange. He *is* God.'

'My God, as well as yours?'

'Of course. Everybody's God. Why not? Yours, mine, everybody's.'

'If we have the same God,' she said, faintly smiling, 'why do the priests here refuse to let me into the shrines?'

The white and gleaming smile flared again, disdainful and amused. 'Oh, priests!' said Subramanya scornfully. 'But I show you everything here. I hold the light for you, and you see something that is your own as much as mine. That is not strange.'

She was silent a moment, pondering. The boy, untroubled, unable to understand what she should find here to trouble her, waited innocently, watching her.

'You have so many gods, though,' she said. 'Some that don't resemble mine at all.'

The eloquent shoulders lifted again serenely. 'Why not? God is everything.'

He felt no need of further explanation, and perhaps he could have provided none. What he knew he knew, but his dealings were not in words. Ganesh, Hanuman, Kali, Gajalakshmi – what did it matter? Even that many personages had themselves many shapes and many names. Parvati was many, Siva many, Vishnu, this sleeper in the rock, many. Many times incarnated, and still to come again. And every avatar, Varaha, Rama, Lord Krishna, everyone was still Vishnu. And Vishnu and Lakshmi and Siva and Parvati and Hanuman and Ganesh and Subramanya, and all the others: all were God.

'But creatures seen so differently,' she said, feeling her way towards this subtlety in him which she had so dangerously mistaken for simplicity. 'So many, and so varied – and all one? Is that possible?'

'Look,' said Subramanya triumphantly, 'I show you!'

He held his lantern momentarily over the majestic face, and then caught her by the hand and drew her with him, circling the long couch of stone to the distant corner of the chamber. He lifted the light high. Only a glimmer shone upon the soles of the large, calm stone feet.

'You see? Is he any less God when we see only his feet?

18

Do you think his face is not still there?'

She was silent a long time, considering that, until Sudha sighed and yawned, and suggested that they had seen enough. She emerged into daylight again still considering it. Subramanya had already put it by and forgotten it; he had no need to remember the logic which lived and breathed in him. He was chattering gaily rather about his parents and his little sister, when he set his lantern down on the stone steps, opened the glass door and turned down the wick. He blew out the flame, and a thin curl of grey smoke spiralled upwards for an instant and was gone. Flame and smoke, light and darkness, lived together inside the cage. Was there any need for a greater diversity than that?

They gave him more money than he expected, and he was pleased.

He walked with them halfway to the settlement, and talked merrily all the way. His father, he said, was one of Cobb Sahib's servants, he kept the garden at the school. But their own house was at the edge of the village; he pointed it out as they went, a low clay shape like all the rest. His little sister was learning to be a dancer. When she was bigger she would go to Madras. If the memsahib was staying here, and if she liked, Shantila would dance for her.

Nothing is rarer than to make a pure human contact; and nothing can happen so simply and naturally when it does happen. By the time he smiled his goodbye to them over his prayerfully-folded hands at the edge of the road, and darted back to his post and his neglected palmyra fruit she knew it was not with her half-rupee that she had won him.

'I made a friend today,' she said to Andrew that evening over coffee, on the verandah of the bungalow he was visibly seeing now as small and inadequate. His manner towards her was becoming, she thought, at once more relaxed and more proprietary. He had produced her to his nurses at the clinic and his staff at the school with the air of one displaying something not yet possessed, but possession of which he was certainly contemplating.

'It's a lucky person who can ever say that,' said Andrew cautiously. 'Who is it?'

'The light-boy at the temple. He showed us round there this morning.'

'Ah, Subramanya! He's not a bad boy. Comes of a Christian family, of course.'

She was startled chiefly by the instant and dismaying reaction she felt at hearing this, as though her recollection of him shrank; as though he had somehow been belittled.

'Really? I shouldn't have guessed that. Not that it arose, actually.' But hadn't it? Was not some kind of answer to that speculation comprehended in the answers he had given to a larger question?

'His father's my gardener,' said Andrew. 'I know the family well. My predecessor here converted the grandfather. Yes, he's a nice boy, quick and reliable. As Indians go!'

Why was it, she wondered, watching him steadily in the yellowing twilight, with the sea-wind coming in cool and fresh after the heat of the day, why was it that when he dropped some such phrase as that, quite simply and without malice, she felt herself recoil in such marked revolt? He gave all his energy to his life here, and his life was helping these people. He was right not to be hypocritical about the failings he found in them. He had as much right to his own standards and attitudes as they had to theirs and certainly more control over them. He had adapted more painstakingly to their ways than they did to his. Nor had she any justification for feeling superior.

She had come here gratefully because he was a refuge to her after too much experience too suddenly swallowed. She had come baffled and irritated by the contradictions of wealth and poverty, by the venality of much that she saw, from the buyable people in high places, through the hotel clerks discreetly black-marketeering in sterling, to the malevolent gangs of children pestering for alms, the servile and insolent room-boys, the predatory priests never content even with the most generous of offerings. From all this she had turned eagerly to an English acquaintance with standards like her own, a feeling for time, a sense of responsibility, and words which meant what they said.

And yet he had only to say something like that, and she knew that they stood on different ground. At that tone in his voice, patient and tolerant though it was, she remembered how much more congenial, on board ship, she had found the Indians than her own countrymen, and how the missionaries, in particular, had clung together in a close little clan, and mixed less than anyone aboard with their different fellow-creatures. She remembered to detach herself from her own prejudices, to distrust her own reactions; she reminded herself that she was the creature of her own upbringing and environment, however carefully she tried to stand apart from them. She saw that all that dismayed her here was at least in part her own creation. And she was willing to wait, to continue an alien, to be rejected, to be exploited, if that was the necessary reverse of all that delighted her, the occasional acceptance, the unexpected communication, the momentary belonging.

'If you want someone to take you about while I'm busy in the clinic, mornings,' said Andrew, placidly unaware of any disquiet in her, 'you might do a lot worse than Subramanya. He knows everybody in the village, and quite a lot about the dig too.'

She took him at his word; and in the few days of her stay she thought much of the light-boy, and spent a good part of her time in his company. With this child, at least, she had no doubts of her welcome, or of the reason for it. He enjoyed her as she enjoyed him. It might be only the courteous brushing of fingers, but at least they touched.

When he invited her into his home she entered with reverence. A small, bare, clean living room, one shelf with a faded wedding photograph, an asthmatic wireless set, a low mat bed covered with a threadbare rug; and behind a drab curtain, the tiny kitchen hot from brazier fumes, a stained clay oven, and two garish pictures, one on either side. Rachel put off her shoes at the doorway and made her ceremonial 'Namaste' to a thin, worn woman who was

Subramanya's mother. Like the field workers of the south, she wore no blouse under her sari, and the folds kilted almost to her knee. She had nothing to offer but a glass of water. Rachel drank it and thanked her, aware of a special and undeserved happiness.

Not until she was waist-deep in the sea that afternoon, braced against the rough waves, did she realize what she had seen in the kitchen. On one side a cheap, highly-coloured paper print of Christ, soft-faced and appealing; on the other a doe-eyed, tender-mouthed Krishna, blue-tinted and womanish, with his flute at his lips.

And she had seen no discrepancy, no contradiction. They were so profoundly alike that there was no distinguishing between them except by the blueness and the beard and the flute – superficial differences by any measure. The very same too beautiful, effeminate, sentimental art, the flowery beauty that poverty and deprivation and wretchedness need. Necessarily, a distant, hampered and imperfect view, perhaps the buckle of a sandal, a little-toe nail, but still a particle of the god. Of God.

Rolled in the ultramarine shallows, refreshed and languid and at ease, she found no fault with this dual vision. All the pantheon of India had begun to fuse into a unity for her. All the pantheons of the world.

She did not realize how strong a tide was carrying her, she went with it and was content. She watched Shantila dance, and listened to Subramanya's monotonously-sung accompaniment, and learned to distinguish *abhinaya*, the mimed interpretation of ballads and songs, from the

23

stylized movements of pure dance. Classical Indian music as yet only confused and excited her, but the popular music of weddings and folksongs she found astonishingly approachable. And how quickly, how very quickly, someone else's fairies and gods become one's own, familiar and dear. She had only to watch Shantila cross her ankles and poise her lifted fingers on the invisible flute, and Lord Krishna was there before her, in all his youth and beauty and antique innocence.

She was changing after her bathe, on the fifth afternoon of her stay, when she heard Andrew come trampling heavily up the steps to the verandah, half an hour ahead of his usual time. Sudha was still snoring delicately under her mosquito-net, for to Sudha the afternoons were made for sleeping rather than swimming. If Andrew called out, he would wake her. Rachel opened the door an inch or two and said softly: 'I'll be out in a moment. There's a fresh lime soda in that covered jug in the cooler. Get one for me, too, will you?'

He was stretched out in one of the cane chairs when she came out to him a few minutes later, still towelling her wet hair. He looked up at her with a brief, preoccupied smile that faded quickly into a grimace of discouragement; and yet she had a strange impression that somewhere at the heart of his unexplained mood there was an odd little glow of satisfaction.

'What's the matter? Has something happened?'

'Oh, nothing I shouldn't have been prepared for, I suppose. It's only too ordinary. I finished early,' he said, 'and thought I'd get the car out and run you over to the south beach or somewhere. I looked in at the village, thinking I might find you there. I didn't, but I found something else.' He was groping deep into his bush-jacket pocket. 'You won't believe it,' he said, sour enjoyment unmistakable in his voice now.

After more than a month in India there was not much she would have had difficulty in believing. She said so, but the serenity in her tone did not seem to be what he expected of her.

'I thought Subramanya's people might know where you'd be, so I called in there. This will show you what these people are really like – unreliable, two-faced, born without sincerity. You think you've got them, and it's like holding water in your hands. You'll understand now what I'm up against. For three generations these people have been professing Christians. And look what they had pinned up on the kitchen wall! Right beside a picture of Christ!'

He whipped it out on to the table and unfolded it before her eyes with a gesture of bitter triumph. She let the towel fall into her lap, and sat for a long moment with her eyes fixed upon the garishly-coloured flamboyantly-printed page, its glossy surface seamed now with sharp white folds like scars. Lord Krishna's flute was bent, his round, girlish arm broken. The delicate, effeminate, blue-tinted countenance with its fawn's eyes was deformed by a slashed cross.

She sat looking at it, and her face was thoughtful, mild and still. She said nothing at all.

'I'm sorry!' said Andrew, stretching and relaxing with a sigh. 'I don't know why I had to take it out on you, it isn't your fault. But you see how devious they are. You can't trust them an inch.'

No, from his point of view perhaps not, and certainly one could argue, she thought reasonably, that knowing what they know, they ought not to profess conversion from one creed to another. What isn't worth keeping, isn't worth giving up, and why change one illusion, one voluntary mutilation, for another? But probably the grandfather had never really understood that his own universality was coming into a head-on clash with something smaller, less enlightened, and as exclusive as it was militant. One more aspect of divinity came graciously enough to him; how could he possibly realize that he was expected to make it, from then on, the only one? Like sealing up against the sun all the windows of your house but for one small casement. Like voluntarily walling yourself into a dark tower with one narrow loophole, when you could be outside lying in the grass.

'You made them take it down?' she asked, smoothing the edge of the spoiled picture with one finger, her voice quiet.

'Well, of course!' he said, astonished, and stared at her blankly.

'Why "of course"?' She looked up. 'They have the right to believe and worship as they please.'

'Certainly,' agreed Andrew, stiffly. 'As they please, and whichever they please. But not *both*!'

Almost pleasurably, as in a half-dream, she heard her own voice saying: 'Why not?'

'Why not?'

He sat up rigidly in his chair, staring at her with dropped jaw and horrified eyes.

'Yes, why not?'

She turned the picture and smoothed it out before him. 'Did you look at the other one carefully? Colour the face blue, forget the beard, and make this fellow put down his flute, and you'd hardly know them apart. Two gentle, plaintive, pretty faces. People made them exactly alike because they needed exactly the same from them. True, we're looking at the likeness on one of its lowest planes, but the same holds good higher up, you know. All that is different in them is the conventions. Why not both? They're one and the same.'

He was clinging to the arms of the chair as if the world had begun to rock under him. He stared under knotted black brows, trying to grasp the magnitude of her blasphemy. His jaw worked, and he couldn't speak. He drew a convulsive breath and whispered creakingly: 'You're not serious! You don't know what you're saying!'

'I am serious. Do you mean you've never really caught a glimpse of it? In four years? Everybody who ever got as far as imagining the inevitability of God was looking at the same sun through his own particular little window. The view doesn't even vary so very much, not until the creeds become business. When the priests move in, and start cornering, and organizing, and retailing what the saints left freely about the world for everybody to enjoy, then the distortions and perversions begin. But that doesn't alter the first principle. Nothing can.'

'You're just being deliberately perverse. I don't see the

27

slightest resemblance between this . . . this thing . . . and the church calendar they've got there on the wall beside it. That's all very facile talk about the two pretty faces. I know our almanacs aren't great art, just as well as you do. But supposing this had been Hanuman, or Ganesh, as it very well might have? What then?'

The heat with which he had begun this outburst cooled quickly, she heard the note of security steady in his voice again, and was sure in her heart that he could not be shaken. In a moment he would be sounding indulgent, reminded to his comfort that she had been in India no more than four or five weeks, and was only running true to beginners' form in knowing everything.

'It wouldn't have mattered,' she said simply. 'I thought this might have made it easier to see, just the fact that it was Krishna. But it makes no difference. They're all aspects and allegories.'

'And a beautiful monotheism embracing them all, I suppose, when one develops eyes to see!' He laughed shortly and angrily. 'Rachel, you're not really such a fool as all that.'

She looked back at him without any answering indignation, even smiled a little. 'Did you ever wonder why Tagore and Gandhi so often wrote simply "God"? Because they meant it, that's why. And long before their day Indians were leaving the evidence for us all over the place, if we cared to see it:

"the loving sage beholds that Mysterious Existence wherein the universe comes to have one home;

Therein unites and therefrom issues the whole;
The lord is warp and woof in created beings."

That isn't one of the desert fathers, that's the Yajur Veda.'

'Well, now come down out of the clouds for a moment, and look around you, and see what goes on at ground level.'

'It was right down at ground level I got all this,' she said mildly. Below ground level, actually, she thought. But of course I had a lantern and a guide. 'Would you believe it,' she said, 'I ploughed my way conscientiously through most of the Vedic translations before I left home? And it never really occurred to me that they meant exactly what they said! "One All is Lord of what moves and what is fixed, of what walks and what flies, this multiform creation." That's in the Rigveda. "Our father, our creator, our disposer, Who is the only One, bearing names of different deities".'

'There's a lofty literature to every heresy and every heathenism,' said Andrew violently. 'But "If the light that is within you is darkness, how great is that darkness".'

She had been ready to continue the argument with goodwill, but that stopped her. After that there was nothing to say; she heard it as an oracle. She lifted her head and studied him with a long, thoughtful, wondering look. His darkness seemed to her impenetrable.

She relaxed with a sigh, and reached for her glass. The scarred Krishna rustled mournfully under her hand. She took it up gently. It was Subramanya who carried a lantern.

'May I have this? As a souvenir.'

'Of course, if you'd like it,' he said stiffly.

He got up, and went to lean on the verandah rail. 'Shall we go out? It's a bit late now, but we could still go down to the Point, if you feel like it?'

But when she agreed that it was a little too late, and remembered that she had a dress to iron before dinner, he seemed, if anything, rather relieved. The whole thing must have been a shock to him. Probably he was already reconsidering about her, drawing back a little, making sure the way of retreat was still open. Maybe it was high time to move on, and leave them both a breathing-space.

She mentioned that evening, over coffee, and in the right tone of regret and reluctance, that Sudha had to get back to Madras, and that she really ought to go with her and see about her flight to Calcutta, before it became altogether too hot to go there at all. Andrew made the right disappointed noises, and cautious feints at dissuading her, but she saw that the news was at least as welcome to him as it was to her. And Sudha, who could always be relied upon to do all things gracefully, sighed her regrets over her coffee cup, and explained sadly that her husband was coming home from New Delhi two days earlier than she had expected him, and she must be in Madras to welcome him.

So that was that. Rachel knew exactly how it would end. They would part on the best of terms; but after the first dutiful letters of thanks and valediction they would let each other drop, gently and gratefully and once and for all. No hard feelings. But it was just as well to have found out in time.

She went down in the morning towards the cave-temple.

The boy with the name of a god was sitting on his heels in the sandstone portico, with a long blade of grass between his teeth. He spat it out when he saw her coming, and joined his long, brown hands beneath a dazzling smile. She sat down beside him on the steps, and opened the flat, cardboard folder she carried.

'Subramanya, this afternoon I'm going away, back to Madras.'

'I shall be sad,' he said, but so serenely that it was plain he would not remain clouded for long.

'I brought you back this.'

She opened the folder between them on the step. She had pressed the picture between the folds of a linen towel, but the thin white scars would never come out. She looked at the mutilated face, and was aware of belated anger. What right had anyone to distrain a poor man's possessions in the name of religion? What happened to courtesy and decency before a fundamentally good man could so forget himself?

'Why did you let anyone force you to take it down? It was your property, you had a right to hang it wherever you liked.'

He looked at her gravely, but without any distress, his large eyes wide open to the sun. 'It did not matter so much. It is only a picture. Cobb Sahib is like a child about pictures. You must go gently with children, when they do not understand.'

'Yes,' she said, for some reason gloriously reassured, even though Andrew would surely remain a child to the end of his self-sacrificing days in this place, and never come near understanding of the thing he had done, or the forbearance extended to him. 'Yes, I suppose so.'

'He is a good man. It would be wrong to hurt him.'

He pricked up his head alertly, looking beyond her towards the road. A car and its attendant dustcloud rounded the curve of the village, the first tourists of the day. Subramanya tightened the cord round his waist, and hitched the lantern expectantly against his hip.

'Lord Krishna is not jealous; he knows, he will wait. Some day Cobb Sahib will stop caring so much about images, and look for God.'

That was perfect, there was nothing more to be said. He had illuminated everything.

'Take my picture with you,' he said suddenly. 'I don't need it. It was mine, I bought it. I give it to you.'

The car had stopped in the arc of gravel by the road; two men were getting out, festooned with cameras. Subramanya rose to go to his duty.

'Not because it is a little spoiled,' he said, turning on her his sudden, blazing smile. 'I like it better now, because you brought it back. But I give it to you.'

'Thank you, Subramanya. I'll keep it gladly.'

'To remember me,' he said, already skipping away from her with one bright eye upon his clients; but he turned once more before he left her, and joined his hands in a last salute.

'Namaste!'

'Namaste!'

He ran away from her as he had run towards her on the first day, headlong and eager, clutching his lantern firmly by the ring at the top. As she drew back into the trees with the cardboard folder under her arm she heard him announce himself magnificently to the newcomers, astride before them at the edge of the sandstone outcrop, with the instrument of revelation uplifted proudly in his hand.

'I am Subramanya. I am light-boy.'

Grim Fairy Tale

Looking back now, I realize that I ought to have smelt a rat right from the start. If I hadn't been as vain as I was green, I should have wondered whatever possessed my boss to take me with him on that business trip across Europe, when he had so many older and abler men at his disposal. My driving was all right, but certainly no better than Smith's or Davidson's, and I couldn't speak a word of German, while Brent was completely bilingual, and they were all senior to me.

But at the time, of course, it seemed the most natural thing in the world that Mr Fordyce should choose me; so it never occurred to me that the real difference between Smith, Davidson and Brent and me was that they were married, and I was single.

Mr Fordyce had a daughter. Lilian was coming with us as far as Cologne, where she was going to spend the two weeks of her father's business jaunt with friends of the family, and we were to pick her up again on the drive home. I didn't see anything fishy in that, either. She seemed a nice girl, and I never noticed anything peculiar about her, such as her being twenty-eight. I was twenty-two myself, and rather partial to the company of girls older than myself, because they were better listeners. All across France and Belgium I enjoyed having my driving admired – so intelligently, too – and my ego gently groomed by Lilian's approbation, and I really missed her when she left us at Cologne.

From then on I don't know which of us talked more about her, her father or me. He must have been rubbing his hands, because everything was going according to plan, and, knowing what he knew, he must have been willing to bet I was as good as hooked. Sometimes I wonder if it wouldn't have been better – I might have been very happy, and I should almost certainly have been comfortably off, because he was the sort to do the right thing by his son-in-law.

But of course, after that night everything was different. I don't know that I had any choice, after that night.

We were a whole week in Frankfurt, where Franz Eisner, the firm's chief agent in Germany, had his office. Then we went on to Stuttgart and Munich, and back by way of Nuremberg. And it was in Nuremberg, when we had just two days to get back to Cologne and pick up Lilian, that Mr Fordyce got a telegram, and announced that a big deal with Canada was coming up unexpectedly, and it was by way of being an emergency, and he'd have to fly back to England immediately. Leaving me to drive the car back across Germany, pick up the girl, and escort her safely home. Which he had no doubt I could do admirably.

Stephen Dalloway was the white-headed boy all right, while it lasted.

I had no doubts, either. I felt a few inches taller, and quite complacent at the idea of two days or more *tête-à-tête* with Lilian, but probably not as complacent as he felt at the way the bait had gone down. It was only after I'd seen him off that I had time to remember little things like my complete lack of German, and the fact that I should have to drive and navigate at the same time on roads I didn't know and through cities where the traffic had put the fear of God into me even on the way out when I'd had the boss and all his experience right at my elbow.

Still, I wasn't the sort to have qualms about my own capabilities. To my way of thinking, there wasn't much I couldn't do, given the opportunity. And of course, it was flattering to have it taken for granted that I could be relied on to manage the journey across Europe like an old hand. I had visions of a distinguished future, Stephen Dalloway, Continental representative of Fordyce's, comfortably installed in Franz Eisner's office in Frankfurt.

It was afternoon when I started, owing to my having to see the boss off at the airport, but it was only two hundred and twenty kilometres to Frankfurt, and from there to Cologne by the autobahn is a morning stroll. I'd memorized the map beforehand, and in any case you'd have hard work to lose yourself between Nuremberg and Würzburg, because once you light out westward across the face of Germany there's virtually nowhere else to go. I'd decided not to stay overnight in Frankfurt itself, but to stop short of it by the odd few kilometres, and sleep in Hanau, so as to face the city in the morning, when I was fresh and at my best.

I had a bit of a cold, just come out that morning, but it was nothing much to bother about, and the sun was shining, and altogether I felt pretty good.

By five o'clock that afternoon things didn't look quite so cheerful. The sky clouded over early, and turned the colour of lead, and there was thunder rolling round on my left flank. Then I picked up a five-inch nail which was just one of the things I'd forgotten to allow for, and it fetched me up on the grass verge of the road, shaken and irritated. And while I was changing the wheel the rain began – not thunder rain yet, just a nasty, wetting drizzle that gradually grew heavier, and had me feeling cold and clammy before I had the sense to grope in the back of my car for my raincoat.

I didn't know the car well enough to have the drill to numbers, and the job took me longer than it should have done. And before I'd gone ten miles farther, my other back tyre ripped open on a piece of glass.

I had to walk two miles into Neustadt to find a garage, and it rained hard all the way, and when I got there it took me twenty minutes of exhaustion to make myself understood.

Once they'd grasped the situation they made short work of fetching the car, patching the inner tube that was still worth patching, and selling me a replacement for the other; but even so, it meant that I had to kick my heels in Neustadt for two hours, and it was past six when I got on my way again.

All it meant was that I should have to drive later than

I'd intended. I put up the best speed I could, but towards evening that road is infested with enormous lorries, eight-wheelers and worse, and they drive hell for leather, and take an age to pass, so the whole run into Würzburg was tough on my nerves, even apart from the falling dusk, which seems to come inordinately early there by English standards, and the frequent and fierce thunder showers.

If I hadn't already been somewhat daunted I don't suppose I should have picked up the hitchhiker with the Union Jack on his rucksack who thumbed me hopefully outside the village of Enzlar. He had a beard, and glasses, and hobnailed boots, a discoloured windjacket, and about half a ton of impedimenta dangling round him, camera, tape-recorder, everything you can think of. I suppose he was rising fifty, and deadly serious. Not my type. But he was advertising the fact that he was British, which meant that he could at least talk English to me, and prevent me from going completely melancholy for want of a human voice.

He talked! The first thing he told me was that he'd come all across Europe without walking more than two miles at a stretch, which made me want to ask why he needed the boots. I'd hoped he was going all the way to Aschaffenburg or Frankfurt, but he was only bound for Kitzingen, on the near side of Würzburg.

'Where are you spending the night?' he asked me, hoping I'd stay in Kitzingen, too, and take him on with me next day.

'Hanau,' I told him firmly. It might have been sensible to draw in my horns and settle for somewhere nearer, but

I was determined not to alter my plans just for a run of bad luck.

I knew what he'd say, and he said it. Straight out of the guidebook. For that matter, it's the only thing there is to say about Hanau. 'Ah, the birthplace of the brothers Grimm!' he said, beaming at me with queer, light, opaque eyes; and he began to talk about the folklore of fairy tales with the gusto of a devotee.

I'd always thought the Grimm fairy stories a pretty grisly collection of horror comics in their own right, but this fellow knew exactly how sinister they really are when considered in all their implications. And what he knew he meant to share with me. The sky sank low over our heads, copper and lead in mottled patches, the darkness came down hours before its time, and the thunder rolled along mile for mile with us on our left quarter, and slashed at us with vicious scuds of rain. And this fellow talked. Like a book.

'You know, of course, what the dwarfs and ogres and gnomes of fairy stories really are, don't you? They date from the dawn of history, when new races were sweeping westward out of the Danube valley. They're the new people's view of the old, the survivors of the old civilization depressed and submerged into decline, pushed out of the fat lands into the hills and forests, where living is hard and precarious. They're the relics of submerged peoples, dispossessed gods, outmoded cults. The stories turn them into grotesques, shrunken in stature, ugly, wicked, because the people who made the stories were afraid of them still. They made them malevolent because they knew they'd given them reason for hatred, reason to be inimical and vengeful. And they *are* malevolent – they *do* hate – they *are* inimical and vengeful. Because they have reason to be.'

His eyes glowed at me gleefully. He talked as if the old war were still going on, and all the guerrillas of innumerable doomed races were lurking in ambush for stragglers from among their supplanters, not half a mile from the road.

'Or of course, in the ultimate analysis,' he said blithely, 'they're the spirits of the dead, who are also dispossessed and submerged, and have reason to bear a grudge against the living. In either case, they're to be feared and avoided at all costs. And all those princesses, and elder brothers, and younger sons who fall into their clutches in the stories – well, in the stories they're always rescued in the end, of course. But how do we know how many of the dominant race went missing to provide all those legends? And *weren't* rescued?'

When I dropped him at last in Kitzingen I had a furious headache, and a mind full of monsters. I've never been so glad to get rid of a passenger in my life.

'It'll be pretty late when you cross the Spessart hills,' he gloated at me through his ginger beard as he took his leave. 'I often think many of the wildest Grimm stories must have come out of those forests. Only a few miles from Aschaffenburg and Hanau, and yet you might be in another world and another age. There are places, you know, where the veil is very thin. Spessart always seems to me to be one of them.'

He went off dangling his plethora of equipment and hunched under his enormous rucksack, and in the half darkness he looked like one of his own ogres.

As for me, I crept through Würzburg feeling uncommonly miserable, and along the narrow road under the ominous shadow of the Marienburg, and out into the rain-soaked countryside again. By eight it was dark; pitch dark because of the low and heavy clouds which brought the night down on me untimely. Then the real thunderstorms began, streaming with rain until there seemed no air to breathe between the slashing jets of it, and visibility was nil.

I slowed down to a timorous crawl, and edged along by feel, through sudden pools that tried to tug me to a standstill. It was plain night now, and a black night, too, hot and heavy and crushing, so that even between the rain-storms the very air seemed solid.

I should have stopped. I should have had sense enough to settle for the pub in the nearest village. But I went obstinately on, determined not to give in to my luck. And in the Spessart hills I lost my way.

It couldn't happen now. The autobahn has been extended right to the outskirts of Würzburg, and you roll along through the wilds on a moving belt. But at the time I'm talking about, only a few years ago, the motorway had only reached Aschaffenburg, and you did the rest of the trip on the old, winding road. After you passed the well-known Spessart Inn it was forest, forest all the way, rising and falling with the road, and not a solitary house to be seen in miles of it.

It was pouring with rain again, my head was thudding like a steam-hammer, and all I could see by my headlights was drowning, drenching streams of water, and occasionally the merest glimpse of the long, unchanging procession of tree-trunks on either side. The road was a river, and had narrowed considerably on this stretch, so that I didn't notice for some time how extreme this narrowing process had become, or how bad the surface was; and exactly how and where I left the road I shall never know.

But at last I realized that there were no more lorries, and that was odd. Whatever my speed, I should either have overtaken one or two, or been myself overtaken. But now there were no more lorries. There were no more cars at all. Nothing but the Ford and me.

I was afraid to stop my engine, so I kept going, but wound down my window and stuck my head out into the saturated darkness. There wasn't a solitary sound left in the world except the indignant note of the car and the slashing fall of the rain. Then the rain stopped, and all round me I could feel the silence pressing in, and the darkness, and the wet, green, earthy, ancient smell of the forest. And I was afraid. Not of being lost, not of an uncomfortable night in the car, not of anything comprehensible or reasonable, just afraid. Perhaps of the immensity and antiquity of the world outside the tiny shell of the car, and of the insignificance and ephemeral nature of the car and its driver, those intruders from a new world. A world which thought it had displaced the ancient one, a world from which I was now a straggler, and vulnerable.

I knew it was nonsense, but the knowledge resided in a part of my brain, the reasoning part, which had shrunk into a corner and assumed the defensive. All the rest of my mind moved now irrationally, by instinct, memory, hypersensitive touch.

I told myself that the rough track on which I found myself was bound to lead somewhere, to a village, or at least a clearing where there would be a house, or to another road which, since I was not conscious of having changed direction in any considerable degree, would surely bring me to Aschaffenburg. So I went on, creeping gingerly along the sodden wheel-ruts as the track grew greener and narrower; but all the intuitive part of my mind, quivering with outspread tentacles like the hair erected on a frightened man's head, stretched outward into the primeval darkness and fended off terror. The old things, the buried things, came into their own by night and in solitude. How many of the dominant race have vanished, to provide all those legends? Cut off from their kind, astray from their daylight world, like me—

That was when the car rocked suddenly sideways into a bigger hole than usual and, grind away as I might, I couldn't get it out again. I got out to try to push it clear, and it did move on to an even keel, but then the engine died on me, and I couldn't start it again. I was quaking with exhaustion, fever, fury, and fright when I stopped shoving to wipe the rain out of my eyes and peer ahead through the sighing darkness; and somewhere, small and distant between the trees, I saw a glimmer of light, steady light, like the glow from a window.

* * *

I don't know why it wasn't immediately reassuring. But I know that it wasn't. The hair rose on my neck and scalp with foreboding. And yet I went forward towards the light, between the thinning trees.

The obstinate rational corner in my mind was still functioning. This must be a house, it said, go and ask where you are, and how to get back on the road to Aschaffenburg and Hanau. And I did what it told me to do, though I didn't believe in its reasoning. I went straight towards the window, for it was certainly a window. There was no clearing to be seen, just a low fence erupting quite suddenly in the streaming gloom, and a bushy, tangled garden, and then the long, low huddle of the house, hardly distinguishable from the surrounding darkness of trees and night.

Only two storeys, with a verandah all along the upper face and a flight of wooden steps leading up to it from one end. A squat, secret, unwelcoming house, low-browed behind its bushes, unbelievably solitary and sinister. A shaded light in one upper window, and that unshaded one below. I walked up to the fence, and there was a little gate in it, rolling open on a broken hinge. I went through into the garden, among the dripping bushes, and crept closer to the house.

It was then that a door opened in the dark face, and let out a flood of light into the garden; and in the light, a grotesque little black silhouette stood, a figure I didn't care to think of as human, though its movements caricatured the motions of man.

I saw no features, only a shape. There was a huge head,

sunken into thick shoulders, a paunchy body that tapered off into skinny little bowed legs. The creature was about three feet high, for it came only half-way up the lighted frame of the door. It stood a moment looking out into the night, and then it went in and shut the door. There wasn't any doubt about it. I hadn't imagined it. It was there, and it was alive.

I don't know what it is in a man that can drive him forward towards something that threatens and terrifies him. Not courage. Courage ought to be reasoning and reasonable, ought to have an objective. There was every reason in the world why I should turn and run for it, feeling the way I felt, and no reason at all why I should creep shivering through the wet bushes towards that lighted window.

But that's what I did. Curiosity must be a passion as strong and fundamental as love, to hold its own with the sort of panic terror I felt blazing up in me. I was incandescent with it, my erected hair giving off sparks into the darkness, all my skin tensed and burning with its heat. And yet I was crawling through the tangled branches, soaked, shuddering, my knees quaking under me, drawn to the window as to a magnet.

The house waited for me, quiescent, biding its time. I reached out and touched the wall beneath the window, drew myself up, and looked into the room.

There were six of them. In that little, wood-panelled, ancient brown room, six of them sat, some at a table, some with their backs to the green-tiled stove with its sunken radiation eyes. One of them was smoking a short briar pipe. One, the one I'd seen in the doorway, was just closing the door of the room behind him, and now I saw his face, and it was ugly, tragic, and ferocious. Two of the others were females. The word 'women' didn't occur to me in connection with them. They were thick-bodied, neckless, with gross lips and broad noses. I swear not one of them was taller than the first.

All the voids in my racial memory, all those dark hollows of ignorance that might so easily, so horribly be peopled after all, swelled into one darkness and filled the night for me. The antique darkness in which the enemy lurked still, and still was dominant, the territory where the daylight laws of reason and credibility were not current, gripped and held and contained me. For my reason denied this, but my senses recorded it. The forest house was full of dwarfs. The very air outside its confines was heavy with their tragedy and hatred.

In the stories, you'll remember, the hero still advances, that indestructible inquisitiveness overcoming his fear even when he knows his enemy. Now I know it can happen, because it went on happening to me. I'd seen them, and still there was something else I had to see. In that upstairs room, too, there was a subdued light burning. I felt along the wall until I reached the wooden staircase to the gallery, and step by step, clinging to the wood with cold hands, I climbed it, and edged my way to the window. The sill was low and one half of the window was slightly open so that a draught stirred the drawn curtains. I put my hand in, and parted the curtains an inch or two, just enough to peer in.

A little lamp, heavily shaded, was burning on a small table beside the bed. It filled all the centre of the room, that bed, and its down quilt billowed like a white, bulbous cloud. Beneath the cloud a girl lay asleep.

She lay on her back, her arms relaxed at her sides, her pure profile bright under the gleam of the lamp. The face was motionless, withdrawn from the world. Long dark lashes lay on the pale cheeks, the soft lips were raised tenderly to the leaning air. Over the pillow, over the bed, her long, long, golden hair streamed unbound. She was more beautiful than I can ever tell you, she was the most beautiful thing I'd ever seen.

Her breathing was deep, regular, and slow, her face marble. She slept an unmoving, an enchanted sleep, there in the house of the enemy. And unless someone awoke her and took her away, there she would sleep for ever.

I had no doubts left in me at all. There was no part of that nightmare of the war between the ancient and the new races that I could not believe. There were places, there were times in the darkness, when the old world reached out after its revenges. There was magical death, and magical damnation. The loveliest, the youngest and best was always the desired prize.

So it was up to me. You can see that. And you'll understand why I unhasped the open window, and climbed into the room, and went and knelt beside the bed, touching her fingers, whispering into her ear, imploring her to awake before it was too late. No noise – there must be no noise. Even to touch her was dangerous. Supposing she should be startled and cry out, and *they* should hear?

There was a perfume in her hair and about her skin

that made my senses fail, and now that I was close beside her, her face was so beautiful that the tears came into my eyes. Are tears a waking magic? One actually fell on to her cheek, but she did not move. And then I remembered what I had to do. Of course, there is only one way, the old, the time-honoured way to awaken sleeping princesses.

I bent my head, and kissed her on the soft, uplifted mouth. It was like a little death. Everything I had been faded and declined in me, burning out, and something new and wondering and unsure, but clear and good, slowly generated and grew in me to replace it. And before I had lifted my lips from hers I felt the long lashes sweeping my cheek, brushing through my lashes. She opened her eyes, which were as darkly blue as gentians in an Alpine meadow, and looked at me, all dewy and astonished and direct as a child, and slowly, marvellously, she began to smile.

And I, drawing back a little from my too impious nearness to her, knocked over the table and the lamp together, and the lamp went out.

Beneath us there was a savage, alarmed outcry of voices and a clashing of doors, and feet thudded wildly on the stairs, heavy, hasty feet, as the dwarfs came raging to retrieve their treasure.

Groping through the darkness, crying to her to come with me, and I would save her, I caught at her hand, and for an instant I swear those soft, cool fingers folded gently upon mine. Then the door of the room burst open and they came swarming in, the powers of evil; small, heavy, loathsome, they poured over me, clinging about my legs, climbing up my body, battering at me, and screaming in harsh angry voices.

I fought my way across the room, trying to sweep them away from her bed, but their weight dragged me down, and their heat clinging to my sweating body was awful, unbearable. I tried to shake them off, but they dragged at my feet and brought me down, and then they were all over me, and I was stifling, dying. Something exploded inside my aching head. Even the darkness went out.

I came to life again, if it was life, lying on a stone floor. My body was ice-cold, but my head was filled with molten metal, so heavy that I could not move it even to ease the pain. At first I thought I was encircled by a ring of tiny fires, then I saw that they were eyes watching me. All the dwarfs were crouched round me, staring; and one of them, who sat beside my left shoulder, held a misshapen, veinous hand above my heart, poising a long, thin knife.

They did not move, nor often speak. They just sat there, and watched me. I kept my eyelids lowered, peering stealthily through my lashes, so that they should think me still unconscious, asleep, dead, whatever it was they conceived my state to be. I saw that the door of the room stood ajar, and that there were stars in the sliver of sky I could see beyond. I regained a tiny, feeble flickering of hope, because there were stars again. The world had not entirely abandoned itself to the ancient evil.

And I remembered her, the inexpressibly beautiful, the captive, the victim, charmed again to sleep in the room above, and knew that I had to get away from here alive, in order that she might live again. Whether I could or no, I had to escape and bring help for her.

I did not know yet if I could move, and dared not try it, because the least tension of my arm would be seen at once, and surprise was the one weapon I had. But between me and the door there was only the dwarf and the knife. If he would once look away from me I might attempt it.

I did not know what inspired in me the fiery and despairing calm with which I contemplated this act of hopeless defiance. I think it was her eyes, newly opened still in my mind's eye, that drowned in their deep blueness the fierce, thin blue of the knife blade. I waited, watching the slight movements it made above my chest, praying for it to be withdrawn, only for a moment.

Then the door was pushed open, and a giant came in out of the night. I felt no surprise. No prodigy could surprise me any more. Only the normal, only daylight, and traffic, and a man shaped like other men could have astonished me now. This man looked enormous, towering above me, towering above the dwarfs, talking to them in a deep, resonant voice, in some language I could not recognize even as German. He had a pointed beard, and high-arched brows, and a handsome, angry face like a devil's, famished and corroded with rage. He stared at me, and swept through to some inner room, and the door closed behind him.

One more apparition out of the submerged world, cast up through the rift of night and storm and solitude. But when he spoke they all listened, and when he had passed they turned to look after him. Even the dwarf with the knife. It was the only moment I could hope for, and I took it. I reached up and caught him by the wrists and, springing up, jerked him backwards off his perch, and jumped over him, and ran.

The shrilling of their voices and clutching of their hands were like a wind that blew me onward, and the pain that filled me was like a fire burning its way forward over a dry plain, and sweeping me with it. I hit the edge of the door blindly, and wrenched it open, and fell into the night; and ran, and ran, and ran, leaping aside from bushes, ducking under the branches of trees, jumping over sodden hollows, fending myself off with outstretched arms from the trunks of trees.

I heard the hunt pour out of the house after me, saw light streaming from door and window for a few minutes, and then sound and light fell far behind me, and I was running off the ground, floating, drifting effortlessly through a void, almost without pain any longer. For a long time it seemed. A very long time. An eternity.

After that I remember a road under my feet, quite suddenly, out of nowhere, and two lights gleaming like eyes on its wet, silver surface, and voices, and men tumbling out from the brain behind the eyes. I remember falling through miles of air into long arms, and gasping out my story and my appeal, between breaths that hurt me clean through to the heart, as though the knife had transfixed me at last. I remember a face above me, big white teeth and great, astonished eyes, and a deep, soft voice uttering sounds of reassurance in English.

'All right, son. All right, now, take it easy!' the incredible voice was purring. And the face – it seemed only the last fantasy of the night to me that this face should be black.

I went down, fathoms deep, into the blueness of remembered gentian eyes, and in the depths there was darkness and silence.

When I came to myself, I was lying in a bed in an American military hospital in Aschaffenburg, where the black highway patrol had rushed me in the jeep that night; and Franz Eisner was sitting by my bed, as round and rosy and ordinary as ever, beaming at me through his thick glasses.

He patted my shoulder, and fed me grapes, and told me where I was, and how I'd got there. And all the time I wanted to know only one thing, the single thing that mattered.

'Did they find her?' I asked, hearing a thin voice that hardly seemed to be mine. 'Did they get there in time? Did they find the girl?'

An odd, embarrassed smile flickered over his face, but he said soothingly, 'Oh yes, they found her.'

'So I did manage to tell a straight tale before I passed out! Thank God! And she's all right?'

'She's quite all right,' he said. 'Don't worry about anything, everything's being taken care of. Miss Fordyce has gone home by plane – you've been here four days, you know, and only just missed pneumonia. You were running a tremendous fever when they brought you in. And the car's all right, don't worry about the car, I've got it in the office garage in Frankfurt. When they found it they found your briefcase and papers in it, of course, and that's why they sent for me. All you've got to do is lie still and get well, and leave everything else to me.'

'Where is she?' I demanded. 'I must see her!'

'She?'

'You said they found her!' I cried, alarmed again. 'Temperature or no temperature, fever or no fever, I didn't make her up, or the dwarfs, either, or the giant.'

'Yes, well – yes, Stephen, they did find her. And the – the dwarfs and the giant, too. You see, my dear Stephen,' said Franz, taking the plunge, 'the giant had sent for the police himself. He said some foreigner had broken into his daughter's bedroom and assaulted her, and then escaped from the dwarfs who were guarding him, and got away in the woods. But he calmed down when he heard that some half-delirious Englishman had been picked up by an American highway patrol babbling at them to go and rescue a princess who was being held captive by monsters in a hut in the forest.

'He saw the joke,' said Franz gently, 'and Fräulein Ulla saw it, too. They dropped all charges against you at once. You've nothing to worry about.'

What he saw in my face I daren't guess, but he went on talking, which was kind of him. How I'd been unlucky in blundering on the inn from the forest side, how I would have seen the car park, and the telephone wires, and the parked wagons, and all the evidences of blessed, everyday modernity, if only I'd found my way to it by the village road—

'But they *were* dwarfs,' I cried, trembling, 'not above three feet high, any one of them! And the other man, the big one – he was tall as the ceiling—'

'He *is* a very tall man,' agreed Franz soothingly, 'nearly two metres, I know, I've met and talked to him. And if you were lying on the floor, as it seems you were . . . and of course, after the others he would seem enormous. They *could* be rather frightening, those midgets of his, seen without warning, offstage like that—'

'And the knife was real,' I persisted. 'I touched it, I know it was real!'

'Oh, yes, the knife would be real enough. They were genuinely alarmed, you know. Schmidt throws them – the knives, I mean. He runs Loeffler's Midgets and his own knife-throwing act. And Fräulein Ulla—'

I was getting the hang of it at last. I said flatly, 'She's the target.'

'Well, yes. But they wouldn't have touched you with it, you know, it was only meant to keep you quiet until the police came. The group always call in at that inn when they're heading for Frankfurt. Schmidt's sister keeps it. She's the widow of a lion-tamer who used to be with the same circus.'

He looked at me with sympathy, and didn't laugh; I've always been grateful to him for that. 'The little fellows don't look so bad by daylight,' he said, 'and still better, of course, when they're dressed up for the ring. But they always give me the creeps, too, I don't mind admitting.'

'I seem to have made a complete fool of myself,' I said bleakly.

'Oh, I don't know! Coming on them by accident, as

you did, and in the state you were in, who could blame you?'

He hesitated, and then added somewhat constrainedly, 'Fräulein Ulla didn't. She sent you a letter.'

My hands were shaking so much I could hardly open it. The single sheet of notepaper was headed from Willy Isserstedt's Circus, Frankfurt, three days previously. It had her scent clinging to it, the breath of a rose, of a memory, of a true fairy tale. I had to ask Franz to translate the few lines for me.

Stephen, she had written, *the treasure you left with me I keep and guard for you until you return. Use these three charms I send you, and by day or by night you may come safely to me, and claim your own again. Ulla.*

The three charms were three tickets for the circus. The performance at Frankfurt was already past, the one at Koblenz was too soon for me to hope to make it, but the ticket for Cologne I could have used. And three is always the magical number, the number of success. And the tone of her letter, its directness, its teasing, its tenderness, ought to have drawn me to her across a world. A daylight world or a dangerous nocturnal world.

But I didn't go. I was too young, too sore, too ashamed to be able to face her. So I made a bigger fool of myself than ever, and hurried back to England as soon as I was fit, and even tried for a little while to make up to Fordyce and Lilian for the way I'd let them down. But I couldn't have gone through with it, even if they'd encouraged me, and they didn't. There was a distinct chill in the air, young Stephen wasn't the white-headed boy any longer.

I left Fordyce's a few months later, and took a job with a firm that does even bigger business with Germany. And I'm learning German for all I'm worth. Some day I'll even be able to understand that outlandish Bavarian dialect.

Because I'm going back there. I'm going to do what I wish I'd had the courage to do then; find her and ask her for my own again. Maybe I shall be too late, maybe in daylight and without the terror her eyes won't be so blue or her hair so golden. Maybe I shall seem so insignificant to her on a second view that she'll laugh at me, as she didn't laugh then. But I've got to try. I've got to know.

Somewhere in Germany Willy Isserstedt's Circus must still be wandering, and if I search long enough I shall find it. In fairy tales every search ends in finding. And this time not her six-foot-six-inch father nor all his three-foot midgets are going to frighten me away from her.

Trump of Doom

After old Eb Langley had his first stroke, he had to loose the hold he'd had on the Worbridge Town Band, and I came in for the job of conducting them for the Sunday School Parade at Whitsun.

If Eb hadn't been flat on his back, nobody else would ever have been allowed to lead that march, and we heard afterwards that when they told him I'd been picked to take over he relaxed in a minute, and let out that baritone cackle of his, and said: 'Wait'll they see what a mess young Les Parkes makes of it, they'll be sitting on the doorstep imploring me to get up off me deathbed.' So it set him back badly when we got through the day in fine style, and I reckon old Lije Weatherly going and comforting him that night didn't help his convalescence much. 'Don't worry about us,' says Lije, 'you lie easy, son! Best performance we ever put up, that's what they're all saying. As if we'd let you down,' says Lije, rolling up his eyes like a lay reader, 'after all you done for us!'

Nearly had another stroke on the spot, they say, and his

poor little meek wife, stone-deaf as she is and him too mean to buy her a hearing-aid, watched their faces and tried to make out what it was all about, and how soon she'd better start shooing Lije out of the room, before the old man burst.

He was by way of being our town philanthropist, was old Eb. For one thing, he was the only one around, barring the doctor and a few elderly survivors from the last industrial boom, who had any money to be philanthropic with, and if he wanted a brass band, and a horticultural society, and a few other local activities to lord it over, he had to provide the money for 'em.

The band was his favourite good work, it gave him more scope than the other groups. Plenty of kids used to come along at one time, keen as mustard to follow in father's footsteps, because ours is a district with a band tradition. Broke their innocent hearts, Eb Langley did. I'm not saying he wasn't a good musician, he was, but he liked nothing better than tyrannizing over all the lot of us, letting fly like a wild man if we made a bit of a mistake in practice, and sarcastic – you wouldn't believe! Had all the youngsters scared to blow at all, and all of a shiver if he looked at 'em. I should never had stuck it myself, those few months after I started, if it hadn't been for Nora Weatherly. She was only seventeen, and so was I, but we knew our own minds before we left school, and I was set on getting in with her old man, so I put up with Eb's bullying better than most. But if you hadn't got a reason as good as mine, you broke down and slunk out after a few weeks of it.

Lije was the only one who used to treat his lordship

with disrespect. After Eb's worst outbursts there'd be a sudden blast from Lije's double-B, right out of the cellar, and even the kid who'd just been chewed to pulp would venture a feeble grin, and begin to get his colour back.

But there wasn't much we could do about Eb, really. He'd had twenty years to get everything well into his own hands. We used to meet in the clubroom at the Black Horse, which was the pub he'd bought after he sold out his dog-hole collieries to the National Coal Board. There wasn't another suitable room in the place, and he'd never charged the band rent for using it – I reckon he got value for his money making us that much more beholden to him. And then there were the instruments. Only a few of the old ones had turned up again after the ten-year interval caused by the war, and the rest he'd provided out of his own pocket; times without number, when we were in funds, someone would suggest that we pay off the debt, and he'd never take it. Oh, dear me, no, a pity if he couldn't help us to a few instruments, and the band his only pleasure! It suited him fine to have us obliged to him still. We should have known! As if he ever gave anything away without being sure he could get back ten times the value some other way! Why, his poor wife hadn't had a new coat for years, and he grudged his lorry drivers a ten-minute break on the road in a four-hour journey!

He got worse as he grew older. They do. We didn't all say it, like Lije, but we were all mighty relieved when he took to his bed, especially when weeks went on with me deputizing, and it began to look as though he wouldn't be coming back. He was better, he'd reached the stage of getting up and thumping about his front bedroom at the Black Horse, and you could hear him roaring at his wife halfway down the High Street. But he'd grown monstrously fat and heavy during the time he was lying up, and his heart wouldn't be responsible for the consequences if he started running about the town again, and finally he had to resign.

Then he comforted himself with thinking how we should go to pieces without him, and if we had he'd have been happy. I didn't know as much about conducting as he did, but I knew more about how to get on with folks, and I was learning the rest as fast as I could. When he heard we were doing well, his bile rose so there was no living with him. He used to spend his days lying in the window of his front bedroom, keeping an eye on everything that went on in the street, and interfering as much as he could with all of it. Looked like a great fat toad, only without the mild expression.

First time we marched up the street to play by the war memorial in the new uniforms we'd been saving up for, I thought he'd blow up. And Lije cocks up the bell of his double-B towards the window, special, and gives him a sour one, deliberate, as he goes by. Nora told him off for it afterwards. Told me off, too, for not stopping him, as if anybody could stop that old devil doing anything, once he took it into his head. If anybody knew that, it was Nora. But it was always me that was supposed to look after Lije, steer him off his monkey-tricks during the Sunday night open-air concerts, keep him sober when we went off to play in contests. That was what I was in the band for, according to Nora.

We started winning a few little local events that summer, and the barman from the Black Horse told us Eb's missus was having a hell of a life with him. Only comfort the poor woman had was that she couldn't hear one word in ten he yelled at her. Then we decided to enter for the county championship in August, and the way we'd been improving I thought we had a good chance of winning it. It got around to him, of course. If he'd been sure we'd go along and make an exhibition of ourselves he'd have done everything in his power to help us – that was the only way he could ever have felt reconciled to having to loose his grip on anything he'd once been running. But he'd heard us play, he knew we were doing all right.

Middle of the next practice he sent his missus down with a note. He was very sorry, but would we mind shifting all our stuff out of the clubroom by the end of the week, because he'd got an offer to rent the place to the auction bloke from the market as a storeroom, and as he hadn't got any regular bookings for it as a clubroom, except ours, which didn't bring him in anything, we would see he couldn't afford to turn down the offer. He was sure we should find another room without any trouble. He was sure! He'd lived in the town all his life, he knew there wasn't a decent room to be booked in the whole place. The old hands argued, and the kids exploded, but there was nothing we could do about it, out we had to go, instruments and all. We stacked them in our back parlour for the time being, and lost a whole week's practice while I ran round the town trying to find a place for us to meet.

We ended up in Alf Parkinson's derelict garage, up on the pit mounds. It was summer, and it didn't matter so much that all the windows were out, and some of the end boards coming loose into the bargain; but it was a long walk out of town for the lads who lived up the other side, and we had to carry the instruments back and forth because there was no proper lock on the door up there. Still, it was a private place, and a roof over us when it rained. We'd have played in the mortuary, by that time, sooner than let Eb Langley beat us.

'You watch,' said Nora 'this won't be the end of it. If the old buzzard's feeling as mean as that, he'll stick at nothing to bring us to heel.' She said 'us' because of her old man and me; if anybody was taking us on, he was taking on Nora, too. 'I wonder,' she said, gnawing her lip, 'what the next move'll be!'

We didn't have to wonder long, because a week or so later he wrote me a letter to say that he was forced, owing to temporary difficulties, to dispose of some of his surplus effects, and as it seemed unlikely that he'd ever be able to take an active part in the band's activities again, he wanted to realize on the instruments which were his property. We were welcome to take them over, of course, if we could do so at once, because he'd had a lot of expenses with his illness, and business being so bad, and all, and if we decided against buying he was obliged to part with the things in next week's regular auction sale at Windlesham. And could he have our decision by the end of the week, please. And he named his price, too. I hadn't got anything to prove it, but I'll swear it was more than he'd paid for 'em when they were new. And anyhow, he knew damned well we'd lashed out on those new uniforms, and hadn't got above a pound or two in hand. All the times we'd tried to pay him for those instruments, and he wouldn't let us!

I went to see him before I dared tell the lads what he'd done. I did everything but go on my knees to him; I begged him to wait till the end of the month, to give us a bit of time to raise the money. He all but wept down my neck with sympathy, juggled with papers and figures to prove to me that he was as good as bankrupt, and for his poor wife's sake he couldn't wait even a week longer. I've never been more meek and humble to anybody in my life, but at the end of it all he still owned the instruments, and still wanted his price for 'em, or else! And we still hadn't got it to give. So I had to tell the boys that night, and a fine row there was.

'Let me go and negotiate for you,' says Lije, blowing gently down his double-B, which was his own, and safe as houses. 'I won't make no trouble, I'll just quietly be the death of him. Eb and me,' he says, 'we understand each other.'

'You keep out of it,' I said, thinking of Nora. 'I'm conducting this band, and it's up to me to think of a way round this. What's more,' I said, 'we'll get our instruments for a lot less than that out of the old robber, or my name's not Les Parkes.'

I talked it over with Nora afterwards, and she went with me to Maddingley to see Tom Lowther, who conducted the Maddingley Colliery Band. They'd been our rivals ever since we started up again after the war, and there was supposed to be pretty high feeling between us over the county championship, but it was all part of the game, as you might say, and anyhow Tom Lowther was a good sort, and wouldn't stand for us being frozen out of the contest that way, it would have spoiled his fun. So we told him all about it. He said it was a dirty trick, all right, but what was he supposed to do about it?

'Tom,' I said, 'if *you* was to go to him, and say as you'd heard he'd got these instruments for sale, and put it up to him that you'd be glad to have 'em if the price was right, I believe he'd jump at it. He'd be so pleased to think he was putting us out of the running and giving our chief rivals a leg up, that I believe you could even knock the price down considerable. If you let on to hate us enough, he'll almost give 'em to you. Nora here and me, we've put together as much as we can raise,' I said. 'I'm betting that from *you* it'll be enough. From us he wouldn't touch it if it was three times as much, he'd have some tale to put us off with. We'll get it back from the band after we've won the trophy.'

That started him grinning. 'You'll never see your money again,' he says, 'if you're relying on getting it back that way. But just to show we ain't afraid to meet you on equal terms, I'll see what I can do for you.'

It's my belief he enjoyed that job. We didn't hear any more until the Friday, and then it was another letter to say that Eb Langley had had an offer for the instruments, and much as he regretted it, he couldn't afford to turn it down unless we were able to say at once that we'd take them off his hands at the terms agreed. If we couldn't see our way to doing that, would we please deliver them at the Black Horse after the practice, because the prospective purchaser wanted to see them and collect them, if satisfactory, next Monday evening. And we did, looking as down-in-the-mouth as we knew how, for fear he should smell a rat, and I could see him peering over the windowsill at us when we left, fairly quaking with glee. He thought he'd done us good and proper this time. He wouldn't have been so pleased with himself if he'd known that the little van that fetched the instruments away on the Monday didn't take 'em any farther than our house.

Tom Lowther was grinning all over. 'I've brought you five quid back, and all,' he says, 'it worked like a charm. And I'll give you the cost of my petrol, I was going up to our Win's, anyhow, so I've hardly come out of my way. My word, I wouldn't like to be within a hundred yards of the Black Horse when Langley gets to hear about this deal! He'll have another stroke, I shouldn't wonder.'

'Come out and have a drink,' I says, beaming at all that nice brass lying about our parlour again. 'We certainly owe you one.'

'Not tonight,' he says, 'I'm driving. After we've blown you lot clean out of the park at Hillingdon Royal, you can buy me a double. Nice stuff!' he says, looking where I was looking. 'What a pity you can't play 'em!'

We let him have that – he'd saved our bacon for us. We put our heads together after that, and did some hard thinking, but we couldn't think of anything else Langley could do to us now. We didn't trust him as far as we could throw him, though, so we used to drift in for a drink by twos and threes, just to find out it there was any funny business going on, but all we found out was that he'd nearly thrown a fit when he got the news, and had been foaming at the mouth for three days, and nobody dared to go near him except his missus, and after all she hadn't got much choice. So after a bit we relaxed, and concentrated on practising for the contest; and what with the stimulation we got out of having won the first two rounds, we were playing well.

We hadn't exactly hired Burke's bus for the trip to Hillingdon Royal on the day of the contest, it was just that we had an understanding with him. Some of us worked Saturday mornings, so we couldn't start off until half past one. Buses were always busy Saturdays, winter with football matches and summer with trips to the seaside or into Wales, so I'd just stuck my head into Burke's garage, three weeks ago, and said: 'Okay for the championship, Bill?' and he'd said: 'Okay, Les!' from under an old Alvis, and that was all the booking we ever did, but I knew it would be all right.

Only this time it wasn't all right, because on the Saturday morning I came off shift early, and there was Bill Burke dancing about on our doorstep like a flurried hen, and he grabs me by the arm and says: 'Les, something awful's happened! I've let you down!'

'What's up?' I asked him. 'What's come to the bus?' It had to be the bus, how else could Burke have let us down? And at this hour there wouldn't be another within fifty miles radius that wasn't booked up. Saturdays are like that in Worbridge and district; when you've got a fine day and

68

time off, you light out as far as possible out of it.

'He's *bought* it!' says Burke in a wild groan. 'I couldn't help it, Les! He owns the ground my garage is on, and the lease has only got a couple of years to run, and he as good as told me I could say goodbye to the place if I didn't do what he wanted. Tried to get me to put the old engine out of commission and pretend I couldn't get it right again, but when I wouldn't he offered me such a price for it – my God, I couldn't believe me ears! I'm no millionaire, what am I supposed to do when I get a windfall like that dropped in my lap? I've got kids to keep! And anyhow, I thought I knew of a bus I could get for you in Hillingdon, where my brother works. There's an old pit one they only use for the charter journeys during the week, it's shabby for parties on the spree, but I knew you wouldn't care so long as it goes, and I thought we could have it both ways. But even that's hired out,' he said, clutching his hair. 'I didn't have the chance to phone about it first, I had to say yes or no to him then and there. And I said yes, and now look where I've landed you! I've been phoning all round ever since, and there isn't a coach to be had in this county. And now what are we going to do? You'd be justified in suing me!'

'We can't afford to,' I said, 'or we would. What are we going to do? We're going to get there, somehow, Heaven knows how, but we are! Have you got a car? Even one car? Can you get the four old 'uns there, and the big drum?'

He had a rickety old pre-war Morris, not big enough for four, really, but our older colliers don't run to size. We got 'em in, and strapped the big drum on the luggage-rack, and started that contingent off with plenty of time in hand for the two or three breakdowns they were liable to have on the way. Then I flew round the rest of the lads, beating up what transport I could think of, and warning the ones I couldn't fix up that they'd have to get out on the Hillingdon road and try to thumb a lift. Young Fred took Ernie Briggs on the back of his motorbike, Sid Peters borrowed his cousin's tandem and took one of the others on the rear saddle, one or two of those who finished work early, and were ready and dressed when I reached 'em, rushed straight out and caught the last possible service bus for the last possible train connection at Maddingley, and the rest of us swore we'd somehow get there in time under our own steam.

'Whatever happens,' said Nora, when she saw us off, 'you stick with our dad, Les, and don't let him get up to anything. And you behave yourself, our dad, and don't you get stopping anywhere for a drink on the way, because there's no time for that.'

'I can have one after we've won the championship, I suppose?' he says, hoisting his old double-B on his shoulder.

'You can do what you like afterwards,' says Nora, 'but if you don't get there in time to play *and* win, I'll never forgive you. After a dirty trick like this,' she says, 'we've *got* to win. And I hope the old so-and-so dies of spite when he hears!'

We were the last two to get started. We went by service bus to Maddingley, and then went and stood on the kerb a little way along the road out towards Hillingdon Royal, and started thumbing. They say there's no future in it with a rucksack these days, but it didn't pay off so badly with a double-B. I suppose it's the novelty. We got a lift for about seven miles of the way with a big Ford, then he had to drop us because he was turning off to one of the farms, and the next bite was only a little Morris with barely room for one, so I put Lije and his double-B into it, and then started to walk after 'em while waiting for another stroke of luck. But I didn't get one. I had to walk the rest of the way, four miles as near as makes no matter.

It would have been fine if I'd had plenty of time, but I had to do it in under an hour. By the time I got to the park gates at Hillingdon Royal I hadn't got breath enough for talking; but Ernie Briggs was there keeping a lookout for me and as soon as I puffed up he says, grinning: 'Take it easy, you've got twenty minutes or so to relax in. We're playing third, and we're all here, now you two have made it.'

'Two?' I said. 'You mean Lije hasn't got here? But he must have done! Four miles back I started him off in a car. They hadn't got room for the two of us.'

'He hasn't shown up yet,' said Ernie. 'I took it for granted he'd be turning up with you.'

It was no use sending anybody out to look for him, we could easily lose another man that way, and anyhow it was just on closing time, so if Lije was where I reckoned he was he'd soon be turfed out to return to his duty. So I left Ernie at the gate to keep a lookout for him, and went to join the others where they were waiting nervously by the bandstand. Much chance I had to relax, with one ear cocked towards the band that was playing first, and one eye rolling back towards the gate to see if Lije had appeared.

Come time for us to go up and play, I thought we'd had it, but suddenly up strolls old Lije from down by the paddling-pool, as cool as you like. Been in the park three-quarters of an hour, he said. Said it made him feel calm and confident watching the kids, we'd ought to have more sense than huddle there making one another nervous. We had to send one of the lads to fetch Ernie off the gate quick. I've never started the band off on a test-piece in such a state of nerves in my life. I could hardly hold the baton, I was trembling so.

All the same, we won. We did it!

We had to wait until late in the evening to hear the result, and after that it was a rush to celebrate. I should have gone back on the last train, or cadged a lift in the Maddingley coach, like several of the others did, only I'd lost Lije again. It's a very easy thing to do as long as the pubs are open. So I sent the trophy back in the coach with Ernie, and started on a tour of all the bars in the town. I daren't go back and face Nora without him.

By the time I found him, leaning on his double-B in front of the museum, having a heart-to-heart with a statue of Orpheus about the relative merits of strings and brass, it was going on for midnight, and there was no more transport until morning, and even then only part way. But if he was drunk, he wasn't incapable, and he couldn't see that there was any difficulty about getting home.

'We'll walk,' he says. 'Do us good, Les, lad! Best part of the day's the night.'

'What, with that?' I said, looking at the double-B.

'Why not?' he says, surprised. 'It's only ten miles, the short way.'

We walked. It took us two and a half hours, and he went like a machine all the way. He's only a little 'un, scrawny and bandy-legged to look at, but tough as blazes, especially when he's got a skinful. He wouldn't even part with his double-B, said it balanced him. It was all I could do to stop him playing it, just to show he'd got plenty of breath to spare. He did sing, several times. About half past two in the morning we were walking down the High Street at Worbridge, in that deathly small-hour hush, and he was so happy he loved everybody, even Eb Langley.

'The old bastard!' he says fondly, beaming at the Black Horse all shuttered up and dark. 'You can't help admiring his spirit. Hold on a tick,' he says, 'I must blow him a kiss, just to show there's no ill feeling.'

And before I could lift a finger he skipped up to the front door, clapped the bell of his double-B tight over the keyhole, and blew a blast that lifted the roof six feet in the air and made the walls bulge.

You never heard anything like it! In that silence it scared me out of my skin. I grabbed him by the arm and dragged him down the shut back of Hollis's, so fast you couldn't have seen us go. And I didn't stop till I shoved him through his own back door.

'You've got an unforgiving spirit,' he was saying reproachfully, 'tha's th' trouble with you. We won, didn't we? We can afford to be generous!'

But I just shut the door on him and made for home as

quick as I could. Everything in the High Street was quiet as the grave, I was thankful to see.

Next day I didn't get up until nearly dinner time, and then I went straight down to Nora's, same as usual on Sundays. Lije had gone out to the Black Horse to fetch some beer, and when he came back with the jug he was fairly busting with news.

'What d'you think!' he says, his eyes bulging. 'Old Eb Langley popped off in the night! True as I'm standing here! They found him dead this morning in his bed!'

'No!' says Nora, dropping the tablecloth she was just unfolding. 'What was it, his heart?'

'They reckon so. Seemingly he must have jumped up in bed, some time in the night, and just gone out like a light. Joss says to look at his face you'd think he'd been frightened to death – looked as if he'd woke up and seen the devils coming for him.'

Lucky Nora was there to do the talking, because I couldn't have said a word. I was watching Lije to see if he was thinking what I was thinking, but his face was as smooth as a baby's.

'He must have been took awful sudden,' says Nora. 'And he never had time to call to anybody? Nobody heard anything in the night?'

'Who was there to hear anything, when you come to think of it. His missus was in the next room, but she's deafer than the wall.'

'Of course, that's right!' says Nora. 'She wouldn't even hear Gabriel's horn! And when you think what I said when you went off yesterday – I said I hoped the old so-and-so would die of spite when he heard the news! How awful! I never thought he'd go and do it!'

I was still watching Lije, and I still didn't know what to think. 'Just imagine!' I said, staring at him, 'it could have happened just about the time we were walking past down the street—'

'Did we walk down the street?' he says. 'The head I've got on me this morning, I'm damned if I know how I did get home. Last thing I remember was that bloke with the long hair trying to swop me his harp for my double-B. What happened after that?'

But I didn't tell him, I just changed the subject. If he didn't know, I reckoned I'd best let well alone. And if he did know, all the more reason why I should keep my mouth shut. And if any of the folks who live near the Black Horse heard any funny noises in the night, all I can say is, they're keeping pretty quiet about it, too.

After all, everybody seems satisfied. We've got the trophy, we're getting our clubroom back next year because Mrs Langley doesn't much like having the place bunged up with sale junk, and nobody can fetch old Eb back, even supposing they wanted to. His missus looked ten years younger at the funeral. She had a nice new black costume, and a hearing-aid, and a smart hat on her new perm. They say Ben Barclay's beginning to cast an eye in her direction. Yes, on the whole I reckon things have worked out pretty well.

The Man Who Met Himself

If I hadn't known Frank Willard for four years without ever really knowing the first thing about him, I might not have felt so deeply involved. I'd played in the same cricket club for two seasons, and lifted my hat to him and his wife after church almost every Sunday morning since I'd come into the district; and yet when they fetched me to the police station that evening, it was as though I saw him for the first time.

He was sitting on an upright chair, with his hands slack between his knees, staring straight ahead of him with blank blue eyes in a stunned face, as though memory and mind had left him altogether.

When I walked into his line of vision he looked through me. His well-polished black shoes and rather worn grey suit were as neat as ever, but the man inside them had stopped functioning. The doctor said he was in a state of shock. Queer the way the human mind works. Nothing whatever had happened to him physically, nothing new had come to his knowledge; the thing that shocked him had been there within his consciousness for over a year; the only new development was that it had just been taken from behind his eyes and set, as it were, in front of them.

Exactly half an hour earlier, the police had arrested him for falsifying the books of his firm on a dozen separate occasions, and misappropriating to his own use something like five hundred pounds.

I had to touch him before he realized I was there. I sat down in front of him, and took his hands, and my grip seemed to penetrate his consciousness.

But when I said, 'Hullo, Frank, what's been happening to you?' he only stared at me helplessly, and said, 'I don't know,' like a child who'd had a fright.

He'd been like that from the first moment, they said. He'd listened to the caution and the charge, and then simply let go of everything. It was too much for him now that it was out in full view. He couldn't grasp it.

All he'd said to the charge was, 'Yes.' And some minutes later, as though he wanted to explain, 'She was used to nice things. She didn't understand about money.'

It wasn't much, but it was enough.

He'd been slightly careless, it seemed, over the last transaction, and the amount was bigger, too. Almost all of it was still in the house; he showed them where, moving like a sleepwalker.

So far as he had any mind left he did his best to co-operate. I could understand that. Thirty-two years old, hard-working, a mirror of unassuming respectability, kindly, scrupulous, patient, precise, his natural place was on the side of the law.

There wasn't much I could do for him at that stage, either as probation officer or as friend. His police-court appearance had to be deferred for three weeks or more, because he wasn't fit to be put in the dock.

For two or three days he continued half dead, and then the numbness wore off and he was infinitely worse, alternating between collapse and hysteria. He spent a week under sedatives, and slowly emerged into a sort of calm, a sort of articulate life.

As soon as he was fit to talk to a solicitor I went to see his wife, to urge her to get him into the hands of a good man as quickly as possible.

I'd never really noticed her before, or I should have understood. She received me in the sitting room of their small, respectable house, in a dress which wouldn't have been out of place at an embassy cocktail party, and wearing a sapphire pendant on a platinum chain. Twenty-eight, very pretty, very chic, with a hard, bright finish. Gold hair and a very short, full, hungry mouth.

She was very voluble indeed on the subject of her husband. It had been a terrible shock to her, and she couldn't forgive it. He'd brought disgrace on her, drawn down a barrage of gossip and calumny upon her innocent person. For innocent she certainly felt herself to be, and deeply injured. It was no part of her duty to associate herself with a criminal, and she didn't intend to.

He could get legal aid, couldn't he? She had her own position to think of. If she left the public in any doubt of where she stood she would be doing herself an injustice.

She meant to give evidence for the prosecution. Oh,

she knew she wasn't forced to by law, but she owed it to herself. Frank must take the consequences of his own actions, he wasn't going to shuffle them off on to her. As for briefing a lawyer, where did I think she was to get the money? She was left to provide for herself now; not that he ever had been very good at providing for a wife. And besides, there was the principle of the thing!

I was glad to get out of there. The room was as much of a revelation, in its way, as Mrs Willard herself. It was most expensively decorated, and full of possessions. There was a cabinet full of very good china, the carpet was Persian, and the piano a magnificent grand. Jade and cut glass ornamented the shelf over the fireplace. No need to ask where the money had gone. I remembered, too, now that I had the clue, a coat which I'd taken for granted as a mere imitation of the fur it seemed to be. With tastes like that, she obviously had no funds to spare for her husband's defence.

It was I who got him a solicitor. He had wanted to plead guilty, but Grant tried to persuade him to change his plea. He was still inclined to go where he was pushed, past caring where our efforts landed him, since his world had already fallen to pieces; but when he understood that his wife meant to take the stand and give evidence if the case had to be heard in full, he made up his mind irrevocably on a plea of guilty. He was entirely ignorant of the obligations and exemptions of law, and thought he was sparing her a terrible ordeal, and we let him think it. There wasn't much else we could do for him.

The police had opposed bail, purely because they were

afraid of what he might do to himself if they let him out of their care. I went to see him shortly before the assizes. He was still a very sick man, he was going to be that for a long time ahead, but in a stunned fashion he could talk coherently and reason sensibly by then. He talked about her; he always did.

'You know, I never really believed in my luck. Someone as beautiful and gay and bright as Eileen – what could she find in a man like me? She could have married whom she pleased, they were round her thick as bees, fellows with plenty of self-confidence, fellows with good prospects. And she took me and my twelve pounds a week, and no hope of getting any farther!

'I got to feeling how badly I was letting her down. She was meant to have beautiful things, they're her proper setting, and she loves them so.

'Oh, you mustn't think she complained! She admired them just like a child, wondering why she couldn't have them, when she wanted them so much. She didn't realize how costly nice things are. Money was something she didn't understand. She just fell in love with things she saw. I couldn't bear it. It was like letting a child starve in front of your eyes.'

Through his labouring voice I could hear hers, that clear, constant, injured voice lamenting that other wives should have things which were out of her reach, reminding him eternally, in oblique ways, that she might have married so-and-so and been well off, that she'd condescended to his hopeless, helpless love, and he owed it to her to maintain her properly. I heard the endless, inescapable implication of his miserable betrayal of her, and her forsaken condition, until everything, even his honour, which meant more to him than to most men nowadays, became expendable in the cause of her happiness.

What he had done was horrible to him, but in the same circumstances he would have done it again. In his own eyes he was damned in any case, and he embraced his damnation if it had given her a few gleams of pleasure.

'I asked her not to come and see me here,' he said. 'I couldn't bear that. Not even to write, until the trial's over and everything's settled.'

I thanked God for that, at any rate, since it saved him from wondering and grieving when she didn't come; for, of course, she wouldn't have dreamt of coming near him.

Always, before I left him, he asked me breathlessly, as though the words burst out of his heart and tore their way to his throat without any will of his, 'Have you seen her? How's she looking?'

I told him she was bearing up admirably. What else could I have done? I couldn't tell him she'd already persuaded the landlord to transfer the tenancy of the house to her, and had been seen out with him in the town on several evenings lately; or that she was reputed to be about to take a part-time job in the box office of the most palatial cinema, whose manager had a somewhat mottled reputation where women were concerned, though to do him justice he never pestered any who were unwilling.

'The first time,' said Willard, thinking back laboriously over the year of his downfall, 'it was the fur coat that did it. I was afraid she might guess how I got the money, but she never did.'

She took good care not to, I thought but did not say.

'And then she was pining for a good piano. She plays well, you know; it was terrible for her, having to be content with a second-rate instrument. I had to get the money somehow. I *had* to get these things for her. You didn't know her – you can't understand.'

I understood too well, but the words that bled out of him were also something I could comprehend and pity.

'The last time—' his blue eyes, still opaque as *lapis lazuli* in a face petrified in bewildered suffering, stared through me— 'it was because of the Hall being sold, and all those beautiful things coming under the hammer. We had been there one Sunday, when the place was on show last summer, and she had never forgotten. There was a set of Meissen china, white and gold filigree, the prettiest you ever saw – she talked about it for months after. And a little inlaid ivory cabinet and a full-length Venetian mirror in a black glass frame. When she knew they were all to be sold she almost fell ill with longing for them. What could I do? I had to buy them for her. I meant it to be the last time – but you always do mean that.

'Mr Benson wrote to me – did you know? Such a kind letter, you wouldn't think I'd been robbing him for over a year. I can't write back. Not yet. I'd like to, but I can't do it. Will you give him my thanks, and say – how sorry—'

I always left when he began to cry. Not because the sight embarrassed me, I was long past that, but because about then he seemed to forget I was there, and to lapse into his dazed condition again. Pure exhaustion. I think; talking, thinking, remembering, even existing was physically tiring to him.

Because of his plea of guilty, and his complete submission, and because for once it needed no lawyer to urge that here was a broken man, he got eighteen months. The governor of the prison where he was sent had a long talk with me about him, and the medical officer, who regarded the term as one of sanctuary rather than penance, was furious about the sentence.

'What in the world do they think we can do with him in only eighteen months?' he wanted to know. 'From what I've seen so far, he'll spend the first six months more in hospital than out of it, and after that he'll need psychiatric treatment for a hell of a lot longer than the seven or eight months we shall have left. Just when he's within hopeful distance of normality again we shall have to turn him loose and, unless he is exceptionally lucky or tougher than I think he is, he'll end up in a mental hospital within a year after that.'

I felt much the same way about it, but we had to make the best of it. And he responded better than had been expected. He was a model prisoner, co-operative, gentle, anxious as ever to give the minimum trouble and the maximum satisfaction. Something he'd never noticed about himself, and didn't notice now, took over his life in prison and helped him to benefit by it: people easily grew fond of him.

His wife wrote him one letter, sharp and cold as ice, condemning his crime, dissociating herself from it, and

stating the measures she was taking for her own mainte-
nance now that he had failed her. It never reached him.

The governor sent it back to her with the request that
she would avoid using such a tone in the future, and confine
herself to innocuous subjects, if she wanted to help her
husband. He need not have troubled, for she had written
merely to break off relations, and had no intention of ever
writing again. So Willard was spared her whips and
scorpions, and he made good progress.

We all dreaded the time when he would have completed
his sentence and would be thrown back upon the problem
from which only prison was protecting him. I felt so
strongly about it that I even went to see his wife again,
prepared to beg for her sympathy and help if necessary. I
need not have troubled, either.

She overwhelmed me with her righteousness. She'd
inquired about divorce, and was amazed and disgusted to
be told that she had no grounds, that the imprisonment of
one partner didn't absolve the other from their marriage
vows. But at least she was absolutely determined that she
would never receive or live with him again. The tenancy
of the house was now hers, and if Frank came forcing himself
on her here she'd slam the door in his face, the dirty crook!

She was brazenly beautiful, indiscreetly jewelled,
expensively dressed, and looked somehow both more
splendid and more vulgar than when I'd last seen her. The
sitting room had new and elegant curtains, and in the china
cabinet there was a new tea service – new, that is, to me.
White and gold filigree, incredibly delicate and thin. I
recognized the Meissen from the Hall by its description. If

Frank hadn't managed to give it to her, someone else had. No doubt the ivory cabinet was somewhere about the house, too, I thought. She was a woman who knew how to get what she wanted.

As I was leaving, another visitor arrived, a large, prosperous-looking man climbing out of a large, prosperous-looking car, and swinging in through the gate as if he owned the place. He wasn't the landlord. Was he the cinema manager? I didn't know the fellow very well, but as far as my recollection went he was younger than this specimen.

The man gave me a very narrow and suspicious look from the doorstep as I went away, and I've no doubt as soon as the door was shut he wanted to know who I was, and what I was doing there. She was getting her personal affairs a little involved, was Eileen Willard. I was thankful I couldn't be classed as a competitor. This type I'd seen on race courses, and in certain pubs where somewhat hush-hush business was carried on over short drinks.

The problem of Frank remained.

No use allowing him to walk in all innocence into the kind of reception she would give him. No use leaving him in his fool's purgatory of hope any longer. The governor would have broken it to him, but I volunteered for the job because, almost without meaning to, I seemed to have drawn nearer to Willard than anyone else, and these responsibilities one can't escape.

We were left alone, and I told him exactly how it was. That it was over, that it was no use hoping to make her change her mind. I went further, since there was no help

for it. I told him she was no good, never had been, never
would be, and that he was well rid of her, though I had no
hope at all of convincing him of that.

I told him there was only one thing to do. And he must
do it: cut her clean out of his life, and start afresh without
her.

He didn't protest, he wasn't angry. When I finished, he
didn't say a word. Until I saw that dead, blank look of
shock in his eyes again I couldn't even be sure whether
he'd heard me, or understood what he heard. It was the
first disaster over again, only a thousand times worse.

As he'd known all along that he was a thief, and yet
been shattered when the fact was dragged into the daylight,
so he'd known all along that she was a bitch, and yet having
her unworthiness laid before him in so many words had
all the impact of a revelation.

He sat looking at me for a long moment in the silence
of despair, and then the numbness faded out of his face
before the absolute, awful conviction of his loneliness and
desolation. His hands began to grope in front of him in
panic, feeling for anything that still shared the darkened
world with him. I gripped and held them, and went on
talking to him, not about her now, about him, about his
future, about his ability to remake his life. He struggled
for a moment, and then he collapsed.

He still hadn't said a word or made a sound.

The MO gave him an injection, and he slept for twelve
hours. He was under drugs for several days. Gradually,
rather more readily than expected, he came back to what

was now normality for him – a dumb, patient, listless resignation, obliging but unconvincing. He'd lost a lot of flesh, and with it, surprisingly, years of his age. He had even become unexpectedly good-looking in a motionless, emaciated way. But grey streaks had appeared in his hair.

He was quite calm now, and he never talked about her. No one could tell what was going on in his mind, but certain queer traits in his behaviour seemed to worry the MO.

People often turn to spiritualism or occultism when bereaved, and I suppose no one was ever more bereaved than he; yet there was a nasty feeling of the abnormal about his new preoccupation with signs and portents, with superstitions we'd never heard of, and oracles appropriate rather to the play of children than to the desperation of men. I think he was still hoping for a sign from heaven that somehow Eileen would be given back to him.

He asked for library books on the occult, and talked with a kind of willing faith about visitations and dreams and their meanings, about sendings, ghosts of the living, and portents of death.

Only once did he mention his wife. He said he had met her in the yard during exercise. She was wearing her mink coat, and she came towards him as though he didn't exist. Just as she began to melt into his flesh she vanished.

But, that tendency apart, he was decidedly better than he had been since his trial and, in spite of all the MO's misgivings, unquestionably sane. He went about the daily routine with more will and quickening interest, still dully, but intelligently. I began to hope that he was at least entering on convalescence.

I'd planned to meet him myself when he was released, but a very awkward case blew up that morning, and I had to send a car to fetch him while I rushed off to the other end of the county. The driver had orders to bring him straight to my house, where I meant to keep him until I saw how he was shaping.

My housekeeper, who is a good soul, and considers my job to be very much her concern, had guaranteed to take care of him until I came home. But I was away all day, and when I got back at six o'clock in the evening she was waiting for me with a long face, and there was no Willard to be seen.

'He gave the driver the slip,' she told me. 'Asked him to stop while he bought some stamps, and then walked out of the post office by the other door.

'There was nothing for the poor man to do but come back and report. He couldn't possibly find him. I thought about ringing the police to look out for him, but after all, we can't force him to accept help, and he hasn't done anything wrong. Only it does make one rather anxious.'

I was more than anxious by that time, but there was nothing I could do about it. She had even gone down unobtrusively and walked past Mrs Willard's house, to make sure there was no one hanging about there, and no sign of any disturbance.

I told her everything was sure to be all right, and we were being silly, and sent her home; but I sat over the telephone all the evening, hesitating whether to notify the police or not.

It was impossible, of course, when it came to the point.

He was adult, sane and, as far as I knew, without either criminal or irresponsible intentions of any kind. I couldn't send out a hunt for him as though for an escaped lunatic.

Towards nine o'clock I took the car, and drove slowly through the town, keeping my eyes open, but there was no sign of him. All the same, I didn't go to bed; I couldn't have slept.

It was just after midnight when something came fumbling at the door, like a blind man feeling about its surface for a latch. A tiny, shuffling, hair-raising sound one wouldn't have heard at all in the day. I opened the door, scared for my life of what I was going to find; and there he was, groping stiffly with one hand, and dangling a gun from the other.

The light made stony, pale pebbles of his staring eyes, and his jaw hung open and rigid. I brought him in on my arm, and he stumbled up the steps and moved like an automaton across the room, wherever I led him. He let me put him into a chair, and lay there, still with that fixed, horrified face. I tried to get some brandy into him, but he choked on it, and it ran down his dangling chin.

Then I tried to take the gun from him, but he held on to it with sudden resolution, and said, 'No, don't touch it! Not you; only me!' And he began to weep, almost silently, without any sobs.

'What's happened?' I asked him, shaking him by the shoulders. 'Where have you been? What have you done?'

'I've killed her,' he said. The voice that came out of him was small, still dazed but quiet. 'I shot her. I'm sorry about your driver, but you see, I had to go and get the gun. And I didn't want you to be involved. I had to get away from you. I was going to kill her, and then myself. And I've done the one, but there's no need to do the other. I'm going to die, anyhow. I've had a sign.'

I wasn't interested in signs, only in facts. I shook him roughly, shouting at him to tell me exactly what had happened, and how he'd obtained the gun in the first place. He said it belonged to an old lag he'd made friends with in prison, who had revealed the fact that he possessed one. Willard had asked if he could borrow it when he went out, and the man had given him a note for his wife, so that she would let him have it. Then he'd gone to earth in a cinema until night, and on to Eileen's house under cover of darkness.

'The door wasn't locked,' he said in the same soft, hopeless voice. 'She was expecting somebody. Not me. One of *them*! The hall was in darkness, and the stairs, too, but upstairs her bedroom door was half open, her light was on. It cast a very faint light down the well of the stairs. I didn't need any light. I knew every knot in the floor, every worn place in the carpet.

'I began to climb the stairs; and when I was coming up to the midway landing I met myself coming down. I'm not mad! I looked up suddenly as I stepped on to the landing, and I was there – face to face with myself – coming down. I'm not mistaken! I know what I saw. I know this face, I know the clothes I'm wearing. And the gun! He – I – had the gun, too. So I knew I'd already done it, and she was dead. And I'm going to die, too. When you meet a sending of yourself, you know you're going to die.'

It made no sense, it couldn't have happened, and yet I was afraid. I bullied him, trying to get straight answers out of him.

'You turned back on the stairs? You didn't go on to her room?'

'What need was there?' he said, beginning to shake all over with horror and the reflection of my fear. *'He'd* already been.'

'But you didn't – did you? When you met him – yourself – you were frightened, you ran out of the house—'

'Yes, I ran out of the house.'

'You didn't go on? You remember that?'

'I don't know! No – I killed her! She's dead!'

'What time was it? Do you know? Did you come straight here to me when you ran away?'

I was only confusing and frightening him even more. The awful sobs came, shattering him, tearing out of him with such violence I was afraid he might die under my hands.

I imagined him feeling his way up the stairs in the half darkness, trembling with despair, and love, and hate, lightheaded with hunger, for he'd surely never thought to eat anything all day. How could he know what he was saying or doing? It would have to wait until he was rested, and fed, and calm, and by then we should know well enough that Eileen Willard was alive and venomous as ever, and all he'd suffered was a crazy hallucination.

I filled him up with sedative tablets, and got him into my own bed, which I certainly wouldn't need myself that night. After some time the tablets worked, and he passed out. He still had the gun clutched in his hand, determined that no print should ever connect me with it, and I hadn't cared to distress him further by forcing it away from him. Now that he was fast asleep at last I was afraid to try to break the death grip he had on it, but even more afraid to leave it where it was.

I got it away from him gradually, gently working his fingers loose, one by one. And just as I was going downstairs to examine it somewhere well away from him, the telephone rang.

It was the police. They wanted to know if Frank Willard was safely with me, where they understood he was supposed to be. I said he was, and asleep in bed. My heart was pumping so, I thought the Inspector couldn't help hearing, but my voice sounded all right, and I was encouraged to ask, 'Why? What's it all about?' Only checking up, I thought. Knowing the state he's been in.

'Just wanted to make sure he was safe in your hands,' said the Inspector. 'Lucky for him! Constable on the beat by his wife's place spotted the side door was ajar about half an hour ago, couldn't rouse anybody with the knocker, so he went in. Found the woman dead in her bedroom – murdered. Glad your man's well out of it. What time did he turn up?'

How fast can you sort out all the pitfalls, and present an impregnable lie, without even knowing you're going to do it? I did it – so far as the circumstances could be reckoned up on the known facts – in half a second flat.

They would easily find out he'd given us the slip this

morning. They might find out about the gun, but that could be disposed of, he could have repented and thrown it in the river. Then, my housekeeper knew he was still missing when she went home at something after six. Had he been seen by anyone during the last hour or so before he came to me? There was no way of knowing, I could only make a guess.

How much time could I give back to him without risking a host of witnesses against us? What time had she been killed? Late? Lovers steal in by unlocked side doors only after dark, and after the crowds have gone home from the cinemas.

'About ten o'clock,' I said. 'Not in very good condition. He's up against a tremendous readjustment, and it's all rather too much for him. I've given him a sedative, and he's dead to the world. Anything I can do?'

'This won't exactly help the poor devil,' said the Inspector sympathetically.

'You're right, it won't. Maybe I can keep him from hearing about it for a day or two. Try not to ring me here, in case he's around. Any idea who did it?'

'No statement yet,' he said, and rang off.

When I put down the telephone I was shaking like a leaf. The gun had gone clean out of my mind, and lay forgotten in the desk drawer all night. I felt sick. I couldn't believe it was myself I'd heard, lying, calculating, obstructing the police, aiding and abetting a possible murderer. I couldn't grasp it. I felt caught like a fly in a web. So that's how these things begin, as smoothly as that, out of pity and rage, out of a sense of an injustice which was certainly not the fault of the law. From whom had Frank Willard received solid help and sympathy, if not from the police and the prison authorities? And yet what I'd done I couldn't for my life have helped doing.

She was dead. She had been murdered.

No use hoping now for a nice, bright, normal morning, the kind that makes midnight fancies contemptible, a bright morning and Eileen Willard passing by, alive and well on the arm of one of her new men. One point in his story was confirmed already; now what, for God's sake, was I to do for him, and for my miserable self? I'd begun something that had to be finished, but to save my life I didn't know how.

I couldn't rest. I prowled about the house until the first light, and then I left Willard still sleeping heavily, and went down into the town. I had to find out more about times and details, in order to know what to say when the inevitable further questions began. Until I knew more I could neither come out with the truth nor go on lying.

The Inspector didn't seem surprised to see me. I suppose some uneasiness on my part was only too natural, since I had the husband in my care.

'What are you worrying about,' he said, with a smile that disquieted me horribly, 'if your protégé was tucked up in bed soon after ten?'

'All very well for you,' I said. 'I have to break the news to him sooner or later, and I know how precariously balanced he is. I want to be able to answer all his questions, and get the miserable business over. How do you suppose he's going to react if a couple of uniformed policemen turn up suddenly to interview him, after all he's been through?'

'That won't be necessary,' he said placidly. 'We won't even ask him to identify the body; she has a brother who can do that.'

With cold sweat crawling down my back I fished doggedly on. 'Thank goodness for that. I'd hate him to have to view the wreckage. She can't be so pretty now – like that, in her blood—'

'Who said anything about blood?' he asked mildly, hoisting an eyebrow. 'But you're right about her not being pretty. Strangled women aren't.'

'Strangled?' I felt my knees give under me, and leaned hard on the edge of his desk to keep myself upright.

'There was a small amount of blood smeared around,' he conceded thoughtfully, 'but it wasn't hers. She put up quite a struggle. The man who did it left most of the skin of his wrists and forearms under her fingernails. An all too usual end for a woman of her type. She's been running at least three men on strings since her husband went to gaol; she was bound to get herself knocked off sooner or later.'

I couldn't speak for a moment, I felt so lightheaded and sick with relief. I'd had Frank Willard's lean wrists in my hands only a few hours ago, while I coaxed the gun out of his fingers; I knew he hadn't a scratch on him. The police didn't want him, weren't even interested in him.

Who was it he'd seen creeping down the stairs, then? A real man, after all; not a hallucination? Had he been right in feeling that she was already dead? Had he run headlong into her murderer? Someone who looked like enough to himself to drive him out of the house in superstitious terror? If so, he might be able to help the police, and the truth would have to come out. Well, I was the only one who'd lied about it, not he; no one could hold that against him.

With difficulty I asked my question casually, 'What time was she killed?'

'Not twenty minutes before the constable found her, most probably. Certainly not before one o'clock.'

She'd been alive, then, when Frank entered the house, alone and waiting in her room for whichever of her admirers was due that night. And, but for the grace of God and the apparition on the stairs, Frank would surely have walked in upon her and shot her dead, and himself after her.

'As late as that? Then the fellow who did it couldn't possibly have got far,' I said, hardly knowing what I was talking about, I was so demoralized with relief.

'He didn't,' said the Inspector simply, and jerked his head towards the door behind him. 'Between you and me, he's in there now, safe and sound, and I hope by this time he's talking. Not that it'll make much difference whether he does or not, his hands and wrists are just about clawed to pieces. They won't have much trouble matching up the debris from under her nails with his injuries. Fellow by the name of Clandon, a bookie. Not the sort of man I'd try double-crossing, if I were a woman, but she was no judge of men.

'An inquisitive neighbour saw his car drive away. We put out a call for it less than an hour after we found her.

And picked him up at Shelworth, heading south.' He added kindly, 'You know, you don't look too well, George. Missed your sleep over that lame dog of yours? I'd go home and snatch a few hours rest if I were you.'

I'll never know how much he knew. Maybe nothing. Maybe he only had a feeling that I'd lied to him. He'd had plenty of practice in detecting lies, and I hadn't had much in telling them. But even if he knew more, even if Willard had left traces of his presence in the house, they weren't interested. They had the man they wanted.

Maybe I wasn't looking well, but I felt wonderful, I felt reprieved. For myself and for Willard, too.

I went home and sat by his bed, and told him every word that had passed, except for my lie and the comments on Eileen. He thawed into sensibility and intelligence as I talked; in those few minutes he came a long way back from wherever it was he'd been heading – disintegration, mental collapse, the abdication of humanity.

He kept saying, 'I didn't kill her! I didn't kill her!' in a voice of stupefied delight. And at the end he said, but quite gently now, 'Then if it wasn't a sending I met on the stairs – what was it?'

'An image of grace,' I said, 'to turn you back in your tracks, and head you in the direction of life.'

And he looked back at me without a smile, but with the grave wonder of somebody waking from sleep, and said, 'Yes. Yes, that's what it must have been.'

But it was only three or four weeks later, when the inquest and the police-court hearing were already over, that we found out the exact mechanics of mercy. Willard was her heir, of course, since she'd never made a will, and when he had to go to the house and look over all the stuff there to see what he wanted to keep and what was to be sold, he asked me to go with him. It wasn't fear or superstition – he was clear of both by then – it was a natural human reluctance to go alone into a place that had so many painful memories for him.

It was evening when we went in, and heavily overcast, and the hall was in half darkness because the bulb had blown. I went up the stairs first, and when I stepped on to the midway landing I came face to face with myself, all in an instant, as the faint light from the first-floor corridor window fell upon me after the comparative darkness below.

Even at that hour of day the effect was devastating. I recoiled upon Willard as he followed me up. And then I saw him spring out of the obscurity at my shoulder, and everything crystallized into mere glass and the trickery of the restricted light.

I ought to have known. She was a woman who knew how to get what she wanted. Everything she wanted. Not only the Meissen china and the ivory cabinet, but also the full-length Venetian mirror, framed in black glass, that was too big to fit happily into any of her rooms, and had to be set up here on the dark wall at the turn of the stairs, where there'd never been a mirror before.

That's one thing for which I shall be grateful to Clandon as long as he lives, in gaol or out. It turned out he was the one who gave it to her.

The Linnet in the Garden

In the courtyard of the Golden Bear, Nanynka was singing as she pegged out the kitchen cloths to dry. The pure, soft notes of her voice rounded to fill the whole well of the yard between the high, stone-faced walls and the single, sickly plane tree in the square of grass quivered with the reduplication of sound.

It was the only place where Nanynka found it safe to sing. If she had ventured to lift up her voice in the corridors of the house, or on the staircase, Madame Groh would have been out of the bureau in an instant, stretching out her long neck and hissing like an angry swan. Once she had stretched out her thick, mannish hand, too, and boxed Nanynka's ears for her audacity. But here in the dingy yard she could let the pent-up notes flow out of her lips and ring against the stone, eddying upward magically large and strange; and no one who mattered would hear. Only the penurious and ineffective had rooms overlooking this narrow well. The old gentleman on the first floor was stone-deaf into the bargain. The shabby but refined lady on the

101

second floor would close her window and draw the curtain to mark her disapproval of kitchenmaids who sang at their work, but she was too well aware of her low standing with Madame Groh, and the precarious hold she had upon her cheap lodging, to make any complaint. And the young gentleman who had the wretched little back room on the third floor – ah, he was different! He would prick up his ears at the first rising notes, and run to flatten against the windowpane his rather long, rather inquisitive, incorrigibly optimistic nose, craning close to try and catch a glimpse of the singer, and remaining there still and quiet until she had gone back reluctantly into the dark cave of the kitchen. For he was the one person about the Golden Bear who recognized Nanynka's singing as music, and took pleasure in listening to it.

Nanynka was thinking about him as she stretched up her slender young arms in their muslin sleeves, and pushed down the pegs over the folds of the great linen tablecloth. Nowadays she thought about him a great deal. His name was Hugo Meyer, and he was a student at the instrumental school attached to the Opera, and sometimes he was even allowed to play in the orchestra when its numbers had to be augmented for some great occasion. He was very young, only about nineteen – Nanynka, at seventeen, did not consider herself very young any more, but that was different: she was a girl, and alone in the world, had had to fend for herself for more than a year now. But Herr Meyer was a young man of education, and had been looked after tenderly by a mother, and perhaps sisters, whom he had left behind somewhere in the country when he came to make his way in the city. He was quite helpless about such matters as landladies, and money, and the laundering and mending of linen.

The first thing she had ever noticed about him had been the cobbled rent disfiguring the skirt of his good grey coat, and it had vexed her so much, and stirred in her so illogical a sense of pity and tenderness, that she had braved Madame Groh's wrath in order to creep up the back stairs to his room one day when he was away at a rehearsal in his everyday blue, and abstract the coat from his meagre wardrobe. She had taken it to her pallet on the attic landing, and there strained her eyes far into the twilight in unpicking his scamped work, drawing threads from the turned-up part of the hem and making a beautiful, flat almost invisible darn which even his mother, she thought proudly, could not have bettered. The young gentleman might not even notice, but some day the mother would notice and wonder.

But he had noticed. On Sunday, when he had put on the coat to go to church, she had seen him come down the stairs, frowning down every few steps at the transfigured darn, and searching his mind for an explanation. And that was the first time he had ever spoken to her. Suddenly at the foot of the stairs he had raised his head, and seen her shrinking back at once towards her stony retirement in the kitchen, her hands hidden under her coarse apron as though the sight of them might betray their part in the mystery which engrossed him; and he had halted, and smiled, and turned back on an audacious impulse, as surprising to him as it was to her, to say directly:

'You are the one who sings in the garden!'

She knew by his startled eyes and sudden fiery blush that he was by no means in the habit of pursuing the maids in the inn, and was at a loss how to continue, or indeed how to conclude, the encounter he had thus initiated. And she herself was seized by such a violent access of shyness that she could only stammer: 'I hope, sir – I hope it don't offend you. I won't do it if it offends you!' – groping behind her for the knob of the door, and averting her eyes in confusion from his face.

'Oh, *no!*' he said quickly and eagerly. 'I beg you, don't deprive me—' But she had darted with lowered head through the doorway, and left him standing there, staring at the closed door.

Now why or how he should have proceeded with such unmasculine logic from her singing to her needlework she could not guess; but the next time he happened to encounter her crossing the flagged passage from the scullery with a pile of dishes, he had taken up the conversation from a new angle.

'Someone has done me a secret kindness . . . Look! Do you know who it could be?' And he spread out the mended skirt of his coat for a moment under her eyes.

'I can't tell, sir,' she said, looking round in a panic in case the kitchen door should be open and the cook listening. 'Indeed, sir, I can't. I work down here in the kitchen. You should ask the chambermaid.'

He made a derisive face at this. 'She is old and sour, and knows I have no money for extra services. No, this is the work of young, keen eyes and elegant small fingers, don't you think? Perhaps I should express my thanks to

Madame, and ask her to convey them to my benefactress?'

'Oh, no, don't do that!' begged Nanynka, in self-betraying dismay, and caught herself back from further protest into indignation. 'If you please, sir, you are hindering me in my work and I shall be scolded on your account!'

All his boldness, which was considerable and unexpected in one usually so diffident, had left him at this, and he had cast down his eyes and begged her pardon like an abused child, and made off very meekly; yet the swing of his shoulders as he went had no very subdued look about it.

That was the episode which had driven her to her landing bed, and the square of cracked mirror she kept on the ledge of the wall there. She had looked into it earnestly, for the first time in her life seeking something more than cleanness and neatness in her own appearance. The pale, young, wondering face had looked back at her almost indulgently, with eyes coloured like periwinkles in spring, and the mouth had smiled very faintly, the lips curling close, like two rose-petals folded together. Under the limp muslin cap she had seen her own curls struggling loose, live coils of sunlight. She was charmed by possibilities which had never before occurred to her. She put away the mirror, still smiling, and reached a hand under her mattress to touch the flat wooden box where her treasure lay.

There had never been anyone in her life before to whom she could even have considered showing that secret and wonderful and fragile thing. Now she foresaw, distantly and half reluctantly, a day when she might take it out of its hiding place and lay it in Hugo Meyer's hands. She was not yet sure; but she had never so much as wondered until now.

'Green woods of homeland, my joy and my pleasure . . .' sang Nanynka, for once not thinking of her lost homeland at all. She watched the foreshortened lozenge of the third-floor window, and waited for the bright, beech-brown crest to appear, and the wide forehead, and the hopeful, questing nose, and the gay, impudent, bashful eyes peering down for a glimpse of her. He wore his hair short, in the new fashion, and it curled so lavishly on his neck and temples that sometimes she caught herself thinking how well it would have looked drawn back into a ribbon, like that powdered hair she remembered so well from another garden, a garden so different from this stone-walled pit behind the Salzburgergasse. But this time the eager head did not appear. It was her ears, not her eyes, which caught the evidence of his presence.

The note of a flute took up the air from her lips, whispered in unison with her for two lines of the song and then took flight in an airy *obbligato* all round her voice, dancing as rapidly and tenderly as the light that played through the leaves of the plane tree. It was as though he had taken her hand. No, it moved her far more and confounded her far less than such a gesture would have done. She was filled with a sweet and violent excitement, a passion of gratitude, to think that he could take up with such familiar kindness an air from her distant countryside. For he was not merely following her, he anticipated the cadences of the tune, embroidering it with confident arabesques. He was playing something he knew. She thought of the talisman in the box under her mattress, and now she was sure. Some day he would be made the confidant in the central secret of her life, and some day he would hear another song.

She had pegged out the last napkin from the bottom of the basket, and she dared not linger. She had hoped that he would appear at the window for a moment when the song ended, but he did not, and she had still to trim all the lamps, and clean the fish, and make dough for dumplings. She picked up the great basket, and crossed the cobbled yard to the arched door of the entrance, and the flagged passage which led to the kitchen.

There was a wild flurry of footsteps rushing down the staircase, and the swirl of coat-skirts at the foot. Hugo appeared panting in the dark passage, the flute still in his hand. His eyes were wide and bright, his lips parted as much with exultation, she thought, as breathlessness. He had quite gone out of his mind. He cried aloud, without a suspicion of caution:

'Miss Nanynka, you must come to my room. There is someone there who would like to speak with you.' And he took the basket out of her hands very firmly, and put it down against the wall, and stood back to let her go before him, in the most absolute confidence that she would obey at once. When she hung back, staring at him in consternation, he put out his hand and took hold of her wrist, and urged her with great excitement towards the stairs, and she was certain that he did not fully realize what he had done.

'But I must not – I have my work to do, I must not be seen above stairs. What can anyone want with me? Herr Meyer, I beg you – I shall get into trouble—'

'The work must wait,' he said, the words tumbling out of him helter-skelter like the notes out of his flute. 'You need not mind them, we shall see to that. They do not matter now. You will see! Only come, please come quickly!'

It was all quite mad, and of course would turn out badly, but she was dazed into obedience by his conviction, and she went with him wherever he chose to drag her, her thin little wrist gripped hard in his excited fingers. He towed her headlong up the three flights of stairs, and into his narrow and shabby little room. There was someone standing with his back to the window, so sharply outlined against the light that he was nothing but an outline: short, broad, hunched, with a head sunk into his shoulders, and a cloud of fine, long, straight grey hair that stirred with every motion of that head.

'The lady is here,' said Hugo, his hand suddenly trembling upon her wrist and his voice so deferential that she stared again, in quickening fright, at this being who could inspire such awe in him. 'This, sir, is Nanynka.'

The figure in the window moved a little nearer, peering intently at the girl; and gradually through the mists of her fright and bewilderment she saw him more clearly. An old man, in a long, old-fashioned, snuff-stained coat, his hands knit behind his back, his foot tapping testily, the features of his face squat, intelligent and irascible, his eyes, under down-drawn brows, large, lonely and distantly, resignedly kind. He gazed at her for a long time, and did not say a word.

In her uncertainty and apprehension she was dimly aware of Hugo's eager voice pouring into her ears explanations and encouragement of which she did not distinguish a single word. But the old man's foot tapped with increasing irritation, and this sound she heard very clearly.

'Sing, indeed!' said the stranger, in a deep, abrupt, impatient voice which might well have belonged to a much younger man. 'You have not left the girl breath enough to speak, much less sing! Did I bid you drag her up the stairs at a run? Sit down now and hold your tongue! She can very well speak up for herself, if you would but let her.'

Hugo subsided meekly upon his bed, and became instantly silent; but when she turned to cast one glance of dismayed sympathy in his direction, she observed by the bright, expectant eyes and the confident smile that he was not at all abashed. He was watching the terrifying old man with eagerness, and appeared to be encouraged rather than mortified by his own summary dismissal into the background.

'And do you sit down, too, child,' said the old man, and watched her unsmilingly as she seated herself very uneasily upon the extreme edge of a chair. 'What is your name?'

'Anna Fiala, sir,' she said in a whisper. 'They call me Nanynka.'

'Speak up! Are you afraid of me? I do not bite. The worst I ever do is to rap the knuckles of young idiots who play sour notes.' She heard Hugo chuckle, and marvelled that he should dare. 'But none of your notes were sour, child, and you are entirely safe with me. Do you know who I am?'

She was not aware that she had heard Hugo utter a name or suggest an identity, but now she found that she had both clear in her mind. Wide-eyed, she whispered: 'Yes, sir! You are the Herr Direktor Sommerhof, who teaches Herr Meyer the flute.' To her this was certainly the essential, as well as the only familiar part of his many functions and she wondered in some mortification why the old man laughed.

'I have that honour. Do you think he does me any credit?'

With more confidence she said: 'When he played "Green Woods" it sounded very pretty. I do not know about music . . . But I like to hear him play.'

'That is only fair, for he likes to hear you sing. That is why he brought me here. He promised me a prodigy. I do not find that his ardour was *all* partiality. Do you know, Anna, that you have a very beautiful voice? Who taught you to sing?'

'No one taught me, sir,' she said, astonished. 'I have always sung – I like to sing.'

'You do not belong here in Vienna? You have no parents or relatives here?'

'No, sir, there is no one now. I lived with an aunt in Döbling, but she died last year and now I look after myself.'

'And your home? You are country-bred, are you not?'
And as she flushed and bit a trembling lip at the suggestion
that her rustic origin betrayed itself so readily, he said quite
gently: 'It shows in the complexion, in the clearness of the
eye and the candour of the glance – not in any want of
grace. You should be glad of it.'

'My father had a mill in a village in the Eagle
Mountains. He was a widower, and had no son to help
him, and it did not prosper. He died when I was seven
years old, and the mill was sold, and I stayed for a time
with my other aunt in Prague, and then I went to Döbling.'

He nodded his head weightily several times, and his
long grey hair stood up on his head like thistledown. Then
he asked abruptly: 'Will you sing for me again? Whatever
you please.'

She heard Hugo draw a deep breath of delight, but she
herself felt for a moment nothing but fright and outrage
and a longing to escape. 'What shall I sing? I know nothing
but our country songs. I have no training, I do not know
music—'

The two pairs of eyes dwelt upon her intently, the old
man's sceptical, patient, considering, the boy's shining
with hope and anxiety and unguarded affection. That look
of Hugo's dazzled and yet calmed her. She saw his fingers
gripping the flute hard, and his lips quivering with the
longing to speak, and an extraordinary protective
tenderness flooded through her heart and left her washed
clean of fear. She could not fail Hugo, who had believed in
her and boasted of her. Everything she had was not too
much to lay in Hugo's lap. She felt the other song, the

111

secret song, bursting like a flower out of its hiding place. She closed her eyes, and let it well up out of her lips as a spring purls out of the earth. Until that moment only herself and its maker had ever heard it:

> The linnet in the garden sings,
> So small, so sweet a pipe she raises,
> Shy as the fluttering of her wings
> And tiny as the listening daisies.
>
> If I should follow, she would fly,
> But if I woo her, will she linger,
> And stoop from yonder autumn sky
> To be the linnet on my finger?

Its brevity, which had once displeased her, seemed now perfection. A pearl is even smaller. When she had shut her lips upon the last limpid note of the tiny, pure, playful melody, she sat for a moment with her eyes still closed, listening to the silence, not knowing if it meant pleasure or perplexity. When she opened her eyes she found she could not see for tears; and when these had slowly cleared, neither the young man nor the old had moved or spoken. Their two faces looked absurdly alike, wide-eyed, still, passionately attentive.

It was a full minute before the Herr Direktor asked in a low grave voice: 'Where did you learn that song?'

'You don't know it,' she said, instinctively jealous for her possession, the only thing she had in the world of her very own. 'You can't know it! It is mine!'

'No, I have never heard it in my life. That is what is marvellous about it. That is why I asked where you learned it. Yours, you say . . . very well, but where did you get it? Can one possess this song? And how . . . how? How is it possible?'

'Did it please you?' she ventured, frightened by an intensity she could not understand.

'It pleased me. Both the song and the singer. I would not have believed that such perfection of simplicity was possible except at the end of many subtleties, but you have it, it seems, by nature, or by some communication which I confess I do not understand.'

Hugo, quivering with excitement upon his bed, broke in eagerly: 'Did I not tell you, sir, that she could sing Barbarina after no more than a month's study? And who knows—'

'I told you to stop chattering, jackdaw,' said Herr Sommerhof tartly; but the hand he clapped upon Hugo's shoulder lit with the casual brusqueness of affection. It was that gesture, so nearly a caress, that won Nanynka. An old man who could be so moved by her song, and who stood in such a paternal relationship to Hugo, no matter how he chose to hide his partiality behind growls and grumbles, was a man to be trusted.

She jumped up from her chair, pale with resolution. 'If you will wait a moment, sir, I will bring the song to you. I have it. It was given to me by the man who made it. If you would like to see it, I will show it to you.'

Once out of the room, she flew up the stairs to her attic

113

bed and groped under the mattress for the wooden box. She brought it back to them gravely, held before her in both hands, as though she carried something holy; and before their eyes she took from it a half-sheet of manuscript paper with a roughly torn edge. Both the notation and the words that danced beneath were mysteries and magical to her. She put it into the old man's hand, and watched him carry it to the window, for the ink had faded to a purplish-brown in the ten years since it had been written, and the hand was so deft and tiny that for all its clarity it needed good eyes to decipher it.

He was silent a long while, staring at it, his back turned upon the boy and girl who instinctively drew close together as they waited for him to speak. There was something here which had outgrown the mere issue of Nanynka's voice, and the future uses to which that radiant little instrument might be put. They felt the strangeness of the moment, and watched the slip of paper warily, waiting for a miracle; and in a moment they perceived how reverently the old man held it and how far beyond their understanding was his stillness and silence.

He turned at last, and lifted his eyes from the skipping notes to Nanynka's face. 'Do you not know, child, what you have here? Did you not realize that it might have a value? Surely when you read what is written here—'

Slow crimson welled out of the folded muslin collar of her dress, and mounted her fair face from chin to brow. She lowered her eyes, and confessed in a whisper: 'Sir, I cannot read.'

'Ah! I see! Then that, too, must be remedied. But, then,

did you never show this to anyone else? In . . . how many years? – it cannot be less than six and I think it must be somewhat more!'

'It is ten years since he gave it to me.'

'And you never showed it to anyone?'

'No,' she said almost inaudibly. 'Never to anyone.'

'But if you cannot read, how did you learn the words?'

'From him,' she said, and the memory caused her to smile so suddenly and brilliantly that the little room seemed to shine.

'Did you know who he was?'

'No.' She lifted her head, and looked at him, still smiling, for it seemed to her that he would understand. 'I did not want to know.'

'Anna, my child, there is more to this than you know. Will you not sit down here, and tell us how this thing happened to you? And then, if you will, I will tell you what it is that you have kept for ten years. Do not be afraid – you will not suffer any loss!'

She sat down obediently, and folded her childish hands in her lap and told them; and now that she had made up her mind, the words came freely.

'It was when I was seven years old, in the autumn after my father died. I told you they sent me to live with my aunt in Prague, but she had a big family of her own and she did not want me there, and was for ever writing to my other aunt in Döbling to see if she would not take me. I was feeling very strange, and missing my father a great deal. There was a big house near to us, with a beautiful garden like a little park and often I used to slip in there to play by myself. The gatekeeper let me in, but he told me not to go too near the house because the lady had important company staying there, and I must not trouble them. But one day I did go near. I kept in the trees, so that no one should see me, and I saw the house. It was not so big as I had expected, but very pretty, a pink house, with a long room with many windows looking out on the garden, and a laburnum tree just in front of it and a railed terrace. After that I often used to go as near as I dared, because there was almost always music in this garden room. Sometimes there would be the lady singing – she sang like an angel. She was very pretty, with curling dark hair, and she laughed a great deal, and wore soft silk turbans in the new fashion, as it was then, and slender dresses with high waists and little flat shoes. And often there were instruments: harpischord, and flute, and harp. I loved to listen, and especially to the lady. I used to notice everything I heard, and try to copy it, and so it happened that I was often singing to myself when there was no one else in the garden.

'And one day I thought there was no one to hear me, and I sang aloud one of the airs I had heard the lady singing. I had no words for it, only the tune. And as I was singing, one of the windows of the garden room opened and a little gentleman stepped out, and looked straight at me, and smiled at me. I was frightened, because I knew I ought not to be there. But when he smiled at me, I stopped being afraid.

'He was quite small, and slender, not nearly so tall as

Herr Meyer. He had a blue coat with a high collar, and a white stock, and his hair was powdered and tied back in a black ribbon. I do not know how old he was, but it seemed to me then that he was just the same age as I was and it was quite impossible to be afraid of him. Besides, he was so happy. He had a pen in his hand, and a smudge of ink on his cheek and his face was like sunshine.

'I could not run away, there was no time, he came so suddenly. And then I did not want to run away. He said – I remember almost every word he spoke to me – he said: "I thought I heard a linnet singing in the garden. Was it really you?" And when I said it was, he asked me if I would not come in and sing to him again, and he took me with him into the garden room, and it was all white and gold inside, with two harpsichords. He played to me, and I sang to him, and then he sang, too, the same song I had been singing when he surprised me, in a small, high voice like a woman's. I did not understand the words; he said they were in Italian and they began, *"Farewell, my lovely flame . . ."* I had never seen anyone like him, I did not think there could be any others. And afterwards, I did not want to know if he was like other people, after all, I only wanted him to remain marvellous to me.

'Then he said I should have a song all to myself, and he sat down at the harpsichord, and he began to shine and to smile as brightly as if the music that sprang up in him had been light. And in a little while he smudged the other cheek with his finger, and threw down the pen and began to play. He played that song I have sung for you, that song you hold in your hand. He sang the words to me, and played and sang over and over again until I could join in with him. That was how I learned it. And when you learn something in that way, something which belongs only to you, you never forget it.

'I was disappointed at first that it was so short, for I had begun to fancy that I could learn something very long and hard. And I frowned, and asked if that was all. He said, "Yes." I said, "It's a very *little* song." And he said, "It's a very little linnet. But you will find that it is quite big enough. When a song has said all it has to say, then it is just the right length." When I had it perfectly by heart I sang it through for him, the best I could, while he played for me, and he said I sang it very well, and that some day I should sing harder things than this for him and sing them just as well. And he wrote on the paper, and gave it to me, and said it was mine.

'I was afraid to stay too long, in case my aunt should send to look for me. And I remember that when I said goodbye to him, he kissed my hand. I liked that. And when I looked back from the edge of the trees, he waved his hand to me.

'I cannot tell you how much I loved him.

'That was all. That day my aunt received her letter from Döbling, and packed me off the very next morning by the coach. I never saw the garden again, or the lady, or the little gentleman. But I kept the song always, and never told anyone. There was never anyone who would have understood, or cared. It was so much mine, I could not share it with someone who would have thought it trivial or silly. And until – until Herr Meyer – he did not mind when I sang, he said that he liked it – and then, today – the flute—'

She lowered her eyes, but not so quickly that she did not observe Hugo's surging blush of pleasure and the dazzling boyish smile, at once abashed and complacent.

'Ah, yes, our friend Herr Meyer!' murmured the old man with instant comprehension. 'And therefore I, of course, was no obstacle – I was vouched for.'

'There was a further reason why I would not confide in anyone. He was to me – my little gentleman – so much more than a man, so different from other men, that I did not want him to have a name. If he was really only a mortal like the rest of us, I did not wish to know it.'

'You need not have been afraid,' said Herr Sommerhof very gently. 'He was not like the rest of us. And he is surely immortal.' He stood gazing at her for a long moment over the talisman he still held in his two hands. 'Anna, how would you like to leave this inn, and look for your future in another kind of drudgery? Do not think I am offering you an easy life! You have much to learn, and if you elect to go with me you will have to work and work and work, until you may well wish yourself back in your kitchen. But you have a voice that ought not to be wasted, and a natural judgement, and youth, and many a prima donna has come to me with less. If you will put yourself in my hands, I will make of you a singer, and of your little gentleman – God be with him, as he is surely with God – a true prophet. What do you say?'

Nanynka opened her lips, and no words came. Her eyes

filled with tears of longing and disbelief, for none of this could possibly be happening. For a moment she saw within her swimming eyelids a world made up all of song, with no more dingy sculleries, no foul-mouthed cook shrieking, no Madame Groh hissing rebukes. Then her tears spilled over, and ran down her cheeks, and suddenly Hugo had her hands fast in his, and was pouring eager, heartfelt assurances into her ears.

'Nanynka, dear Nanynka, it's true! Herr Sommerhof would not deceive you. You can do your part, and you need not fear that he will not do his. You must not be afraid to venture! You must not be afraid of anything! I shall be near. I will take care of you.'

'My good sister Agathe will take care of her, I thank you,' said the old man dryly, 'and you are not in her good books, Master Hugo, so if you wish to be admitted to Anna's acquaintance in future I advise you to walk circumspectly. Well, child, I am waiting. What is your answer?'

Clinging convulsively to Hugo's warm, kind young hand, Nanynka gasped: 'Do you mean it? Is it possible? Oh, I will work and work, I will do anything, if only I can really learn to sing. You shall never, never have reason to complain of me. But are you sure? – for I have no training, and no one to vouch for me—'

'No one to vouch for you? Anna, Anna, you do not know what you are saying! Listen! – here is the voice that commends you to me!'

And the old man lifted the fragment of manuscript paper to the light, and read aloud, reverently and tenderly, the inscription which followed the song:

To the linnet in the garden, in gratitude for her first performance, and expectation of her many future triumphs, from her most humble, devoted, obedient servant,

WOLFGANG AMADEUS MOZART

How Beautiful is Youth

She opened her eyes upon the dusky golden light in the curtained room, and through the dissolving mists of sleep she saw the new dress, last night's triumph and fiasco, lying where she had let it fall, a pool of iris-grey cloud in the easy chair with the glint of gold tissue shining through, like a fierce dawn breaking through an overcast sky. It appeared to her, in spite of everything, the kind of dress a man ought to notice when it crossed a room beside him, but Mark had never given it a glance, much less made any comment upon its splendours. Heaven knows, she thought, lying motionless in the enormous bed as she studied her folly through half-closed eyelids, I'm sufficiently inured to the allurements of splendid gowns in my profession, why should I have built any hopes on this one, more than all the rest?

She had only to stir a hand upon the coverlet or her head upon the pillow, and Morgan would be suddenly, softly in the room drawing back the curtains. She must have looked into the room half-a-dozen times already, and refrained from taking a step within for fear of waking her mistress, though she had probably been aching to snatch up the dress and put it reverently upon its hanger. No rehearsal this morning, so Barbara could have what Morgan always comfortably termed a long lie-in. No doubt Morgan would add, as smugly, that she had earned it, for the concert at the Mozarteum had been a triumph. It was the private part of the evening that had been a fiasco.

Her songs had been all Mozart, and perhaps that was enough in itself to account for Mark's preoccupation, for he was still, after three months with her, mortally afraid of accompanying her in Mozart. Other people, he said feelingly, cover up for you, but only the pure in heart can play Mozart, for every flaw shows up like a deformity. She remembered the strained whiteness of his face as he took his seat composedly at the piano and played delicately and perfectly, a fine sweat of nervousness all the time dewing his upper lip. Only when she had taken him by the hand, at the end of her last group, and drawn him to his feet to share the ovation, had he relaxed and broken into one of his wild boyish smiles. She had felt, through the touch of his hand, which clung to hers tightly, his whole body trembling.

Perhaps it was this hypersensitivity of his, these stresses he never confided, and for which he asked no consideration, which had startled and melted her into loving him. Perhaps she was of a nature which must love protectively if it was to love at all. At least it had happened, unlooked for, inescapable, invading her heart secretly like a silent army treacherously loosed into a city by night; in the morning of her awareness the stronghold was already lost.

And how were the mighty fallen! She had halted in Paris to choose a dress all for him, to dazzle him, to awaken him to her as a woman; and he had escorted it home in the car, loved the voice which floated out of its misty folds, and never so much as seen gown or woman. He was proud of her, he was devoted to her, he adored her, but he didn't love her. It had never even occurred to him as a possibility.

The sun was high, she traced its climb through the brocade curtains. She would have to get up. Tonight, *Rosenkavalier*, and to survive the Marschallin she must be in perfect condition and perfect mood. Sighing, she stretched and turned in the bed, and silently, slipping over the carpet like a fat, grey tabby, Morgan came in.

First the curtains, then a finger on the bell, then the benevolent smile and the discreet morning greeting, 'A lovely morning, Miss Barbara, dear! Did you sleep well?' And with the tap at the door which heralded the coffee-tray, the day might fairly be said to have begun.

Smoothed reverently into decorum on its hanger, the grey-and-gold dress looked suddenly unsuitable, or else its failure had caused her to regard it with revulsion. It was simple and beautiful, but for her a disastrous mistake, an error of taste due, no doubt, to over-anxiety on her part. She felt an aversion to the idea of ever wearing it again.

She slid out of bed, drawing on her housecoat before the mirror and studying herself with the heavy, still look left over from sleep. She saw a tall woman of forty, statuesque, handsome, with a clear pale face and a profusion of glossy hair; the woman Mark never saw.

Thank God she hadn't put on weight! She was spared the sagging fat, at any rate; all she had to contend with was the more subtle thickening here and there at neck and shoulder and cheek, the faint weariness of the lofty white eyelids, the resignation of the settled lines of the mouth. These had never mattered until Mark came, nervous and ardent and twenty-four years old, almost sick with awe of her at first.

Three weeks of his company and twenty years of success and satisfaction in her career melted and ran out of her hands. She had had everything, but now suddenly the sum of all she had had was nothing. And the devil of it was that when he looked at her he saw and adored Astrofiammante or the Countess Almaviva, or the embodiment of the voice that breathed into them, but never, never Barbara Tremayne.

'The young lady slept late too, poor love,' said Morgan, busy running the bath. 'She was terribly tired when she got here, after that long journey.'

'Oh, lord!' said Barbara, whirling from the mirror in dismay. 'Theodora! I forgot all about her! The poor child!' Her own sister's daughter, newly arrived from England on her first trip alone, and her unfeeling aunt could forget her very existence. 'Do go and ask her to come up and talk to me while I dress, if she's up now.'

'Yes, Miss Tremayne, she's up. I took her breakfast up to her room thinking she'd feel a bit strange if she had to go down alone just at first. You get your bath, and I'll send her in.'

When Barbara came out of the bathroom, Theodora was

sitting in the light from the window, beyond the panes of which the Mönchsberg loomed stonily above the tilted roofs. She was eighteen, and in a simple cotton frock looked even less. Her smooth short hair was as sleek as Barbara's own, her round face had the texture of a new flower, never touched since it had unfolded, and her full lips, plaintive and tender, curled together with the candour of rose-petals, ready to reflect every motion of her guarded spirit. She looked up warily with speedwell eyes, and the very curl of the lashes had a cool, fresh sensation, as if the dew was still upon them.

Kissing her was like kissing the air of the morning. Barbara thought, with a pang which lay somewhere between jealousy and nostalgia, so that's what I was like! That's what I had, and never had the wit to recognize until it was gone. I wonder if she's any brighter!

'Darling, I'm sorry I slept so late. After tonight, I've got two clear days, and we can see more of each other. Did Morgan look after you properly?'

'She was awfully nice,' said Theodora, in the composed voice of a vulnerable young woman.

'Did you sleep well? And how do you feel this morning? Ready to look at Salzburg?'

'Oh, yes! Can you come with me? Mr Creed said you're singing in *Rosenkavalier* tonight, so if you want me to take care of myself, that's all right, I can do it, you know.'

'Is Creed downstairs already?'

'Yes. Do you want him to come up?'

'Not just yet, he'll keep. I have to see him, though, he wants me to go on east after the Festival, but I'm not sure yet if I want to.' She shook out her shining hair, and let it fall over her shoulders. 'There'll be a box for you tonight, if you'd like to go. And an Austrian escort, a handsome one. No need for you to wonder who's going to keep you company while I'm engaged.'

Theodora's demure eyes took on a vigorous sparkle. She burst out: 'All my clothes are so *schoolgirlish*! You know what Mummy is! Will you help me to choose a frock here? I *can't* wear my cottons to the opera, honestly. Wait till you see them!'

'Cottons are in, you know. But if you don't like them, we'll fix something else for you.' She looked up suddenly, and saw how the dazzled blue eyes clung to the grey-and-gold dress upon its hanger, with open and resigned envy, without any hope or any malevolence at all. She thought: 'So I still have something she thinks she would like!'

'Try it on!' she said. 'I've worn it just once, and it's simple enough to look right on you.'

'Oh, no, Aunt Bar, honestly, I didn't mean—' But her ravished eyes widened and grew moist with desire.

'I know you didn't, but I do. Go ahead, see if it fits.'

Theodora's belt flew, her slim arms crossed and swooped for the edges of her skirt and the cotton frock billowed to the carpet. The waves of gold and grey surged over her head. She shook herself, and the dress settled upon her as though she had grown it.

'How do I look?' She knew very well how she looked, she was flushed and shining with incredulous delight.

'The waist's large for you, but Morgan will soon put

that right.' Barbara walked round her niece, critically touching the folds into place. 'Yes, you'll look very well in it.' So that's what was wrong with it on me, she thought. It's twenty years too young, for all its sophistication.

'I've never had a dress like this in my life! Are you sure you don't want to keep it? Oh, Aunt Bar, you are an angel to me!'

Morgan, called back into consultation over the fit of the shoulder, flew for pins and cotton, and began to spin Theodora before the mirror like a top. The delighted little face appeared and disappeared as she revolved obediently, dreaming of a gilded box for her gilded gown and a beautiful young man attendant at her elbow.

Barbara left them to their labours, and went down to talk to Creed, who had several engagements eastward waiting for her approval, and as many good reasons as his finger-ends why she should accept them. He was waiting for her in a retired corner of the lounge, already half-obscured by the steam of coffee and the smoke of cigarettes. They talked business with the amicable rudeness of two old friends who have outlived the necessity of stepping gently with each other.

'Well, have you made up your mind to be sensible and go?'

'No, not yet.'

'All right, we won't argue about it today. But it seems folly not to make the most of your journey now you're here. You're in excellent voice. You've never been better than you were last night.'

It must be true, for Creed never flattered anyone; and

where music was concerned, what he said was the law and the prophets.

'Oh, and Eduard rang up for you. I took it because you were still asleep, and we didn't want to wake you. He can't come and play with your little girl – his mother's apparently having one of her imperial tantrums again, and he had to rush back to Vienna by the morning train. He was spouting apologies like a fountain. One would have thought he was the only personable young fellow in these parts. Who would you like me to call up in his place?'

She detached from her letters no more than a passing thought, like a shed leaf, to follow Eduard home to his mother's tedious bedside, and said, before she realized what name would inevitably come first to her lips: 'Call Mark and ask him to stand in.'

As soon as it was said she wished it back. Yet she could have taken it back, without incurring even the raising of one of Creed's thick black eyebrows, and she did not. Never go back? There's always a reason, somewhere far back in the mind, for a wilful utterance like that; don't revoke it until you know why you said it in the first place. I wish I hadn't started it! she thought, trying to compress the panic and pain within the heart for fear it should break into speech. But she could have stopped it, then and there, and somehow she knew that she was not going to.

Creed moved to the telephone at the other end of the room, but in a moment she was at his side. 'Let me! Poor boy, I make such shameless use of him, the least I can do is ask him myself.' She grudged every word of Mark's to another ear than her own.

'Hullo, Mark? This is Barbara. Were you planning anything for this evening?'

Distant, the unmistakable voice said, rather indignantly: 'I'm going to the opera, of course!' She ought to have known that he would be there to hear her, he was hurt that she had not taken it for granted.

'Well, be a darling, and get rid of your ticket – unless, of course, you were going with someone else?'

'Well, no, just alone. But—' Dismay was in his tone. He was afraid her commission was going to rob him of *Rosenkavalier* and yet he couldn't deny her anything she asked of him.

'I'm scaring you for nothing,' she said remorsefully. 'What I'd like you to do, if you will, is share my box with my niece, and be nice to her. She's eighteen, fresh from England and she's very sweet, so it won't be any hardship. Will you?'

'Of course I will!' he said, relieved. 'What's the drill for a brand-new ex-schoolgirl? Have I to dress?'

She thought of the fitting going on upstairs, and laughed. 'You have indeed, my poor child! The full regalia! But if you've nothing on all day, why don't you come and fetch her now, this morning? Take her to the Cathedral, and the Glockenspiel and the Marionettes! Then you can judge for yourself whether she rates a white tie.'

'If I come round in an hour, can I take you both to lunch?'

She drew back at that, imagining the ordeal of sitting cheek by cheek with that vernal freshness for an hour and more, while his honest eye analysed the difference between them. 'No, but you may take Theodora and my blessing.'

'All right, I'll settle for that,' he said cheerfully.

She went back upstairs, marvelling at her own madness, to select a dress from amongst Theodora's cottons, and see that she did nothing, in her ardour, to spoil the dewy loveliness of her face. Theodora was secretly relieved at the exchange of an Austrian for an English escort; to appreciate so much foreignness and newness, she needed one present link with home.

'What's he like?' she wanted to know, shaking out her white net gloves from their packing folds and turning the nape of a neck as slim and urgent as a boy's, so that Barbara could fasten the back buttons of her dress.

The tongue which would gladly have told her all Mark's beauty and brilliance said instead: 'He's a very nice boy, and a fine accompanist.'

'How old is he? Is he nice-looking?'

'Twenty-four. I don't know – I suppose he is, reasonably.'

She could feel Theodora resigning herself, after such faint sales talk, to receive a disappointing young man with a large intellectual forehead and no light conversation at all. She wondered why she was going to so much trouble to startle them into delight when they met.

When the moment came, and Morgan brought him up to the drawing room, and Theodora sprang involuntarily out of her chair, with astonished lips parted in a dazzled smile, Barbara wondered if the convulsion she felt was of triumph or agony. The only absolute satisfaction she had was in knowing that it was of her own making. Whatever was going to happen, she would have a hand in making it happen. If it killed her!

The back view of them as they went down the stairs held for her a pain which she thought must be almost like a lesser death. Mark was a good head taller than Theodora, as thin and bright as she was rounded and tender. They were talking already before they reached the first turn of the stairs. She closed the door quickly and went to the piano, in order not to hear what they were saying.

A floor below, they halted, hearing her voice raised in song. They looked at each other, half smiling, listening to the liquid Italian floating upon the air, the well of the stairs carrying it more clearly than she had realized, for what she was singing was not meant for them:

> 'Quanto è bella giovinezza
> Che si fugge tuttavia!
> Chi vuol esser' lieto, sia;
> Di doman non c'è certezza—'

'What is it she's singing?' asked Theodora, looking up at Mark in absolute confidence that he would know.

'It's a song of Lorenzo de' Medici's, from one of the masques. The setting's her own.' He looked down at her, and smiled, serenely blind to the implications of Lorenzo's lament in that adored mouth:

> 'How beautiful is youth, how bright,
> Constant in nothing but in flight!

Who would be merry, let him be,
Of tomorrow there's no certainty.'

Theodora, impressed by the prompt translation, let it ripple
through her mind with a gentle, delicious melancholy, and
emerged from under the waves of its pessimism like a
duckling, her new young feathers unpenetrated. Youth
meant nothing to her; she simply had it.

'She's wonderful, isn't she?' she said impulsively.

Her quick glow passed to his cheeks as naturally as a
reflection. 'There's no one like her! She's been marvellous
to me – she is to everybody!'

They went on, inextricably interwound in her praises,
down the stairs and into the sunshine.

He did not bring her back until early evening, when it was
already time to dress. Barbara had taken a light meal and
was resting, but she roused herself to superintend the
assumption of the grey-and-gold dress. Theodora emerged
rosy and tender from her bath, and put on womanhood
only with her finery, growing tall, regal and mysteriously
grave as the dress billowed down to her feet. She had
chattered volubly about Salzburg, but not about Mark. Mark
was already, it seemed, someone not to be chattered about.
One likes to have one's opinion endorsed, thought Barbara,
turning in her heart the dual knife of pain and pleasure.

She left the hotel before Mark called for Theodora. In
her dressing room she put on the voluminous filmy laces
and silks of the Marschallin's morning toilette, and Morgan
knotted up the great glistening fall of her hair into the

artfully artless array of a great lady fresh from her bed. How many Marschallins, she thought, can play the part at forty without a wig? She hadn't a grey thread yet. Only in the full, clear flesh of her face, when she was tired, slight loosenings of middle age began to show. 'I'll make them remember tonight,' she said to her reflection. 'I'll make it unfashionable to be young. They shall never forget me!'

She stood up, her face completed, and shook out her lacy train shimmering round her feet before the long mirror. The flush of resolution on her cheeks might easily have been the flush of rising from the Princess's happy bed, the sparkle of her eyes was bright enough for both royalty and love, and the sadness of her mouth, remembering Mark, might well have been carrying the shadow of foreboding for Octavian's loss. I *am* the Marschallin! she thought, with a stab of something that seemed to her more like artistic triumph than private pain.

Her arms full of her skirts, she made her way down and through the wings. The stage, immaculate eighteenth-century, with its great draped bed and its enormous Venetian glass toilet-table, cast off hastily two or three last hangers-on and received her graciously into its spacious emptiness. Her Octavian came on composedly, in white wig and ruffled shirt and champagne-coloured silk breeches, a handsome, tall girl with a natural swagger and a pair of magnificent eyes. They disposed themselves calmly into the attitude of love, his cheek upon her knee, her hand blandly gentle upon his hair.

The curtain went up, the dark hushed cavity of the auditorium rushed in upon her consciousness, mysteriously peopled with its thousands of half-seen, intent faces, and the beneficent transformation which never failed took place in an instant. The almost unknown girl at her feet became the impossible beloved, whom she had and had not, whom she could not keep for ever, whose eyes she could not hope to fill for many years more with her waning beauty. Octavian was Mark, Mark was Octavian. The curls of the white wig under her fingers became the dark waves of his hair which she had never touched yet, the hands that held her were his hands.

She knew now what she had to do, and understood by what sure instinct she had already set it in train. What she could not keep with grace she must give with grace, as largely, as generously, as though it had really once been hers. The essential thing was to keep one's own greatness. The Marschallin had understood that. It was something to have been trained in the grandest of grand manners, to have sung herself into the personality of this high baroque lady, who knew how to maintain her impeccable style when her happiness went down into ruins.

At first she did not look towards the box where Theodora and Mark sat, but she was sensible of their nearness every moment; and in the middle of her great monologue she suddenly lifted her eyes and sought them out of the darkness. Two rapt faces, very close together, gazed down at her, great-eyed, and compassionate. Theodora in her new dress shone softly, lambent within her own freshness; the boy's normally composed and guarded face was wide open to the heart with admiration and sympathy. Barbara sent up to them what seemed to her all too clearly a cry of

protest against the cruel pity of the young. She poured out
to them the truth of herself, '*the old lady*, the Field-
Marshal's old wife', finding it time to set free her little
lover and remember her old age, and yet clinging with all
her possessive heart to the boy's devotion. It was a joy to
be telling them everything, openly, in front of thousands
of witnesses, even if they would never understand. No, it
was a joy *because* they would never understand, because
she was safe for ever, in the armour of her art, from the
indignity of being understood.

She left the stage at the end of the first act as though wafted
to her dressing room upon the gales of her ovation. She
knew already that she was singing the Marschallin of a
lifetime, which these people might as well reconcile
themselves to remembering, for they would probably never
hear the like of it again. She stood before the mirror gazing
at herself in wonder, her breast surging, her eyes brilliant.

'Shut the door, Morgan! I don't want to see anybody.
Tell them I don't want to break the thread. Tell them to
come after the performance, but I can't see anybody now.'

The flush on her cheeks might have been merely from
the warmth of the room, but it felt more like a flame of
exultation. The high beat of her heart might have been
indignation and pain, but it had an impetus which
suggested, rather, triumph.

'Every Marschallin should be in love with her baby of
an accompanist,' she said to her mirror, as she pulled out
the ribbons from her hair, 'and have a charming niece for
a Sophie to fling at hìm! I must get myself a faithless

husband before I sing the Countess in Vienna next month!'

Morgan, fending off importunate admirers in the passage, put her head in at the door to say doubtfully: 'Mr Creed is here, Miss Barbara.'

'Oh, good, *he* can come in!' She was kicking off her shoes when he entered, her mane of dark hair fallen over her face. She swept it back with one round white arm, and looked up at him with alert and shining eyes. 'Well, was it good?' But she did not wait an instant for the answer she did not need. 'Listen, can you get on to Vienna tonight? I've decided to go. Accept the Mozart parts – all three of them if they're still holding them. It's too tame to go home just when I've struck the real vein.'

Creed was smiling, a little smugly. 'And what about Linz? Is that too much to pack in? I don't want to overwork you, but they offered two recitals.'

'Accept them! Accept everything!' It was the only way to live, after all. She felt the strong tide of her power flowing, coming to the full.

'You're sure you want to take them all? No need to rush until you've made up your mind.'

'I'm sure. My mind *is* made up.' She began to shed laces like snow. Somewhere at a distance the interval bell pealed. Creed went away well pleased, leaving her to Morgan's attentive care.

The second act had been running for ten minutes, and Morgan was out of the room in search of a spirit lamp, when the door opened again, very quietly, and, looking up into the mirror, Barbara found herself staring into the eyes of Mark.

She was startled to realize that for almost half-an-hour she had scarcely given one thought to him, but at the first glimpse of him now her heart mel`ed into piteous tenderness.

'I know you don't want me,' he said apologetically. 'Morgan wouldn't let us in before. I just dodged her. But I won't stay, really, I only wanted to tell you—'

Her face in the mirror wore a slight, strained smile. No doubt the note of discouragement in his voice was due to the fact that he had misinterpreted it as a sign that she was being unwillingly patient with his intrusion. All the same, he persisted, approaching until he stood behind her chair, a hesitant smile on his lips. His face was flushed with pure musical excitement, he wanted to pay her desperate, fervent compliments, and was convinced that she wanted nothing so much as to pack him off to his box and be rid of him. 'If he only knew,' she thought, 'how I long to put my hands up and draw him down to me!'

Her shoulders burned with the awareness of him, standing so close. She could not keep the heavy, destroying tenderness out of her eyes and wondered that he did not see it.

'You were wonderful!' he said, letting his hand stray towards the cool coils of her hair. 'We – I had to sneak back and tell you. We thought we'd better not both come worrying you, but – you're not angry, are you?'

'No,' she said, her voice equable and low, 'I'm not angry. But I think you'd better go back to her now.' She saw the thin dark hand twining its fingers into the strands of her hair and her own hand, unable to resist the longing, stole upward and closed gently upon it. His lips quivered, and swooped to her wrist and fingers. She felt him trembling, as sometimes after a long recital, when he had excelled himself in the teeth of extreme nervousness.

The shock of his touch brought her to her feet, and suddenly she was dazzlingly aware that the incredible happiness was within her reach, that she had only to put out her hand and take it. He was hers if she cared to claim him, but he did not know it; he need never know it, unless she opened his eyes. She drew breath deeply; and on the threshold of the unlooked-for triumph she stood motionless, smiling at him indulgently. Now that the way was open, she knew that she could never go in.

'Silly boy!' she said, like one talking to a credulous child. 'It's only a story, you shouldn't get so worked up about it.'

That made him laugh, as it was meant to. 'Theodora's worse than I am!' he said in his innocence. 'She adores you.'

'She's very young, and very generous. And you're supposed to be looking after her.'

'I know!' he said guiltily. 'I'll go back.'

'And she's very beautiful – isn't she?'

The sudden flush of Theodora's sweet companionship burned high in his cheeks. 'She's *so like you*!'

'Then go and be nice to her. Don't wait for me, afterwards, you take her home and I'll see you both tomorrow.' Enraged at the calm of her own voice as she declined a kingdom, she felt a momentary frenzy of pity for herself and jealousy of the girl, and to evade it she took him by the shoulders, like an overgrown boy, and kissed him briefly and admonishingly in dismissal. She meant the kiss for his forehead, but as though the role in which she had cast him was implicit in her touch, he turned up his mouth to her like a schoolboy humouring a well-loved aunt, and received her lips upon his with perfect unself-consciousness. The light embrace, which left him unshaken, transfixed her with painful delight. She pushed him hastily towards the door, before worse should happen to them both.

'Now go back to her – quickly, before Morgan catches you.'

When he was gone, she smiled into the glass and did not know whether her smile was more rueful or relieved; but it appeared to her that it had at any rate the pride of rectitude. One should take only one's due, and she had never been a greedy woman.

She had the whole of the second act in which to dress, and the result was what she meant it to be, a masterpiece. She stood gleaming in the fabulous silver gown, showers of lace at breast and shoulders and elbows, her hair drawn upward into a turret of silver sparkling with stones; the great lady, the Princess von Werdenberg, in full panoply for the evening, the hoops of her skirt filling the room. Meeting her own eyes in the glass, she smiled with triumph and slowly, royally, she swept to her apotheosis.

There are victories the young cannot yet hope to win. The tension held. How could it fail, when every word, every note, came out of her life and her heart? In the anguished raptures of the trio, drawn aside from the young lovers whose happiness only she, if she pleased, could make possible, she looked up into the box where their counterparts sat. In the subdued light she could see them plainly. They were very close together, Theodora's shoulder curved tenderly within the protective hollow of Mark's, their young, entranced faces almost cheek to cheek. Theodora's hand lay on the rim of the box, and Mark's was closed comfortingly and tightly over it. They had a brief, a touching, a vulnerable beauty, a generous ardour, tears on the girl's cheeks, the boy's eyes wide and grave with emotion.

Ecstatically, devotedly, they gazed at their Marschallin, as her voice soared into the heights of renunciation. Afterwards, they would wonder how any singer could possibly simulate a passion so poignantly; now, they simply believed in it. The light glittered in Theodora's adoring tears.

All Souls' Day

Josef Slavik did not go back to the hut until the pub closed. It was not that he loved the beer or the company so much; so close was escape and renewal now that he was almost unaware of them, and sat for three-quarters of an hour over one drink, unwilling to spend even a few more coppers from what seemed to him the price of the future. It was rather that now, at the end, he could not bear the sight of the empty room, the camp bed and the box covered with white paper for a table, the borrowed crockery which must go back to the Shanes in the morning, all the bare, clean evidence of departure.

The promise was so close now that to feel it still out of reach of his hand was torture. Had he hated England, that it hurt him like a skin he must slough or die? The emptiness of the Nissen hut threatened as it reassured, and he did not want to have to sit in it with the silent women, and wait moment after moment with the fear that even now something could go wrong.

Almost over now! Before the end of next week they

would be in America, where the initiative was, where the future was. Uncle Petr was waiting for them, there was a good job in the firm for Josef, a share in the house for Hilda, and surely a quiet corner for his mother, perhaps some light work, too. She was not really old; it was only because Hilda had the prior claim to be known as Mrs Slavik that the neighbours had added to Slava's name the qualifying 'old'. She needed work of her own, something into which she could dig her strong fingers and vigorous mind; it was only for want of that that she had thinned and faded here, and receded from him into so remote and shadowy a silence. In America, where there was hope, and expansion, and power, where the core of the world had moved and fixed irrevocably since the war, everything would be different. He had waited and hoped for it so long, and now it was almost a reality, almost in his hands. Tomorrow they would return the borrowed pots and pans, and Tom Shane would fetch away the camp bed they were giving to him, and by noon they would be in the train, going south, away from this half-life for ever.

Once it had not seemed to him so bad a life. The job was all right, even if a camp hut was all they could get for a house. But after the years of war, the precarious flight into France, the frustration and corruption and indifference there, the second escape into England, and the long, waiting struggle of that army of exiles, any honest work for a fair wage was temporary heaven. Dissatisfaction came later, when things should have been levelling out to normal, and still there was no advancement and no house. In the new world everything would be different. There a man could get on. There he would not continue, after years of honest service, an alien and a stranger.

When closing time came, he walked home by the field path as slowly as he could. He did not want to see his mother sitting with her hands in her lap, staring at the sky through the curtainless windows. But when he opened the door all was as he expected it to be. Hilda put out his dinner on the white paper tablecloth with her usual placidity. She was growing rather plump and heavy since the baby's birth and death, but she was still as pretty as when he had married her in 1943. She would be better in America, too. She would have other sons, who would not, like their first unaccountably puny mite, die before their tenth day. She was too practical and too unimaginative to waste time in grieving over the lost child; all her thoughts were for the ones they would have thereafter, in the world of promise where opportunity was generated with the newly born, and grew with them until it ripened in their hands. She had not even been up to the churchyard again to look at the little grave. The living would always matter more to Hilda than the dead. She had flushed with excitement as she chattered with him about their plans, and sung as she packed the trunk they had sent ahead on its journey. Where there was room she would make a life, and never look over her shoulder at what was left behind.

She came and put her arm suddenly about his neck as he ate, and kissed him. 'Soon now!' she said in his ear; and he said: 'Very soon!'

'You won't believe me, but I've been scared all along that something would happen to spoil it.'

He said sharply: 'Hush!' for he was still afraid, and did not like to be reminded of it.

'Oh, it's all right now! Only a few more hours, and we're off.'

They spoke in low voices, and did not look at his mother who sat on the camp bed making fast a loose button on his overcoat against the long journey. But he made a slight motion of his head towards her, and looked questioningly and yet evasively into his wife's eyes. She shook her head at him with a slight frown, and lifted her shoulders. 'It'll be all right. When we go – when we begin to see new things—'

Hilda came of a farming family, centuries settled in the district. Once, after the war ended, he had taken her on a visit to his own country, and she had moved through its golden summer with her fixed and assured serenity, mildly entertained, as at a circus. Then he had known that she could not be transplanted, at least into that soil. It had never entered her head. Had he not been in England for five years, and wasn't he doing a good, steady job there? What should he do but stay there with his English wife, and accept the status of an adopted son? In her mind it had always been quite settled. Perhaps she would never have accepted even the idea of going to America, if the coming and passing of the child had not shaken her a little aside from her fixity for a while; but now she was as firmly in motion upon that track as she had been embedded in the English scene. It was not she who hung upon the project like a motionless and silent cloud of denial and regret.

He remembered that visit home vividly, for it was then

that he had begun to understand, and to make his mother understand, that things were changed, that he had moved on, and that if she wished to keep him she must move after him. He did not want to leave her alone there; his father was dead since 1940, and his little brother Oto, his wild, gay, indestructible little brother Oto, had fallen foul of the Germans, and died obscurely in the fortress at Terezín, like so many of the young and brave. Among the hurried and shallow burials of the last few thousand dead, when there was no more oil for the crematorium, the liberating army had found and identified his slight and angry bones. There was no one left there to make a home for Slava. It was natural, it was best, that she should come to England, to her only living son and his wife, to the generations which would follow them, her grandchildren, the fruit of the future.

When he turned his head cautiously and looked at her as she sewed, he saw now her face had aged. The look of stillness which she wore had descended on her then, when he had asked her to come back to England with them.

He remembered the occasion as if it had been yesterday. She had just come back from Olšany, from lighting the lamp on his father's grave. He had not been with her, but he knew from many such nights how the long plateau of the cemeteries would look with all its faint, steady, guarded lights holding off the perilous night and affirming the permanence of the spirit, its blaze of flower stalls along the grey stone wall, its sighing trees. In the triangle of the graves of the murdered, before the gates at Terezín, the lights would be burning, too, a little stray draught in the hinge of the lantern making the flame dance over young Oto's photograph, waking him to the old irresistible laughter. Her mind must have been full of these two as her last son spoke to her of himself and his future. For her Olšany and Terezín were stems of the future, too. It was possible that at first she did not even understand what he was trying to say. Then the veil of silence and reserve came down upon her face, and though she made no protest, and asked only a few clarifying questions, he began to talk volubly as if she had argued against his plans.

'Hilda's family are there, and she hasn't even thought of leaving them. For me it's easier. I've had to pull up my roots already. I've got a job there. The prospects are good. After all, things have changed. We've had to make a life where we could, and now I belong as much there as anywhere. And for you, Mother – it'll be better for you there. You'd always have a home with us. And you'd like it there, it's a good country—'

She did not say a word against him, but only looked at him with that remote and silent and guarded look.

'She married me when I had no country,' he said feverishly, 'and let me share hers. I have to consider my wife, haven't I?'

'Yes,' said Slava quietly, staring at him with the large, commanding eyes which were exactly on a level with his own. She was tall, and had been beautiful, and until then she had seemed to him proudly, immovably young. 'Yes, of course you must consider your wife.'

'I know you thought I should come back and settle down here again, like before. I thought so, too. But you can't just pick up again after so many years. You change – things happen to you in that time. You have to go on from where you stand – there's nothing else to be done. It isn't something I can help,' he had cried, putting out his hands to her in protest against what she had neither said nor implied.

'I know,' she said, and took his hands. But she looked over her shoulder towards the cemeteries of Olšany, for one brief instant asking advice from the other half of her being, before she relinquished all counsel but her own.

'Mother, I can't leave you here alone. Mother, come with us.'

She had come with them; she was here. She sat now sewing the buttons firmly on to his coat, so that he should not lose any on his way to the New World. 'Mother, come with us!' To the ends of the world, silently, without protest, she was coming. Why did he still want to argue with her, to answer what she had never said? Why did he turn on her uncomplaining silences, accusing her of not wanting him to have his best chance in the world?

If the baby had lived it might have been different, she might have made herself content then. But it had lived only to be hastily baptized on the eighth day, and then flickered out like a pallid little candle, and was buried in the new annexe of the parish churchyard, up on the windy and treeless hill, where the neglected graves never ceased to offend Slava's sense of family, and no one ever displayed neat framed photographs of the dead, or lit lamps for them to testify to their immortality. Sometimes she walked up there and trimmed the rough grass, and took flowers to put into the little vase, because the baby had been, for however short a time, a member of her family, and therefore his place in it was permanent and assured, and his resurrection past doubt. Hilda did not think like that. She had lost the baby, he was an incident closed now, and best forgotten. She did not think of him as having existence any longer, all her hopes were fixed on other sons.

'Mrs Nash wants us to go in to them for breakfast in the morning,' said Hilda, spreading her fair round arms along the makeshift table. 'It'll make things a lot easier. We can return the stove tonight, and there won't be a thing left to do tomorrow except get ourselves and the hand luggage down to the bus. Tom Shane's going to take the key in for us, so you won't have that to do.'

'I wish it was the morning,' he said.

'You've no call to, it will be, soon enough. What are you so nervy about, all at once? Everything's gone fine. We didn't even have so long to wait as we expected, thanks to your uncle. You take it easy! There's nothing to worry about now.'

She saw his quick, involuntary glance in his mother's direction, and shut her hand over his with a reassuring pressure. 'I tell you, it's all right! Everything's going to be all right.'

But the hours hung upon his heart with an intolerable reluctant slowness, as if time had stopped; and when his strung nerves searched for the origin of his unrest he was aware of it as proceeding from his mother. She wanted time to stop; she wanted the morning never to come. If he accused her of it, there would be no denial, only the slight

150

stiffening of her body, the lift of her head, the steady silence of her hollow, unquiet eyes upon him. She wanted the morning never to come, because it would take them away westward, while her mind and spirit leaned always back towards the east, towards the little flat in Malěsice, half suburb and half village, to the living room with its green-tiled stove and its heavy lace curtains; towards the irrevocable centre of her life, where she had lived happily with his father, and raised her sons to their divided destinies.

Since it was natural that this should remain for her always the pivot of her life, why could he not accept that, and be content to know that for him it was different? Why must he hide from her thoughts and feelings, as if she had spent these few years in England only in reproaching him, she who had never uttered one word of accusation? They were two generations, their paths could not be identical. But he turned his face away from her, and could not bear his awareness of her antagonism.

All the afternoon and until after dusk he made for himself needless errands about the camp, returning the last borrowed things, saying goodbye to some who would be away to work early next day, making a round of feverish visits, anything which would keep him out of Slava's presence. So few hours were left now, surely they must pass, and at last he would be safe.

Hilda did not understand. She thought he was suffering from reaction after too much excitement, and that he needed only to be left alone, and not agitated further. After all, he was a foreigner, with a foreign temperament. He smiled, a little wryly, when this thought came to him, but he knew that was how she saw him. It was true, she loved him as fully as her nature made love possible; you can love even exotic little dogs, they also have the charm of novelty.

He was coming back in the twilight of the early November night, when he remembered for the first time what day it was. On this Sunday of All Souls all the lamps would be lit in Olšany, all the mysterious groves of quietness full of little sheltered flames; and before Terezín the great triangle of white gravestones, themselves lambent in the dusk, would glow and scintillate with thousands of points of light, soundless and strange under that level northern sky. Slava must have been thinking of this all day long, though she had said no word. He thought he would go to her, and say something warm and affectionate and not about himself, something to remind her that he was also her son, and had not forgotten his duty; but when he went into the bare room Hilda was sitting alone.

'She went out,' said Hilda, seeing how he looked for Slava. 'Only for a little walk,' she said. 'She hasn't been out all day. I was glad for her to go.'

He looked at her sharply, and asked: 'Didn't she say where she was going?'

'No, why should she?' She came and shook him rallyingly by the shoulder, a slight shadow of impatience touching her face. 'What are you so jumpy about? She's all right, I keep telling you. She's been quiet about going, I know – she feels it, naturally, going so far to start afresh at her age. What do you expect? But she knows what she's doing, and she took on to go with her eyes open. She's *your* mother! Have *I* got to tell you she knows her own mind?'

'It's the way she looks,' he said. 'Sometimes she's made me afraid. If anything should go wrong now because of her—'

'Nothing will go wrong – at least, not because of her. You ought to know she doesn't go back on her decisions, especially when they mean as much to you as this does. It's *you* who scare me, not her—'

It was something he did not want to hear, and he broke away from her to avoid the look which searched him through as she said it. 'She never wanted it. She holds it against me. What is there here for us, I'd like to know?' He flung away to the window, and stared out at the twilit desolation of the camp, but none of the few moving figures was Slava returning.

An hour passed, and he grew afraid, though he did not know why. She was a woman in the full possession of strong and determined faculties, who never gave way to fate. What unnatural weakness could drive her to harm now? But when the second hour was passing, and still no sign of her, he could not bear it any longer. He seized his coat, and went to the door.

'Where are you going?' asked Hilda, in the quiet, forbearing voice she used to him only when his foreignness was borne back upon her by some alien act to which she could not adjust her understanding.

'To look for her. There's something queer – why should she stay out so long now?'

Hilda got up and followed him, leaving the door

unfastened, for what was there now to steal. Feeling her at his shoulder, he went on saying laboriously, as if he were trying to convince himself: 'At her age, women sometimes do strange things.' But Hilda's patient, wary silence only asserted unmistakably: Not your mother. They did not talk any more. In silence they walked to the margin of the camp, where the cement-coloured road curved away pallidly in the dark towards the village. The old man with the game leg was just limping home from the pub, but he had not seen Slava. They did not meet her on the road. Josef was frightened, and did not know what he feared. He quickened his pace until they came to the edges of the village, and the low stone wall of the churchyard with its vague, dappled pallor of gravestones inside, and its occasional darker night of yews.

Suddenly he stopped, for he knew where his mother was. Far up the churchyard, small as the glimmer of a cigarette in the night, but pale gold as a star, there was a little light burning, the tiny, sheltered candle of his baby's soul. Flickering a little in the small wind, Slava's ceremonial farewell to the child they were abandoning burned bravely in the vast and quiet darkness, an assertion of permanence and immortality where everything was apparent change and loss.

He stood gazing at the distant point of flame, and it seemed to grow into a field of fire, all the seasonal fires of Olšany in one infinitesimal gleam. He was almost startled when he felt Hilda stir beside him. He did not want her there. She knew nothing of the traditions of life and death among his people, she would not understand. He spread his hand forbiddingly along her arm.

'Go back to the hut. I'll bring her – she'll come with me. You go! It's all right now, leave her to me.'

She went without any protest beyond a shrug, for she knew that Slava needed neither man nor woman, and there was no need to cross him in this mood. Tomorrow the crisis would be past, and they would all stop looking behind them, and begin to crane ahead, into a new era already begun. She went away and left him; and when he was sure that she was gone he went in by the lych gate, and threaded a slow and hesitant way between the graves to where Slava stood, looking down at the candle. She had set it on a flat stone, under a broken tumbler which at once sheltered it from the wind and allowed air to feed it. She was gazing at it quietly, and when he said: 'Mother!' she turned her head with no surprise, arching her fine neck at him and showing him, in the candle's wavering light, a face of assured and appeased calm. He trembled at its large tranquillity, as at the sudden meeting with a mirror.

She began to smile, and then she saw his eyes. They lifted from the tiny grave to her face, and clung there desperately. He wanted to say to her: 'Mother, I know you don't want to go, I know you think I've been wrong to do this, but what is there for me here?' But before the first words had formed in his lips he knew that he was arguing only with himself. He knew what she had always known, what she had tried with her silence and her stillness to hide from him. He knew why the child had not cared to live, born as it had been without heritage or identity. He knew that there was nothing for him here, nothing in

155

America, nothing in the barren other places to which he would thrust onwards in his pointless agony hereafter. The things which were for him had been left behind already, no journey round the world would ever bring him to where he could claim them again.

Before her brimming, compassionate eyes he began to tremble with the revelation. The candle was the last lighthouse glimmering for a few miles across the sea of his banishment, for, wherever he went searching, he would never find what he wanted again. Others might find it. The forcibly uprooted may light on it upon any kindly coast, name it in any language, possess it even by the roadside while they are nomads. But the self-exiled have had it and chosen to be rid of it. He had not even sold it, he had only thrown it away.

The look which he had never understood melted into a helpless sorrow on her face. She held out her arms to him, and he stumbled into them and hid his face in her breast, muttering and crying to her for what she could not give him:

'*Matko ma,* I want to go home! *Maminko moje,* take me home!'

The Cradle

The cradle was carved in limewood, on polished rockers with the heads of horses at either end. The round face and arched wings of a cherub sheltered the pillow, and there were flowers and birds all round the rim. Shut away from the sun in the attic, kept dusted and immaculate by Cousin Sybil's meticulous housekeeping, the wood had never darkened; it looked as if it had been carved only yesterday. The christening robe of lace and lawn in its silver box had yellowed at the folds, the painted toy horse had lost the brightness of his original red saddle and blue bridle, and the hair of his mane had dried and grown brittle with the atmospheric changes of twenty years; but the cradle was always new.

The Rector could never pass by the door without opening it and looking at the hoarded remains of his arrested life. He had never intended that the things he and Gillian had amassed for their eagerly awaited son should be stored up here and turned into the furnishings of a shrine; that was something that had happened of itself. The toys, clothes, the little wooden things he had carved, like the cradle, with his own young and skilful hands, had been left here untouched in deference to his silence and stillness, ever since that moist green December evening twenty years ago, when Gillian had died in childbirth.

People had thought he wanted everything left as it was; in truth he had wanted nothing, except simply not to be, not to bear the responsibility of his own life, not to feel or remember. On that desire, feeling and memory feed and grow strong beyond bearing.

It was worst at Christmas, but still he could not pass by the closed door. Unto us a child is born, unto us a son is given. And the child had been born, and it had indeed been a son; but in the moment of birth he had turned back, frightened, into the darkness and snatched Gillian away with him. And the Rector had been left alone.

The disaster had been too complete and absolute for him, he had shrunk away from human sympathy into the sealed world of his own pain, withdrawing to bury the shrivelled remnants of his life among the relics of his brief fatherhood. The round of his parochial duties the shell of a man faithfully fulfilled, making superficial contacts daily with his fellow men; his mind compiled sermons, his tongue delivered them. But all that was real of him lay shut in here with the symbols of his loss. Out of his inability to act he had left them all in their places, the fragile, intractable things bought and made for his beloved son; and others had respected what they took to be his wish. Dusted and preserved, polished with the caresses of his hands and heavy with the weight of his withdrawal, the cradle stood in the centre of the attic like an altar. Or like a coffin on its catafalque, part of a burial arrested for ever.

Why had he not taken it under his arm that very Christmas Day, and given it to the first expectant mother whose name came to his mind among his parishioners? It would not have been difficult, there were always plenty of births early in the year, the first fruits of last spring's weddings. But he had missed his opportunity, and the small, commanding thing, permanent in its place and for ever barren, defied him to touch it now. If it was a coffin, the body it held was the mummified remains of his effective life, self-buried here. The limewood walls, crested with flowers and birds, were higher and more impassable than the walls of a prison. Humanity moved and breathed in daylight on the outer side of them, but he was within, in the narrow darkness to which he had withdrawn voluntarily, and from which long disuse had sealed every way of escape.

The cracked mirror banished from the guest room showed him his own face, long and pale among the shadows, soon to be old; even age would have no meaning for him. It was too late now to wish to return to life and his own kind; the effort was beyond him, he had been self-buried too long.

And yet it was Christmas again, and the living world was all around him, within touch of his impotent hands. The house was full of the smell of baking, fragrant with the vanilla sugar without which his new housekeeper could not conceive of celebrating the feast. She was down there in the kitchen now, her sleeves turned up to her elbows, wrapping her biscuit animals and angels and flowers in silver foil for the tree; and beside her, cutting out lacy paper decorations according to old tradition, a pink tongue protruding at the corner of her earnest mouth, was the child. The strange child, the girl with the outlandish name, Katrena Iwasckiewicz. They spoke English, mother and daughter both; he could have talked to them if there had not been an invisible barrier between.

He had thought it might shatter when the child entered the house, but she walked gravely on her own side of it, and watched him through the bars with wary brown eyes, and made no attempt to reach him. Perhaps, like all the rest, she had no inkling that he was shut away from her. They exchanged words sometimes; why should she suspect that it was only an automatic physical reaction that provided the responses to her respectful greetings and polite questions? She thought a man had answered her.

The Polish woman had been engaged by Cousin Sybil, before she left on her year's visit to her sister in America.

'In your position,' she had said firmly, 'I think you should set an example, with International Refugee Year only just over, and everything. Mrs Iwasckiewicz has very good references. She came from a Jewish family, and was smuggled into Sweden as a child during the war, and afterwards she married a survivor from a concentration camp, who died a few years later from his experiences, and left her penniless with this baby.'

She had been hurrying on past this supposed danger point, but he had turned from his desk to look at her with widening eyes. 'A baby?'

Of what had she been afraid? That he would object to having a child in the house? She had rushed to diminish the promise at once.

'Oh, she's not a baby now, of course, they've been in a camp for some years. Katrena will be eight years old now, and a very quiet, well-behaved child. I've seen her. I can assure you she won't be the least trouble, and I've impressed upon her mother that she mustn't disturb you or make a noise in the house.'

All the same, he had hoped for he hardly knew what, for a golden shout to bring down the limewood walls, for a tremor of warmth in his atrophied heart, for a breach carelessly trampled in the frontiers of his exile. He, too, was a displaced person; this dispossessed little girl might find her way to him as by right of kinship.

But they came, he spoke to them, he was even moved by them to the depths of that part of him which had communication with the ordinary business of living; but no miracle happened. The mother was silent, gentle, a loving housewife, absorbed in a new and distrustful happiness now that she had that shining, well-equipped kitchen as her kingdom. Sometimes he saw in her dark eyes the fear she had that it would again be taken away from her, but he did not know how to assuage it.

The child was small for her eight years, but sturdy and square, and not timid, as he had thought she might be, but bold and even aggressive, perhaps in reaction against the insecurity of her circumstances. A funny little thing she was, plain of face, brown-eyed and dark-skinned, with two short, stiff little brooms of hair that jutted one on either side of her round head. The gap in her front teeth still further complicated her laborious but determined English. She was full of energy and duty. A born organizer, so her Sunday-school teacher said; bossy, so her fellow scholars said. Yet they played with her willingly, which argued no dislike, and mutinously but good-humouredly fought out with her the clashes of will which she usually won. When she was defeated she was astonished but not resentful, and accepted her diminished role thoughtfully until she could resume her leadership. Outside she had a voice of brass and a shrill laugh; but indoors, mindful of her instructions and no doubt afraid, like her mother, of banishment, she walked delicately and spoke in a whisper.

Just as he reached the foot of the stairs, she came out of the kitchen fresh from her tea, with her baby doll in her arms. She had only two dolls, a blonde creature with washable hair which Cousin Sybil had given to her before she left, and this battered but cherished infant, with its painted blue eyes staring and a chip missing from its burnished nose. She clutched it tightly to her chest, and raised to the Rector a face powdered round the mouth with vanilla sugar.

'If you please . . .' said Katrena in her subdued indoor voice, hissing through the gap in her front teeth. The brown eyes looked up at him with a clear but remote stare. She was not personally in awe of him; she kept her distance and walked warily because she had always had to placate circumstances and people, but as long as she observed all the regulations and performed every duty zealously she felt herself to be safe with him.

'Yes, my dear?'

He always felt constrained to offer her some conciliatory endearment, and yet he never addressed her in such terms without feeling ashamed, as though he had stooped to an unworthy falsity in feeling his way towards her. She was neither his nor truly dear to him; he only wished she could be, but she existed in another dimension from him, and they had no real relationship at all.

'If you please, may we gather some holly and ivy from the garden? We have to make our Bethlehem for the Children's Corner.'

'We have to make it!' That was partly a matter of literal translation from her native language, but partly also her sense of conformity speaking. She knew the proper ceremonies, and it was right to ask for what was needed for them.

'Of course, Katrena,' he said. 'Take whatever you want for the crib.'

She thanked him, a spark of ambitious speculation kindling in her eyes, and ran off into the kitchen to tell her mother. The battered baby doll would certainly be cast for the Child Jesus, but where would she find figures for the Virgin and Saint Joseph and the shepherds? The children of his Sunday school had never done more than decorate with evergreens, but if Katrena's sense of the appropriate dictated a crib, a crib there would be. She never neglected her duties.

But had not he been neglecting his? She was a child in his household at Christmas, and he had provided nothing to put under the tree for her this evening. There would be only her mother's present for her. He could at least add some sweets; perhaps it was not too late to find something else.

He watched her whisk away, the bustling back view all elbows and bouncing braids, before he went on towards his study, to the still unfinished Christmas morning sermon on his desk. The advent wreath in the hall, to which Mrs Iwasckiewicz had added a new pink candle every Sunday, had been changed for the new Christmas Eve one; the tree was fully dressed, with candles and lamps and frilled paper sconces, and coloured balls and crystals of glass. There were even some sparklers tied to the tips of the branches ready for lighting. He had forgotten how elaborate and loving the preparations for the Continental Christ can be. The child's father had been a Protestant of some austere sect, but the adornments of their festival were the traditional graces of a Catholic country. Katrena, with her following of local children, sceptical yet impressed, would see to it that the Children's Corner had its crib, even if cut-out figures drawn on cardboard had to do duty for Mary and Joseph.

He sat over the pages of his sermon for a long hour, sensible of his unfitness to lift up his voice in their festival. Christmas, like the people who kept it, belonged to the desirable outer world to which he longed to return, and he shared in its celebrations only as a shadow. He had not even thought to provide a present for the child, and there was nothing in the house he could offer to her.

He laid down his pen suddenly, and sat staring before

him. There had been a child in that house once, for a few minutes, a living child on whose pleasure a wealth of toys had waited, though he had never played with any of them. Nothing to give to Katrena? There was the wooden horse. Was she too old for that? There was a big ball made of stitched segments of coloured leather. There was a little blue and white sailing boat. Surely that would be suitable for an eight-year-old?

He rose, and went slowly up the stairs, and hesitated with his hand upon the knob of the attic door. He was afraid; the palms of his hands were wet with fear. What would happen if he displaced one of the fixed trappings of that frozen shrine? To change the pattern of its mysterious power might be to shatter even the shell of life that was left to him, after twenty years he might well be afraid. How would he pass by the cradle and take the boat from its place? It would be like climbing out of his grave.

Nevertheless, he opened the door and stepped into the room.

On the worn haircord mat in the middle of the attic showed the marks of two rockers, flattened grey grooves in the dark brown pile. The cradle was gone.

He could not believe it. In twenty years it had never been disturbed from its place. Who would remove it now? Then he felt, with some inner sensitivity in him that still reacted to the instruments of his captivity, the aching emptiness where other things had been, and looked round the room to discover the sources of his wonder and unease.

The wooden horse was gone; the barrel-shaped indentations of its four tiny wheels showed where it had stood.

The silver box that had held the christening robe lay open on the shelf, the layers of pink tissue paper turned back carefully from its emptiness. And whether because of the clearer floor space, or whether by reason of a brightness bursting within his dazzled eyes, there seemed to him to be more light within the room.

He stood gazing where the talisman had been, and he did not understand, he was not even concerned with understanding. He felt only that the wall of his prison had been breached, and there was light shining into his open grave. If he could lay down his dead son out of his arms he could surely arise and go. Both the living and the dead could go their appointed ways, each of them at peace. He felt himself struggling to release the child, but twenty years had bound them inextricably into each other, and to be born twice is too much of pain.

The Rector closed the door of the attic behind him very softly, almost stealthily, and went down the stairs.

'Mrs Iwasckiewicz—'

She looked up sharply from her pastry. He had only to raise his voice a note, and she was instantly on the defensive, ready to excuse and placate, she who cared for every detail of his household with a starved proprietorial affection even Cousin Sybil had never been able to match. He saw how like the large dark eyes were to the child's eyes. He remembered, and for some reason at that moment he felt pride in the thought, that he was the only person in the parish who had taken the trouble to learn how to spell and pronounce her name correctly. That courtesy at least he could offer her.

'You haven't been tidying up the attic this afternoon?'
he asked mildly.

'No, sir!' She drew breath carefully, so as not to betray
her anxiety. 'There's nothing wrong there? I hope there's
nothing wrong!'

'No, no!' he said quickly. 'It's only that some of the
things there have been moved, I merely wondered.'

Her lips were trembling. 'Katrena was looking for some
things, she said you told her she might take what she
wanted for the crib. I hope it was not wrong? She meant
no harm, she wanted only to make her Bethlehem fine for
you.'

'She did no harm,' he said reassuringly, 'no harm at
all. I did tell her to take whatever she wished. That's
perfectly all right. I must go and look at this crib of hers.'

In the darkness of the garden, with the thin wet film of
snow whispering dismally under his feet, he walked like a
man in a waking dream. She had taken him at his word,
then. She had understood him by some blessed intuition
which had penetrated him more deeply than thought. If he
had tried to express to her the needs of his spirit she would
not have known what he meant.

The Victorian Gothic windows of the church shone
across the snow, dimly lighted, their heavy colours
scattered in his path like fallen flowers. He heard the
voices of the children, busy and animated, as he entered
the porch. Their exchanges always began in hoarse
whispers, because they were in church, but ended shrill
and excited, because they were engaged in a work of

creation, and could not contain their delight in it.

'No, not like that!' Katrena had come with treasures in her hands, and Katrena was calling the tune. 'The lamb goes *here*. The donkey *here*. There, now they can all see Him.'

'I'n't it lovely!' breathed the verger's freckled daughter. 'It's got real rockers – look! It dun't even creak.'

'Look at the lace on His frock,' whispered the little girl from the nursery gardener's, and the Rector knew by the awe in her voice that she was fingering the yellowed hem of his son's christening gown.

They fell silent and drew off a little when he came in. In the candle-lit alcove of the Children's Corner, ringed round with its garish little pictures, they had made a bower of holly and ivy round a wooden box propped on its side for the stable. Dolls had provided the Virgin and the shepherds, somebody's golliwog was the black King, Saint Joseph and the others they had cut out from coloured religious pictures and gummed untidily on to cardboard. Toy animals clustered round the crib; the wooden horse had regained his brightness in the candlelight, the incongruous red saddle shone bravely. In the centre the beloved doll in its robe of lawn and lace was just being tucked into the limewood cradle, between the arched wings of the cherub. Katrena's arms were thrust maternally to the elbows in the foam of lace, settling her child to sleep. She looked up at him over the cradle without doubt or fear, and waited to be praised; she knew she had done well.

Death, birth and resurrection are all linked, he thought.

I relinquish my dead, and I recover them; there is no other way. Love can be kept only by letting it go free, as life is incomplete without the unreluctant acceptance of death. The cradle is filled now, with life, not death; even with everlasting life, far beyond my design or my desert.

'It had to be better,' said Katrena, using another of her literal translations, and leaning across importantly to smooth the horse's mane, 'but we had no boy dolls except black ones. Do you like it?'

Ask the prisoner still pale from his dungeon if he likes the light of the sun.

'It's very nice, children,' said the Rector lamely, 'very nice indeed.' And he watched the small, none too clean hand tenderly rocking, and thought how precious a thing it must be to her to have a secure place to sleep. There were things he could give her, after all, some tangible, some intangible; he was not empty-handed any longer, he understood the gifts that would be to her mind. Cousin Sybil's return from America should not send them away.

'Shall we sing you a carol?' offered Katrena, sensing her advantage. And she marshalled her motley choir with much nudging and pushing into line, and, standing before them pale with solemnity, launched her little, croaking voice into something remotely resembling 'Away in a Manger'. Uncertainly she led, and valiantly they followed; the brave, brazen noise matched in potency the trumpets at the walls of Jericho. Like courses of masonry, the years of silence within him shivered and fell away.

He led her home afterwards by the hand, though whether he had taken it or she had given it he did not know. In the chilly darkness of the garden, the lighted window of the house glittering before them with the silvery cargo of the tree, he said suddenly, in a hesitant voice: 'My dear—'

It was strange, but he no longer felt that stab of shame at employing this mode of address. Not mine, he thought; but dear – yes, very dear.

'My dear,' he said, aware of her large eyes raised to him patiently and hopefully in the darkness. 'I shan't be able to put your present under the tree for you this evening. If you'd like it – it's just the right size for your doll – I'd like to give you the cradle.'

My Friend the Enemy

I have asked for this second interview, General, because it has come to my notice that in spite of your very fair and accurate reporting of the conversation we had ten days ago, my actions are being widely misinterpreted and misunderstood in the European press. It is no more than I had expected; they are using the only language they know. They are saying that I have changed sides, that my morale has been sapped during captivity, that I have done things here which make me afraid to go back to England, that I have succumbed to political indoctrination, and have gone over to the enemy. These, they assert, are the reasons for my declining repatriation, declining even passage to a neutral country, and electing to be turned loose here, here where I am, as a – civilian is a word which has no longer any meaning for me, though no doubt it would be their word. Let us say simply, as a man.

It was the same at the end of the Korean business, you'll remember – yes, you, of all people, will remember, for some of your countrymen had the same task to complete then as now, and carried themselves as incorruptibly and mercifully to the same unsatisfactory end. That was when the process came into use in the first place. Already it seems as if it had always been with us, this problem of the uprooted armies who do not want to go home. Already we begin to know the ropes, and even our answers are expected to fall into a certain pattern. Those which do not conform are always suspect.

That is why I have asked for this interview. I do not want you to think that I am concerned with the world's misinterpretation; their good opinion is nothing to me. But the truth is that my real situation is one of which they ought to take notice, before it is too late, and because I know they will not listen to explanations from me, I ask you to be my prophet. Also, for my own happiness, I should like you, of all men in the world, and your country of all countries, to understand what has happened, and think of me in a way which bears some relationship to the truth of what I am, and the circumstances in which I find myself.

What happened to me happened in the winter of 1959, before my captivity, and I must tell you about it in order to establish what kind of captivity mine was, and how little it contributed to the metamorphosis which befell me.

We were in the foothills of the mountains then, fighting our way back and forth over a few miles of shattered country, in a cold you must have learned to know well by this time. The period was already past when the United Nations Command were trying to put an end to the trouble economically, and we were already using all the methods we had, short of atomic bombs. They were too precious to be used on such a comparatively small affair; our forbearance was a matter of meanness rather than scruples. As usual, it turned out to be an affair by no means so small as we had hoped, and we felt deeply aggrieved at the enemy's tenacity, and his refusal to realize that he could not win. By the time of which I'm speaking we were using napalm again, and our bomber force was heavier than anything we'd used in Korea. We had before us a stretch of country as vacant and pitted as the craters of the moon, and we lived in the fringes of this devastation as moles live. No doubt you've seen such country since your mission here began.

It was in a night attack that this thing happened to me. We had taken two days to shove forward a few hundred yards, burrowing from hole to hole, and on the second night we launched a full-scale attack, after a barrage that seemed to me wasted on such a dead world. It went much as it always went: we reached the place where they should no longer have been, and they were still there, and they gave back before us only as they died. And we died, too, in considerable numbers, but that was all in the estimates. We were calculated losses, we could be envisaged. At the end of it both sides fell back and settled down into much the same positions as before, and began to plaster the ground in between with a double barrage. From the tales my father used to tell me, it became more and more, not less and less, like 1915.

As for me, I never made the journey back – not then. I was under a few scattered hundredweights of earth and stones, in a ready-dug grave under one of the hills. I had no broken bones, but was badly bruised from waist to heels, and crazed with concussion, and had very little left in the way of wits or memory for the first day. When I came round it was evening, and by the time I'd dragged myself clear the night was dropping again, the way it drops here, like a hawk, like a driven pile, like a stone.

It was deathly quiet. They must all have been tumbling back and licking their wounds still. The gunners might have been dead. I clawed my way out of the crater, and tried to get on my legs, and couldn't for numbness and pain; and I lay there listening, with my head up, trying to see as far as I could in the blazing darkness, from which all the smoke had cleared away, leaving that night glitter of the frost, like black diamonds scintillating with the refractions of ebony light, that's different here from anywhere else in the world. I could see the frozen undulations of the land, crusted into waves and troughs like an angry sea, and an occasional crouching thing that might once have been a tree. I couldn't hear a sound, a movement, a breath except my own. They were all gone. The night was on me, the cold was eating my chest as I breathed, and I knew that before morning I should die unless I could get to shelter.

I couldn't walk at first, I could only crawl, and I didn't know where I was facing, and had no more reason for going in one direction than in another. I was too dazed to think of using the stars. But it was better to move than to be still, and after a while some of the use came back into my legs, and I got on to them and went on like that, reeling about between the craters, falling into them and struggling out, like a drunk coming home through a ploughed field. It makes a lot of difference to a man to be erect, even when he can barely maintain it, and would be better off crawling.

I stumbled round and over a lot of dead men. It never occurred to me that any of them might still have retained a crumb, a glimmer of life, I was so used by then to the idea that I was the only living creature in those parts. When I fell over the low parapet of frozen earth into the foxhole, and half-stunned myself again upon rock, I looked round me with that crazy want of surprise that marks concussion, and took in the deep rock hollow behind, the embers of the fire, and the man crouched by it, as though they were no more to be reckoned with than the dead men outside.

That was probably why I didn't shoot him then, because he was wearing the kind of clothes I'd been taught to fire on at sight, and my reactions were fairly quick, even for a sergeant and a Regular. But he wasn't real, so real bullets had nothing to say to him. I just lay on the earth floor of his dugout, gathering myself slowly and staring at him, wondering why he moved when none of the others moved.

He could have killed me then without any trouble. He did put his hand out to his rifle which lay along the rock beside him and then, as if he'd realized that guns were only good in another dimension from this, he took his hand away, and sat staring back at me with his mouth a little open, and his eyes half-closed.

What is there special to tell you about him? You know how they look, he was one like all the rest. Middle-aged, shaggy, a bit bulkier, perhaps, than most of them, his face a shade broader, and curiously good-humoured and agreeable, as though he had some Tibetan blood somewhere in him. He had bad teeth, but good eyes, bright as buttons. There was a dirty, bloody rag round his neck, and the padded uniform was gone colourless, or dirt-coloured, with mud and filth and blood. All told, he looked much the same as I looked. And there we sat, studying each other until we knew every line, as though we were man and mirror, and had only one personality between us.

It was a real fire, though there wasn't much of it. I couldn't think of anything else, and I forgot the necessity for being afraid. You've been here on January nights, you'll understand. You find a fire, or you die. I began to inch myself towards it, and he looked at me, and then he moved round from between me and the miserable little gleam, and made room for me to come close to it.

The queer thing is that I knew a few phrases of the language, but I never even tried to use them. I knew they wouldn't be enough to do anything more than take the edge off the situation, and that, you see, wasn't necessary. I had no edge. There we were, and there was no third party to suspect, or discern, or create any constraint between us. I suppose in the next few days and nights we spoke perhaps three times in all, and then it was deliberately for the comfort of hearing a voice, not for communication. Between the thunder of guns and bombs a voice was sanity regained. The words didn't matter.

I had some emergency rations on me, chocolate, and compressed fruit, and biscuit. I took it out and offered him the contents in return for the fire. He understood perfectly. He had a flask of water, and so had I, and he added to our pantry some blackish bread and some hard grey cheese. We ate a little, and fed the fire sparingly, because he had only a small heap of wood and sticks in a corner of his cave. You'd be surprised how difficult it was to find anything burnable in those wastes, where trees were few to begin with and all shattered long ago, where the rare huts had been abandoned more than a year previously, and their thatch and wooden walls hadn't survived a month after they were once deserted. In winter here fuel is just as much life as water is, or food, and just as hard to come by.

The small hours came on, and the cold went into the bone, driving us into the fire until we crouched and touched over it, trembling. We drew nearer, edging flank to flank. Sleep is something that doesn't happen in a cold like the cold of this country.

After a while we huddled together, lying along the ground, body against body, hugging each other for the warmth given and received; and when he felt how comparatively thin my clothes were, he unfastened his own loose skin coat, and wound it round us both, and we lay shaking in each other's arms, and breathing into each other's faces, and all of him was welcome: the strong smell, the pressing flesh, the cheese-heavy breath. I daresay he suffered my stench as gladly. We survived the night, and hour by hour we fed the fire just enough to keep it alive, because we could afford no more.

The light came, and we had not slept, but even the coming of winter light seems to refresh a man who has lived through the killing clasp of a night like that. It was still quiet, too, only a few planes passed over. We uncoupled ourselves painfully, almost too stiff to move, and I think he meant to make a break for it that day, for he began to divide the food we had, pushing a scrupulous half towards me. But I was too sick and weak to be able to go anywhere alone, I could hardly make my legs go one before the other for the agony of the cold in my battered muscles after the fall of earth on me.

I lay and looked at him, and the tears ran out of my eyes and froze on my cheeks because I thought he was going to leave me, and then I knew I should die. He waited for me, looking back at every slow step, until he saw I could not follow him out of the foxhole; and he seemed for a little while to be wondering what to do, but in the end he put back the food he had rolled into the front of his padded jacket, and when he climbed out of the cave it was only to scour the ground around for more wood or dryish grass, or anything that would burn. He brought back the first twigs he found, to show me that he was not departing. He nodded and smiled, and shook his shaggy hair at me, and then I had courage to claw my way out after him somehow and help him in the search.

It took me infinite ages to crawl across the fifty yards of frozen ground, ridged like petrified sea; but my nearness to the earth was my aid, and it was I who found a place where a conduit had once been shored up with wood, and dug out some of the splintered fragments with my nails, and took them home in triumph.

We did well that day, we had a better fire, and at least enough water and food to keep us going, if not by any means enough to satisfy us. We looked at each other's

178

injuries in the middle of the day, when the incredible sun was out for a little while and the ferocity of the cold was tempered by the very look of it. He had two or three ugly but not dangerous flesh wounds, and had bled a good deal. I used my emergency dressings on the worst of the gashes, and cleaned up the rest as well as I could. In return he worked on me, chafing and kneading my back and legs until I actually fell asleep. Yes, it was a pretty good day. Early in the afternoon he shot a bird, some species I didn't know, though I've seen it often enough since. I never noticed the birds until then. He skinned it, and we cooked it in a hollow in the side of our fire, in thick ashes.

I had my mind back before night, only my body was still unwilling to exert itself, because of the curious, intricate pain he had been busy working out through my clothes with his hard, grimy fingers. I thought that by next day I could make an effort to get back to my own people.

It never occurred to me for a moment to suppose that he would try to stop me. A great many things were clear to me about that man. I never knew his name, he never needed one, no one else will ever be simply 'he' to me as *he* was. Never since I became a separate being have I lived in such close proximity to anyone, brothers, or parents, or wife, or children, as I did to him.

That night the guns began again. At first it was only theirs, and the range was short, and only the reverberations, shaking down loose earth and stones, tormented us. Then ours began to reply – I use the old terminology of ours and theirs purely to make myself clear – and soon they were both plastering that belt of waste territory with high explosive, because neither of them knew if the other was still entrenched there. You know how prodigal of bombs and shells the United Nations Command became about that time – anything to end it quickly, but of course it did not end.

But have you ever been a mole in the target area, as we were? It went on at tremendous pressure all night, and by day the bombers came, flight after flight. The earth groaned and quaked, and our walls silted down over us, but we dared not go out of cover, we could only dig ourselves free and wait for it to end. And it did not end. By dawn our fire was out, and we could not hunt for fuel all that day, nor recover the second water-bottle, which lay under the wreckage of our softest wall. We rolled together into the ashes of the fire, scorching our clothes but finding no warmth, smelling the smell of our own burning while we died slowly of the cold.

There was another day of this, and another night. Have you heard enough? If we had not clung together closer than lovers we should both have died.

I loved him as you love only someone you have tried to the limit, and found sound, and he loved me as his own flesh, and kept the life in me as jealously.

The next day it became almost quiet, only a few planes combing the area, so it seemed both sides were satisfied the ground was vacant. We came out of our burrow like sleepwalkers, and gathered enough wood to make a last fire, and thaw our half-dead and wholly stupefied bodies into movement. The noise in our heads never stopped, but it did not prevent us from hearing the little sounds of our own clumsy motions, as if we existed in two planes. We had nothing to eat, and no water, but we could walk. We knew that we had to get back to our own people, but even then it felt to me like a paradox, for no man had ever been mine as he was mine. Compared with my enemy, the men of my own company were strangers, speaking another tongue.

We separated about ten in the morning, having come some way together. He knew the ground better than I, and his head was clearer; he set me on my way with an emphatic pointing gesture of his whole arm, and made me a ceremonial bow, and I returned it. Then we went away from each other without breaking the silence which had been our only communication throughout.

I wandered for several hours, walking the way the sun was declining, before I made contact with a patrol, and came back into camp with them. After that it was almost as if it had never happened at all. An attitude soon recaptures you, once you have regained the ground on which it seemed valid. I didn't even go sick; they were moving up again over the same old ground, and I went back with them. It didn't strike me as absurd at the time.

But for all this recovered normality, he was still there in me.

The night of the preliminary probe I was out with a patrol, and we touched off one of theirs. It was nothing much, just a brush and they drew off again, and so did we. But the contact came with rather a shock, and all at once a man heaved up out of the darkness in front of me, and it was he. I recognized him, and I shot him.

I've often tried to work out the real sequence of what happened. He had his rifle trained before him, and he didn't fire it; I've wondered about that. Did he not know me, and quite simply never have time to pull the trigger? Or did he recognize me, and still intend to shoot, but react too late to save himself? Or did he recognize me, and deliberately refrain? You see my difficulty. I've tried to determine whether recognition came first with me, or the instinctive tightening of the finger, and I think that I knew him before I fired, and still fired. I was conditioned to react in certain ways. He was wearing the clothes at which I knew I had to fire, and I fired. Recognition, though more instantaneous still, had to fall back on thought, and thought was too slow.

I believe I am being honest, and that is the truth of it. But in any case, it does not matter. It was relevant for an instant, then it fell away into something much bigger.

He dropped, and lay still, and when I reached him he was dead.

I stood looking at him, and there was one moment of intense personal grief and regret, but I lost it very soon, because there was something else happening in me. I saw that this had been from the beginning inevitable, because it was necessary in order to complete the experience that I should kill him or he should kill me. We were not creatures of thought. It was only then that I began to see what had happened as ground for thought, only then that the seed which might have died off in the ground began to germinate. Perhaps it needed the blood of one of us; and after all, it mattered very little which one, we were one flesh.

I do not know that I believe in survival, General, but I know that I am at peace about it, and that seems to me more than enough. I know that while I exist, he exists, and while he endures, I endure. I know that it was never part of any will or desire of mine to kill him, and that my membership in him did not cease when I fired the shot. And what I know, he also knows. No words of mine can truly comprehend the complex paradoxes of our duality and our unity.

The same night, as we went back towards camp, I detached myself very quietly in the darkness, and walked away from them. I dropped my rifle into a ditch, and went back empty-handed towards the enemy, and after a long while I was fired at. I showed my empty hands and still went forward towards them; and they accepted me as a prisoner. It was desertion, I know, and desertion was foreign to my well-trained military conscience; but it was the only certain way I could think of never having to do that again.

We have nearly arrived now, General, for you can already see, being the person you are, how my present position arises from this, and how naturally. I was a prisoner of war for nearly a year, until the armistice delivered me, with all the rest, to your door. I think I lived usefully in the camp. There were constrictions, there were hardships, but I had no gun, and I possessed myself for the first time. And when it was my turn to be asked the question, I declined to be repatriated to England, declined to travel to any other country, wished and wish only to be here, where I am, and here to live as I may.

For why should I put anyone to the trouble to convey me across the world, or waste the weeks of the passage, in order to get home? I am home. Not because this was his country – don't misunderstand me, there is no dedicated sentiment about me – but because my home is where I am, at any moment of time, in any place. Language is no limitation to me, frontiers do not contain me. Oh, yes, I can be hated, here or anywhere, I can be killed, if need be. Divergents have a thin time anywhere, and to be without country or nationality is to be outcast everywhere. I can be killed, but I cannot be violated. And while I live, work and people are everywhere, here as well as in any other place.

Tell them, if they ask you, if they say I have changed sides, that I have reached the simplification of no longer acknowledging that the taking of sides is possible. If they cry that I have deserted my friends and my family, say that they are here with me, that my family are all who have need of me, and my friends all whom I meet in the street.

Tell them all this, not for my sake, but because they need to be shown, while there is still time, that there is in reality only one side, that they had better stop playing with guns, because bullets are boomerangs. Tell them that if they do not open their hearth to the enemy they will soon be without fuel. Say that if they hunt together they will get enough to keep them alive through the day, and if they sleep in one another's arms they will survive the killing cold of the night, and if they do not they will die. It is as simple as that.

But do not bother to defend me, for I have joined the ranks of the most despised and persecuted of all racial minorities. I am the Jew, the negro, the aboriginal. I am the enemy. My race is the human race.

The Lily Hand

The day Felipe died the women stopped the traffic in New Bond Street, weeping and fainting and having hysterics round that classy shop of his almost as if he were another Valentino.

I was there myself, covering the story.

During his lifetime, of course, Felipe had done everything he could to build himself up into a legend. There were all the tales about his lavish public life, his fabulous clothes, his beautiful friends, and the bare room where he hid himself when he went home, like a monk's cell, with a fine ebony coffin standing beside the bed. His fans refused to believe this was a publicity stunt. They said he was sincere, a religious mystic: it was the other side to his profession as a great cosmetician.

They found him in that coffin, lying composed and quiet, in evening dress as he'd come home from his last party. He'd been having trouble with his heart for some time, it turned out; this time he must have felt it coming, and lain down there to wait for it.

187

Round the window in Bond Street, the noise was like keening, only rather more ladylike. Sophistication will out. Believe it or not, that scene and the noise that went with it were quite something, even in a reporter's life. I began to think how little anybody really did know about Felipe, and to wonder what else there was.

That window of his, for instance. It was smallish, and just draped with soft silks, usually pastels, sometimes sudden dark silvery greens and almost-blacks. Nothing at all in it, ever, except the most beautiful small arrangements of flowers and the silver lettering of his personal sign along the foreground, with the sign itself just behind: 'The Lily Hand'. Everybody knew it, it was unique, probably the most famous trade sign in Britain. A classic pair of hands folded together, dignified and sure. In white jade, made to his own drawings, so they said.

And I got to thinking, well, why? Was there a real woman in his life, a special woman, that he'd never been able to get out of his mind? Because the more I came back and looked at those hands, the more certain I was that nobody could have dreamed them up. They'd got the mark of portraiture all over them.

So who was she? There might be more of a story in that, if only we knew it. The more I thought about it, the more I wanted to know.

My best line, I decided, was the smart, black-coat-and-skirted secretary. I hung around until the grief squad had finally dispersed; then I inveigled her out for a drink.

'If you've worked for him for ten years,' I said, 'you must know more about him than pretty well anyone else.'

'That wouldn't be hard,' she said, 'and you still wouldn't have much if I told you the lot.'

I said: 'I suppose he *did* have parents?'

'If he did, he took good care to shed them a long while ago, before he got into the big money. I came to him when he first opened his London salon. He'd already made his effort. Before he launched himself he had his personality all ready-tailored, and the day he took that place he put it on. I doubt if anyone's ever seen him naked since – even himself, in the bathroom mirror.'

'And the sign?' I said. 'Did he have that ready, too?'

'No, he started work on the drawings for those hands during the first months after he knew he was a success. I know, I saw him at it in his office sometimes, there was no secret about it.'

'Then he didn't have any model for them?'

She shook her head. 'No, there was no mystery beauty sitting for him, if that's what you're thinking. I've often wondered myself.' She paused and I ordered another drink.

'You know,' she said presently, 'I used to wonder if it was just that that was wrong with him. Felipe made a point of being seen everywhere with beautiful women but none of them ever got past the reception rooms of his life, so to speak. You can take it from me he lived like a frigid old maid. That's the first thing about him that's always made me feel there was something odd in the whole setup. And then there's the little matter of his past, as you said. He buried it, all right. Nothing gets lost as completely as that just by accident. He came here to London when he was ready to go to the top, and whatever had stuck to him from before he brushed off then – once and for all. And then there's the third strange thing . . . You knew he had religion?'

'I know he was supposed to have it – badly.'

'He had it, all right – as bad as you'd need it. I give you my word 'there was nothing normal and rapturous about *his* religion. He took to it the way hypochondriacs take to patent medicines, or drowning men to driftwood. Because it was sanctuary – and there was something after him.'

'Something out of that past he didn't have?' I said.

'Something he'd done – to somebody, sometime, how should I know? Something he spent nine-tenths of his lifetime shoving underground, and one-tenth repenting. When he talked about guilt, he meant it. *Mea culpa, mea culpa, mea maxima culpa*—' She emptied her glass and put it down with a tiny crash on the tray.

'And what do you deduce,' I asked, trying to look very different from the way she was making me feel, 'from all that?'

'I deduce the same as you do,' she said. 'A woman. Back there, in the time we don't speak of any more, the time he wanted forgotten, a woman he played hell with and walked out on – how do I know what he did to her? Only it was something pretty final, to haunt him ever after. And if you ask me, it's because of her that he couldn't get away from female beauty, but had to make it his life work – and because of her he could never let himself go with a woman again. Her face kept getting in between, I suppose – and her hands, I saw you looking at the hands,' she said. 'You were only thinking what

I've thought many a time – *that was a real woman.'*

I covered the funeral. That was pretty much of a high-class female riot, too, in a quiet way. They were all the same kind, clients of his, groomed out of their lives. There wasn't one of them who looked as if she had a story. Then right at the end, when the crowd had gone, I saw one who didn't belong.

A little stooped, middle-aged body she was, provincial down to the toes, very neat in black and violet. She came toddling up humbly, and put a little bunch of violets at the foot of the grave, and stood looking at it for a few minutes and then she turned round and made off demurely.

I went after her, caught her up at the first crossing, and gave her the treatment. I told her I was a reporter but she wasn't in the least put out.

'Oh, dear me, no,' she said, when I asked her, 'I'm no relation of his. It's only that I had him as a lodger once, a long time ago, before he was such a great man. It's quite something to remember, for an old woman like me.'

I took her to tea, and pumped her like mad, and she liked it. She'd lost her husband a year ago, and come to settle with her sister in London, but before that she'd kept a boarding house in Liverpool, and twenty years ago and more she'd had a boy of eighteen staying with her there, a young man who worked for a chemist who had three shops in the town, and manufactured cosmetics in a small way. And that was Felipe! Only his name was just Phillips then – plain George Phillips.

She gave me the chemist's name, and I brooded about

it for days, and then, after all, I took a trip to Liverpool. Because there he'd been at eighteen, it seemed, without any girl trouble, living in lodgings, which suggested he'd got only a loose sort of family at best; and then here he was, Felipe, with his name made, and the woman – yes, the undoubted woman – somewhere already in the past.

The chemist had handed over the business to his sons some years before, but the old man was still alive and messing about in the warehouses, getting in everybody's way and giving them half-senile hell. When I told him who I was and what I wanted, he wasn't impressed. The great Felipe meant nothing to him but a name, but he did like reminiscing about the old days. So he talked, and I gave the talk a push now and again in the direction I wanted to go, and picked out the bits I might want from the flood.

Luckily it was the kind of old-established shop that prides itself on keeping records back to the year dot. He turned up the books from way back, and there was the boy all right, straight from grammar school, George Phillips, and an address in a motley quarter down towards the docks; and then, not three months after he started work, a switch to the old lady's ultra-respectable boarding house. Yes, as soon as he felt secure he'd made a bolt from the low lands. He was on his way up already. Somewhere on his journey between Liverpool and Bond Street, there'd been a casualty. The longer I thought about it, the more sure I was that she'd been a fatal casualty. I kept seeing the hands, and they'd begun to look to me like a piece of exorcism that had gone wrong.

'I remember him all right,' said the old man, pawing

over his years and years of books with pleasure. 'A bright lad he was, I'm not surprised to hear he got on. He meant to. Worked hard, and spent all his spare time trying out new experiments. I always thought he'd make a go of it.'

I said: 'He didn't waste any time running after girls, then?'

'He did not, and if they ran after him they never got far, I can tell you. No, if anything he seemed to fight shy of women. He looked at them, if they were worth it – but he kept his distance.'

'You never met his family?' I asked.

'No – never meddled with my employees unless they invited it. No, he did his work, that was all I asked of him. I always had the feeling he was pretty much of an orphan, but there might still be some remnants of 'em,' he said indifferently, 'down there in the docks.' He gave me the name of the firm the boy had joined on leaving his employ, and I went off rather satisfied with myself, and as I'd got quite a lot of time to spare I went down to the docks and looked for the house.

It wasn't there any more. Neither was the street. There was nothing there but one of those blank spaces you find in so many towns since the war. If I hadn't still had over an hour to fill in before I could get a train, I probably wouldn't have troubled to take it any further, but as I had, I went to the municipal offices, and asked about the people who must have been moved from that road after the bomb fell – where they'd been housed, and whether anyone named Phillips had survived. It seemed there was an old widower of that name, who'd escaped because he happened to be a retired seaman, back on Mersey tugs for the duration, and away on duty when the street got flattened. They gave me an address for him, in a colony of prefabs out of the town, where all the survivors had been rehoused after the war. As far as they knew, this must be the Phillips I wanted.

I went there at once; it seemed a pity not to get a look at Felipe's father, or whatever he was to him, while I was here; after all this work that wasn't going to pay me, for all I could see, in anything but satisfied curiosity.

I found the right number and knocked on the door, sure he'd be out, and then there he was, staring at me across the step. Quite a presentable old chap, a regular marine type, neat as you like, clean-shaven, and the colour of teak, and almost as tough to look at. The little house shone behind him, real seaman-style. Also he had that self-sufficient look of a man who lives alone, and has done for years; but tempered by something in his eyes that made it a different kind of self-sufficiency from the kind a bachelor has.

I told him I was a nosey reporter who couldn't get somebody else's business out of his mind, and he didn't throw me out. I think a visitor was a luxury, in a small way, and he was willing to enjoy me. He let me come in and sit with him, and I offered him my cigarette case, but he liked his pipe better. It was a very modest household, but kept better than many I've been in.

I said: 'Unless I'm making a mistake, your son died recently, and he was a great man in his way. That's what brought me here looking up his early days.' And I looked at him to see if he knew what I was talking about, because

194

very likely pictures of Felipe didn't come his way very often, so the old man might easily have missed the connection. But he knew all right. He knew a lot of things he never talked about. He knew about the woman. I could tell by the way he was looking at me, without any surprise, because he'd been over all that ground himself before me, and locating the exact spot at which I'd arrived was child's play for him. And it was then I began to feel the ground giving under me, simply because he knew. How could he know? It couldn't have happened until long after George Phillips left here.

I talked a lot, because I had to have something to fill in the time until I got my bearings. He listened without saying anything, and when I dried up he knocked out his pipe, and said:

'So you came looking for a romance. You won't find one. He was the only son we had, and we did our best for him. And when he was working, he suddenly turned round on us and said he was getting out – for good – and we let him. We could have stopped him for a few years, I suppose, but he was gone already at heart. He knew where he was going, and he meant getting there, and we were his handicaps, so he left us behind. You can't stop the heart. If that's the word for what he had. I shouldn't bother to look for any other story but that one; you'd be wasting your time.'

I didn't know what to say. He was doing the talking now. There wasn't much of it, I could feel the minutes slipping from under me, and soon I should be out on the doorstep. He looked at me, and said: 'He might have lived me down, you see – but not his mother. She was the nearest perfect of any creature you're ever likely to know, and she loved him like women do love their only sons when they've lived their lives round them for eighteen years. And the minute he had a pay packet he could live on, he turned round and told her he was done with her, that she wasn't going to ruin his chances. And he went, and she let him, but she was never quite alive again. He broke her heart – did you know people still die of that? She didn't last quite a year after. The last letter I ever wrote him was to tell him she was dead, but he never answered it. He went right ahead, and became a great man, the same way many another has – over other people's faces.'

His mother! It hit me so hard I couldn't take it in all at once. It was something I'd never even thought of, and I wanted to ask him why, why, what sense does it make? But there are things even I can't do. All I could manage was to babble a sort of apology, and a promise to drop the whole thing, and then try to get myself out of there and leave him alone. I got on to my feet, and he didn't try to stop me, and all the time I knew I should be eaten alive by that unanswered why, as long as I lived. To know so much, and not know *why*!

He said at my shoulder, as I was going: 'Don't take it to heart, son. It's the world's fault as much as his.' As if he thought I understood, but I didn't understand.

And then I saw the photograph. It was a big one, standing on a table near the door, where I'd seen only the back of it as I came in. It was a woman, three-quarter length, with her hands folded in her lap.

After that, I did understand, I understood everything. Especially the price he'd paid for it. *'Mea culpa, mea culpa, mea maxima culpa!'*

My God, but she was lovely! She was one of the loveliest things I've ever seen, even this much of her, and it was old and a bit faded. After all, she'd been dead going on for twenty years. A youngish woman in a hand-knitted jumper and dark skirt, with great gentle black eyes and curly hair, and in all the lines of her bones that extreme, spare delicacy you see sometimes among the women of the ports. She had the warmest and kindest of smiles, and the look of her eyes was something children would have run to. And the hands, linked so tranquilly in her lap, had the very folds of those hands Felipe had made famous all over the world, trying to get her off his conscience, and her beauty out of his eyes – the white jade hands of character, the lily hands.

Only these hands were black.

A Question of Faith

The last train was due at 9.50, and the walk from the station to the prison gate took about a quarter of an hour. From the moment when he heard the train whistling its way distantly round the curve, the Governor became a little distracted, and his replies to his friend's questions shrank to monosyllables. When the clock pushed an indifferent hand over the rim of ten and caught its breath for the chime, he began to listen with an intent and sharply-focused eagerness which made conversation impossible.

Wyndham sat back into silence and watched him steadily for several minutes, but whatever it was he waited to hear, the night still did not provide it.

He was young to be in charge of a regional training prison, and in himself he was as much an experiment as the closed stone world he ruled. To be three years in office and still on trial is a tightrope act for any man to have to perform. The Governor showed the signs, Wyndham thought, studying him affectionately after two years of absence, in his too finely drawn thinness, the instant passion of his reactions to sound and movement, his burning weariness of eye.

No doubt they had argued, when he was appointed, that a young and enthusiastic man was needed for such a social revolution as this, a man with a vocation, as well as legal qualifications and academic honours. This kind of life ate men. The Governor was a keeper who fed himself daily to his animals, but, like all sacramental meals, his substance remained inexhaustible.

The clock smoothed its face as complacently as a cat, and now it said a quarter past ten, and still the expected, whatever it was, did not happen. The Governor leaned back from the fireside chair to take the telephone from its cradle.

'Excuse me, won't you? One of my fellows was due in by that train. Hullo, Willetts, has Bayford checked in yet?' His face mirrored the negative reply. 'Yes, I heard it – it seemed to be well on time. He may have missed the connection at Lowbridge. No doubt he'll be in later on. No, we'll give him a few hours grace. I'll call you.'

He hung up, and sat frowning into the fire for a moment under his tired eyelids.

'One of your home leavers?' asked Wyndham.

'Yes. He has two months of a five-year sentence left to run, and he's been home on the usual ice-breaking trip. It saves them from dying of gate fever – terror of not being wanted back, not finding any place waiting for them.'

'Supposing one of them failed to report back?'

'No one ever has.'

'What's the matter, then? Are you afraid this fellow might be the first?'

'Oh, no. I have absolute faith in him,' said the Governor simply.

'It's a lucky man who can say that of his best friend. What's he like, this chap Bayford?'

'Oh, young – unlucky – unhappy. His care history reads like a tract for the times. He's illegitimate, never knew his father. Mother was never much use to him. When he was three she got the county authorities to take the kid, and went more or less candidly on the streets. Married some miserably bad lot of her own calibre, and when Harry was in his last year of school and looked as if he might be profitable, they suddenly began taking an interest in him.

'You'd hardly credit,' said the Governor, in a detached tone which was belied by his shadowed eyes, 'how easy it is for worthless parents to win their children back again. Every boy wants his mother, I suppose he'll go to quite a lot of trouble to shut his eyes to the suspicion that she might not be worth having. And he'd never been officially taken from her, she had only to claim him and he was hers. Only the boy himself could have saved himself, and then only if he'd been the most exceptional of boys. They lived on him, and neglected him, and knocked him about for three years, and by that time he could hardly keep his eyes shut any longer.

'So he looked for a bit of companionship and pleasure somewhere else, and found it in the wrong places, like so many others. At eighteen he went to Borstal. He'd already been on probation and made a mess of that. The magistrate went out of his way to lecture him about what the younger generation owes to its elders, and how it's letting them down.' A faint smile touched his lips at the thought.

'At twenty-one he got five years for his share in a gang job. The only piece of luck he ever had was that the gun failed to go off, otherwise it might have been murder. Two years ago he was transferred to us.'

'And you think you've done well with him? He doesn't sound desperately promising material to me.'

'He's earned full remission since he's been here. It's been hard going, but it was worth it.'

The Governor recalled with a flash of intense pain the closed, inimical face, so young, so withdrawn, and the burning of the half-veiled eyes, terribly resigned yet more terribly vulnerable, which had confronted him at his first interview with Harry Bayford.

'He was intact morally, you see. He'd understood everything he did; there was a mind there to appeal to. All that was really necessary was to be utterly honest oneself – not always an easy thing to do.'

'I'm not completely sold on this idea of agreeing with young thugs who plead that the whole world's against them.' Wyndham softened his dissension with a smile, for they were old friends.

'He never pleaded anything, he just endured us. But the whole world *has* been against him, you know. I did what might have been the wrong thing with another man,' confessed the Governor. 'I grew fond of him. With Harry it was the right thing. It surprised him when he'd thought he was past surprise, and it disarmed him when he'd thought his armour was complete. Generosity is Harry's vice and virtue – he pays you back double whatever you offer him, whether it's trust or violence.'

'Well, if you have absolute faith in him, what are you afraid of?'

The Governor did not attempt to deny the anxiety which filled him, but only looked up under his thin hand with a wry smile, and said: 'To tell you the truth, I have not quite so absolute a trust in society as I have in Bayford.'

'I can quite see,' said Wyndham, laughing, 'why you still have the twenty-foot wall. It's to defend your children from the world outside.'

A quarter to eleven, and still nothing, no ringing of the telephone bell, no knock at the door, to break the tension of this waiting. Wyndham wondered if it was like this every time one of the prisoners went out to take his first distrustful look at the world again, and how, if it was, his friend's constitution could stand the strain. He wished a message would come soon, before the Governor disintegrated before his eyes.

'It would be a serious blow to you, apart from your concern for the boy himself, if he should fail to report back,' he said sympathetically.

'There are plenty of people and organizations waiting for something like that to happen,' admitted the Governor. 'I doubt if one lapse could provide enough capital for them to damage us, but I'd rather not give them the chance to try.'

He started up abruptly from his chair as the telephone

rang, and scooped it from its cradle with an eagerness he did not attempt to disguise. 'This will be him. Excuse me!'

He identified himself briefly, and then sat listening, the relief in his face stiffening into a new and grave anxiety. He was silent for several minutes with the receiver at his ear, and then he said sharply: 'Please hold everything until I get out there myself. Yes, I'll come at once. I should appreciate it very much if you'll let me talk to him.'

Wyndham was on his feet and at his friend's elbow as he pressed down the rest and held it there for a minute. 'What's happened? Not an accident?'

'No. No accident.' He lifted the receiver again. 'Get my car out at once, please. I shall be away a couple of hours or so. No, thanks, I'm driving myself.'

And to Wyndham he continued, as he hung up once more: 'The police picked him up for housebreaking at Hampton's Corner, about an hour ago. Householder caught him on the premises, apparently. He's gone to earth inside himself, and won't say anything. I've got to go.'

'But my dear chap, what can you do about it? If he's let you down like that.'

'I'm not convinced that he has. That's why I've got to go.'

'But Hampton's Corner – that isn't on his way here from Lowbridge at all, it's on the Stapleton road. And if he was actually caught in the house.'

'Yes, all that! The place is ten miles out of his way; the police are sure of their man. Only I'm sure of my man, too. But even if I believed we'd got all the facts, I should still have to go. Look, don't wait up for me, old man, I

may be some time. I'm sorry your first night here had to
be broken up like this.'

'Like me to come with you?' offered Wyndham, out of
sheer unwillingness to see him drive off alone with his
bitter disappointment.

'That's uncommonly kind of you, Tom, but no, thanks,
I'd better go alone. Wish me luck!'

But so far as belief in his luck was concerned, he knew
that his friend's wish was fruitless. And as he slid behind
the wheel of the big car and drove it out through the slowly
unfolding gates in the high wall, he knew that he was the
one creature in the world who believed in Harry Bayford's
innocence of all intent to offend. His loneliness did not
frighten him; he was used to being alone. No wife, no
family, no hierarchies of friends; he belonged to his
vocation more exclusively, more rigidly, than any monastic
to his cloister.

In his anxiety to have all the details, to confront and confute
them, he drove at considerably more than thirty even
through the town. Speed was terribly important, for he
was like a vital witness trying to forestall an execution; all
he knew was that Harry Bayford, whatever his past record,
would not, for any inducement which could have been
offered him, have committed a crime this night. But he
knew that so well that it was all the evidence he needed.
Others, the sceptical Stapleton police for instance, who
did not love the new prison methods, would need a great
deal more convincing.

The little town was half-asleep already, but within the

police station there was a bright, gratified wakefulness. They were waiting for him, they ushered him in at once to the Superintendent, who tempered the triumph of his smile with a sympathetic regret, so far as he was able, and told him the whole story.

'It's a large house, right on the corner there, where the lane from the junction comes out on the high road. The constable going off duty was cycling by the gates when he heard somebody blowing a police whistle, and he dived back and in at the gate just in time to see this fellow Bayford vaulting out of a ground-floor window, left of the front door – it's the living room. The lights were on in the room, and the householder – he's our local bank manager, name of Simpson – came to the window after him, still blowing away for help. Our man collared Bayford, and between them they got him back into the house.

'This was just about ten o'clock, according to the constable. Simpson says he was just putting on some coffee in the kitchen, which is at the back of the house, and waiting for his wife to come home from a bridge party at a friend's up the road, and when it struck ten he thought he'd stroll along and meet her – it's only a hundred yards or so. As he came through the hall he heard somebody moving about softly in the living room in the dark, and having his suspicions he went and got the whistle before he crashed into the room and switched the lights on.

'Bayford was at the bureau, but as soon as the lights went on he streaked for the window, which was open.

Obviously he got in that way. That's all. Nothing missing, so far as Simpson's been able to judge yet – seems he was interrupted too soon.'

The Governor, balancing his hat with absent care upon his crossed knees, asked in a mild tone: 'And what does Bayford say?'

'Hardly a word. At first he did babble that he wasn't stealing, that he hadn't taken anything, but by the time they got him inside again he'd turned dumb and sulky. All he'll say now is what's the use, nobody's going to believe him. He's made up his mind he's had it, you know, sir. I'm sorry, this is a bad letdown for you. We got his name and record from the papers and letters he had on him, and that's why we got on to you. But he won't add anything. We've been trying to get him to tell his side of it for half an hour now.'

The Governor nodded resigned understanding of this silence.

'I appreciate your calling me, and letting me butt in like this. I'd like to ask you to try and keep an open mind about Bayford. That's all I'm asking. I don't expect you to take my word for it that if he says he wasn't there to steal he's telling you the simple truth. But I will ask you to take my word for it that if he says that to me, *I* shall believe it. And I'll ask you to do us both the justice of assuming that I have solid reasons for feeling so sure of him. I've known him intimately for two years now, and what I feel about him is the result of experience, not sentiment.'

'That's understood, sir. I respect your evidence, and in

return you'll realize that I have my duty to do, on the facts as I know them.'

'Good! Would it be in order for me to talk to him alone?'

'Certainly, if you think it's any good. He's in the next room.'

'But first,' said the Governor, checking at the door, 'may I point out one thing? This boy was on his way back to us after a five-day home leave. He should have caught the connection at Lowbridge at 9.25, and by his being here at all he must have fulfilled his bargain up to that point. When he didn't arrive I assumed, as I'm still assuming, that he missed that connection. Now he turns up here, ten miles out of his way by your reckoning, but, by mine, on the nearest point on the road between Stapleton and Mordenfield. There's a bus from Stapleton at 9.45. My estimate is that when he missed his train he begged a lift on the first car he saw heading in the direction of the Stapleton road, to try and catch that bus.'

'It would make a good story,' agreed the Superintendent, solidly entrenched against believing in it.

'In which case it should be possible to trace the car.'

'If he'll give us a description, we'll try. But I'm afraid he's going to need more that that.'

'That's evidently what he thinks, too,' said the Governor, and went into the room where the boy was.

His heart chilled with dismay at the sight of him. He was sitting compactly and resignedly upon an upright chair, his feet planted neatly together, his hands clenched tightly upon the brim of the new trilby in his lap, his eyes roving with narrowed, stoical despair from the constable who kept him company to the window and the door. These were not possible means of escape to him now, they were tunnels to the other, the forfeited world.

He had receded far down the subterranean passage from freedom to the dark anonymity out of which he had been coaxed with so much pain, and so extraordinary a delight, during the last two years. The thin, intense face, lately wildly responsive to every recognition, had congealed into a formal mask of withdrawal and loneliness, as though he defied anyone ever to touch him again; but the alert eyes were frenzied with despair.

Even when he saw the Governor enter his expression did not change; only the eyes fixed on the newcomer hopelessly, almost indifferently, as though from a great distance.

This was the very face they had seen turned upon them when first he came to Mordenfield. Could everything be undone in one hour, like this?

The constable looked over the Governor's shoulder into the Superintendent's face, and got up and went out, closing the door after him.

The Governor said: 'Hullo, Harry.' He had never called him that before, and after tonight he probably never would again, but there is a time for everything, and now it seemed so inevitable that he did not even notice it. 'You'd better tell me all about it,' he said. 'I'd tell you some of it myself, but they might not like it that way round, so you tell me.'

The boy said in a slightly lame voice, as though the effort of silence had already partly disabled him from speech: 'I bet they've told you all that matters to them. I got picked up in a house where I'd no right to be. What more do you want?'

The Governor lifted a chair, and set it opposite to the one on which Harry sat. When he found himself compelled to meet someone else's eyes so closely, the boy turned his head away, but the gesture, instead of being defiant, was indescribably revealing, and more like a convulsion of pain than a gesture of rejection.

'I want to know *why* you went in there,' said the Governor. 'I could make a guess, but they wouldn't be interested in my guesses. So you tell me. Why did you go into the house? Because, of course, it wasn't to steal.'

The head turned again, abruptly, the eyes flared wide. 'I haven't said it wasn't, have I?' His thin hands, nervous as a girl's, tightened violently on the brim of the hat.

'You don't have to say it. I know it.'

'You think you can kid me with a confidence trick like that?' said the boy unpleasantly. 'I've had all that once. I'm over it.' But he began to shake, and had to dig his heels into the floor and his teeth into his lip to suppress the weakness.

The Governor didn't argue; he said instead: 'You missed your connection at Lowbridge, and went up the lane to see if you could hop a car to Hampton's Corner, to try and catch a bus. I don't suppose you made a note of the number – why should you? – but you could describe the car and the driver. It should be possible to find him, and the station

210

staff will be able to confirm how you missed your train. All right, so we've got you to Hampton's Corner. The bus had beaten you to it, after all, and you were still eight miles from home.'

The boy had begun to breathe hard, and the frozen calm of his face was shaken with painful tremors of hope.

'It wasn't a car, it was a van. A bloke from the beet factory – they work all night in the season.'

'Better still! Finding the man will be easy, now we know just where to look. Go on from there, then. You were eight miles from home, and getting worried, because it was getting round to the time when we would be expecting you, and you didn't want us to think you'd welshed on us—'

Harry shut his eyes and rolled his head back as if from a punch. 'What's the use? They won't believe me! Nobody'll ever believe me! I could have told them, but what the hell's the good? Let me alone, can't you? I was all set to take it, and you come beggaring in here and unwind me—'

'You wanted us to know,' said the Governor patiently, as if there had been no interruption, 'that you were on your way, before you walked the eight miles, or hitched a lift if you were lucky. You're making me tell it all for you, Harry. You might make just a small contribution yourself.'

The thin hands came up and clenched the short dark hair at the temples and out of the trembling mouth speech came pouring in jerks and recoveries, like arterial blood.

'I wanted to phone you and tell you why I was late – and that I was coming as quick as I could. There's no call box all along that road, and anyhow, I didn't have any coppers. I saw the phone wires went to that house, so I went up to the door and rang the bell, to ask if I could use their line – but nobody answered, and there was this room, with the curtains not drawn, and a bit of fire still in – and I could see the phone in there on top of the bureau. I tried the window – I know it was daft. I wish I'd never touched it, but I did – and it went up, and I thought, it'll only take me a minute, so I shinned over the sill and went and started to dial. I know I shouldn't have gone in – but it looked so easy, and there was nowhere else to ring from, and I thought for sure there was nobody in. They never answered the door, and all the front lights was off.

'But I no sooner got a couple of numbers dialled when I heard him in the hall, and I put the phone back, quick, and stood still, hoping he'd go away. I knew then I'd been a fool – I was scared to go out and come clean to him. And the next minute he was in on me, whistling like mad, and the lights all on, and – and I run for it. With my record, what else could I do but run? Nobody's going to believe *that* for a tale – not from me! With my record, what else could I do but run?'

Listening to him bleed, himself weak with an exquisite, singing relief, the Governor thought: Now it's up to me to get him out of this!

And he found time, between the pulsations of his gratitude, to be deeply afraid; for it was certainly he who had stripped the boy's armour of loneliness from him, and unless something better could be put in its place he might die of the cold.

To know truth when you hear it is one thing, to prove it to the police quite another. And what kind of evidence had he to offer, except the station staff at Lowbridge, and the van driver, though the latter was certainly a godsend? He prayed that Harry might have talked about himself to this chance acquaintance in the dark, but he knew how unlikely that was.

No, it was up to him to put out his hand, and pluck proof out of the air. If one has faith enough, it ought to be possible, and he had claimed an absolute faith. His mind began to read over, word for word, all the things Harry had told him, looking with particular industry for the minute revelations he did not know he had made.

'You must repeat all that to the Superintendent, just as you've told it to me.'

'What's the use? There's nobody to bear me out, after I got out of the van. And *he* doesn't know but what I come there just to lift whatever was lying around.'

'You'll tell him, all the same. Do as I ask you. You know you can rely on me.' He did not add, but he knew that Harry heard: 'As I knew I could rely on you.'

'I am promising him a miracle,' he thought to himself, 'and he believes me. And now I have got to produce one.'

He went to the door and opened it. The Superintendent looked up knowingly from his desk, rather surprised, even rather disappointed, that the enthusiast should have given up so soon.

'I wonder if you would hear Bayford's story now? He's ready to tell it.'

The boy went through it again almost word for word,

his eyes returning always to the Governor's face, and resting there with such trust and such terror that it seemed altogether too much for one man to carry.

'We'll certainly make enquiries for the driver of the factory van,' said the Superintendent at the end of the recital. 'For the rest of the story, it holds together, but you'll allow there's been time for thinking it out, and I should have been more impressed if it had been told immediately. It's a pity there can't be independent confirmation. I'm sure you accept it, sir, and I take it for granted you're in good faith in urging it upon me. But I have to deal with evidence, and you'll agree there's very little possibility of finding any to support this version of what happened.'

The Governor said, aware of the eyes which held fast to him as to life: 'I think I can supply you with two pieces of evidence which will go a very long way towards confirming Bayford's story. I start with the advantage, you see, of having no doubts at all about his honesty in the matter, so I can explore the details of what he's told us even more closely than he can, in his present state. You know this man Simpson? He isn't, by any chance, deaf?'

'Good Lord, no,' said the Superintendent, astonished. 'He hears as well as any of us.'

'And he was in the house when it was entered, so he must have been there when Harry rang the bell. Make no mistake, if he says he rang the bell and got no answer, that's exactly what happened. I don't expect you to be sure, but *I* am sure. Therefore I think it very probable that you can tell Mr Simpson something he doesn't know about his own house. The front door bell is out of order. At least you can send a constable round to test it, can't you?'

The Superintendent gave him a long look of mingled patience and derision. 'We can settle it from here. I'll ring up Simpson, and ask him to try it.'

'But I'd rather the constable went and did it himself – with all respect to Mr Simpson, but in fairness to Bayford. And at the same time, would you ask him to look into something else there? Knowing Bayford as I do, I know something he hasn't even remembered to tell us. He says he went into the room to telephone, and had already begun to dial when he was interrupted. It didn't occur to him to say that he fully intended to pay for his call, but I tell you so for him—'

The boy's face had suddenly flushed and softened into a wild relief. He opened his lips with a gasp, but the Governor restrained him with a quick pressure of his hand upon the tight fingers that clutched the new hat.

'If he had already begun to dial his number, he had already paid. The price of a call from Hampton's Corner to Mordenfield is fivepence. Somewhere in that room, unless he had time to pick them up again as he ran for it – which I very much doubt – your constable will find five pennies.'

'Sixpence!' stammered the boy, faint and sick with eagerness. 'I told you, I didn't have no coppers – it was a sixpence. I put it inside the top drawer of the bureau, and I never thought about it afterwards.'

He clamped his knees hard together and clenched his hands, to prevent himself from trembling all over.

215

'If your constable finds the bell out of action, and the sixpence in the drawer, Superintendent—'

'If he does,' said the Superintendent, politely tempering his incredulity, 'it looks as if we shan't have to detain Bayford any longer. That would be clear enough.'

He rose and went out, and they waited in silence, without looking at each other, because there was nothing they had to look for with any uncertainty, it was only other people they had to fear now, and ungentle circumstances.

The Superintendent came back into the room, and sat down again at his desk, staring at the telephone. And once, when the silence had lasted almost ten minutes, he looked up suddenly into the Governor's eyes, and seemed about to ask him something, but thought better of it.

It seemed to him criminal recklessness to go about the world staking your life on other people, like this, but it was none of his business, and the bubble was due to burst any moment, without any pricks from him.

The telephone rang.

They sat breathlessly still, watching and listening as the confident hand lifted it, and the sceptical voice said: 'Well, what results?'

Then there was a silence. 'All right,' said the Superintendent flatly, 'that's all, you can come on back now.'

He laid the telephone resentfully in its cradle; it offended him to see the probabilities disarranged.

'Well, I should have lost my money. The bell doesn't ring. The sixpence was in the drawer. Bayford, you'll probably never know what a lucky lad you are!'

The boy sat with his eyes closed, and the colour ebbing and flowing in his thin cheeks, and all the lines of his body growing languid and eased.

When he opened his eyes, the Governor was leaning over him, smiling, a hand under his forearm to lift him gently out of the chair.

'Come on, Harry! We're going home.'

The Purple Children

The outrage took place at eleven o'clock on a moonless night, before the stars began to silver the white walls of the church with their mysterious and tender twilight. The policeman on guard at the side door of the Town Hall was cut off from the rear entrance into the courtyard by one high wing of the building, and heard nothing until the alarm sounded. It was the sentry at the rear gate, an eighteen-year-old, new to the town and ill at ease with his enforced duties there, who was singled out as the weakest spot in the defences. Half-dozing on his walk back and forth across the gate, he heard the most innocent sound in the world, a girl's voice calling softly: 'Puss, puss, puss . . . Here, pussy!'

As he started into wakefulness with the exaggerated attention which made the walls seem higher and the night darker, a little figure with the light running steps of a child darted towards the gate, and halted with her hands locked upon the bars. He saw how slight she was, and how young, not more than fifteen. Her frock was dark, probably black like so many of them here, and her thin, small wrists issued pale and strange from the sleeves, afloat from her body, as though they could have passed through the bars with ease, and left him helpless behind. But they did not. She turned on him a face which was only a silvery oval and a dark shining of eyes, and he thought he saw about it the shadowy movement of unkempt locks darker than the darkness.

'You can't go in there,' said the sentry gruffly. 'You ought to be in the house at this time of night. Don't you know there's a curfew?'

'I *was* in the house. I only came out because of my cat. She got out when I went to bring in wood, and I couldn't catch her. She's only young, she runs away. It's no use telling *her* there's a curfew.'

'She'll come back in the morning,' said the sentry awkwardly. 'They always do. You go home, like a good girl, and don't you risk running about here in the dark. Somebody might think you were up to something.'

'But she might not come back. She's never been out at night before. She sleeps on my bed. I could get her now, if you'll let me. She ran through there into the courtyard. Won't you please help me to catch her? I'll take her straight home if you will.'

The boy felt the small, cold hand laid entreatingly on his arm. She was only a kid, she hardly came up to his shoulder, and she was beginning to sniff ominously. He couldn't see any harm in it. He'd got orders to treat the natives politely and considerately, as long as they weren't making trouble, and what trouble could this waif possibly make?

'I shall lose her,' said the girl in a quavering voice. 'I've had her from a little kitten, and now I shall never get her back again. Oh, *please*!'

'I *can't* let you in there, I should get into trouble if anybody found out—'

'Well, who's going to find out? All I want is to get my cat. You'll be there close to me every minute, you can see every move I make. And you've got a gun – I don't see what you have to be afraid of. Oh, do please help me! Only a moment. If she won't come to me, I promise I'll go home.'

He hadn't meant to do it, but somehow he had set his hand to the bars beside hers, and thrust the gate open before her.

'Well, be quiet about it, can't you, or somebody'll hear us. Come on, quick, and get her, and get yourself out of here.'

She slipped past him like a shadow. The only sound was the light, hasty tread of his own feet keeping hard on her heels. He turned his back on the gate and the silent, dark lane outside, and pressed at her shoulder as she flitted into the most obscure corner of the yard, where the shabby outhouses leaned together in a huddle of shadows, and the steps plunged down to the cellar. Behind them the tall bulk of the Town Hall shut off the awaking stars, and the ropes of the flagstaff creaked faintly in the wind which never stilled in the upper air.

'There she is! You see, I told you!' whispered the girl triumphantly, and darted forward and was lost among the deeper shadows under the wall. And there really was a cat, the sentry saw with relief and satisfaction, a thin little tabby shape skipping from darkness to darkness, evading them with the light, unhurried insolence of cats everywhere. It took ten minutes to run it to earth at the foot of the cellar steps, against the closed door.

The girl snatched up her quarry and held it struggling in her arms. She looked up at the sentry under the black tangle of her hair, with a wild smile.

'Thank you! Now I'll go home. You were very kind to let me come in.'

But she did not move, she stood looking at him still, her lips parted, her eyes enormous and shy and wary. When she looked at him like that he felt how alien he was in this place, and even her thanks could not compensate him for the quiet, patient hatred of her people. She let her body touch his, her sharp little shoulder leaning for a moment into the hollow of his arm, which moved of itself to hold her. It was like holding a willow sapling, so pliant she was, and yet so unmoved, so immaculate, as if her body did not understand, and felt no awareness of his disquiet. And then they both heard, clear through the silence, the sudden light impact of feet, as though someone had dropped from the high wall.

The sentry span round and went up the cellar steps three at a time, just in time to see the figure of a boy disentangle itself from the severed ropes of the flagstaff, and run head-down for the gate.

He would have kept silence if he had not lost his head; but the shout of rage and alarm was out of him before he knew it, and after that there was no hope of keeping it all quiet and pretending that no one had got past him during the night. The only chance he had was to get at least one prisoner to show for it. He hurtled after the racing boy, hauling the loaded spray-gun round from his shoulder in flight, to bring it to bear upon the fugitive.

He heard the girl scream, and was startled because the sound came from only a yard or two behind him, where silently, wildly, she was running, too. When she saw him check for an instant to ready the gun, she ran past him and flung the cat sprawling and clawing in his face. He threw up his left arm to cover his eyes, and swerved aside, firing the gun blindly.

The spray spattered darkly over her cheek and her spread hands, but she had gained the few yards she needed for herself and her partner, and she flew through the gate and pulled it to with a clang. Before the sentry could fling off the cat and wipe his eyes clear of the blood from his scratched forehead, both the fugitives were snatched away into the silence and darkness of the little streets.

People came pouring into the courtyard from three doors now. They found the sentry mopping his face, a long, violet stain upon the ground, and the coils of the severed rope dangling at the foot of the flagstaff. They got the Major out of bed, and the sentry reported to him with every excuse he could think of, though the sum of them all sounded thin enough.

'She was only a little girl, sir, a kid about fifteen, I didn't think she could be up to anything. She was looking for her cat.'

The Major had been in the country for over a year, and was accustomed to the local style of warfare, to the ugly demands it made upon him, and the satisfaction he sometimes felt in their ugliness, which frightened and depressed him more than anything else. He stood gazing at the boy without rancour. After all, he was only three years older than the enemy, by his own estimate; for him this game might still be able to dissemble its ugliness.

'They are always kids of fifteen,' said the Major. 'Haven't you learned that yet?'

'But there was a cat, sir, that was the truth, anyhow.'

'That skinny tabby,' said the Major wearily, 'belongs to the caretaker. I imagine its appearance was a stroke of luck. On the other hand, she may have seen it before she made up her story and began calling. She certainly never owned it. Well, you seem to have spent practically a quarter of an hour being civil to her, I take it you can pick her out again?'

The sentry, who was not good at thinking, obeyed his instincts. He was too frightened of his own side, by this time, to retain much resentment against the enemy; his fear even drew him into a kind of distant alliance with them. He said: 'No sir, I don't think I could. She had her hair over her face, and she kept in the shadow all the time. It was pretty dark there under the wall. I don't think I should know her again. There's scores of them that same build, thin as a monkey.'

'And scores of them,' said the Major, looking almost affectionately at the long violet stain like blood upon the stones, 'with purple hands and faces? At least you had the sense to fire your charge. That ought to give her one distinguishing feature, don't you think?'

The sentry looked at the dye in his turn, and was filled with a treasonable but unmistakable regret.

'I'm sorry, sir,' he lied. 'It was just then she threw the cat, it put me off proper. I reckon I missed her.'

'Then why,' asked the Major gently, 'did she drip violet dye practically all the way to the gate?' He marked the last infinitesimal spot in the light of his torch, and, searching back and forth along the stones, could find nothing more. 'A pity! A heavier charge, and we might have been able to follow her all the way home. Did you mark the boy, too?'

'No, sir. He was well out of range, only he turned back to catch hold of her hand.' It was the first time he had fully realized all that he had seen. Regret rose in him like a tidal sea. 'They haven't done anything all that bad, sir, it's only a flag.'

The Major smiled, thinking that when this boy was forty instead of eighteen he would no long make the absurd mistake of speaking of 'only' a flag.

'Whoever it was worked extremely fast. He's left about ten feet of the flagstaff coiled round with barbed wire as he came down, and it seems to be stapled in half a dozen places. You must have been very absorbed in your cat-hunt. And he must have spent a longer time practising the movements involved before he could reproduce them at that speed. Yes, I should like to congratulate that boy. But when we've found her we shall have found him, too. We'll try the grammar school first,' he said, smiling to himself, beginning to feel the terrifying satisfaction of hate reacting against hate. 'If she isn't there, we'll visit the homes of all those girls who don't answer the register. We shan't have to look any farther.'

In the shed behind Niko's father's shop, Ariana knelt over a pan of water, scouring with a handful of wet sand at the backs of her hands. The water lay in her palms as she rinsed them, as clear as it had come from the well; only the wreaths of sand lay in the bottom of the pan, stirring idly as the drops fell. Cristo held the torch close, keeping his body between its light and the covered window. Andreas crouched on his heels, his head bent close to Ariana's, his cheek brushed occasionally by her swinging hair.

'It's no use,' she said, letting her hands lie quiet suddenly in the wet skirt of her dress, and looking up at him with enormous black eyes. The misshapen blotches of purple ate away half her face into shadow. Behind her all the silent, intent partisans drew closer with a long sigh. 'It won't come out,' she said with the calm of despair. 'Now they have only to look for me – I can't be hidden. Andreas, what am I to do?'

'If they find you,' he said, taking her stained hands in his, 'they find me, too.'

'That's foolish and wasteful. You'll be needed again. And besides, they'd beat you. They'll only imprison me. No, it was great luck that you were not splashed like me. Don't be so ungrateful as to throw it away.' Her voice was violent and resolute, but she was very frightened. He felt the small, wet hands, hot with scouring, tremble in his own.

'I will not let you bear it alone. We were all in this act

226

together. When we drew the lots we drew the danger with them, as well as the privilege.'

'They'll come straight to the school,' said Cristo. 'But if only one girl is missing they may not notice it, and no one will betray you. Perhaps if you stay at home and take care not to be seen—'

'For how long?' said Andreas shortly. 'You see the marks won't come out, they'll have to wear away gradually. Do you think she can be hidden for months?'

'But they may give up in a week or two. She need not be hidden from our own people, only from *them*.'

'If they do not find me in the school,' said Ariana with authority, 'they will want to see the register and find out who is missing. It is only another way of being set apart. I think I would rather be there to face them. It is not I who will have cause to be ashamed.' But her body shook and her hands contracted in the boy's hands, because she knew she would still be afraid.

'If we tried linen bleach,' said one of the girls timidly, 'do you think it would move it?'

Niko shook her head. 'No, it's an old vegetable dye, nothing will fetch it out, it has to wear off. My uncle is a dyer,' she said sadly, 'I know.'

Andreas stood up slowly, still holding the thin marred hands in his. All the intent and anxious eyes settled upon him and clung.

'Yes. I had forgotten,' said Andreas. 'Yes, of course, your uncle is a dyer. Does he still use this dye?'

'There's no substitute for it if you want this purple, and it's faster than the modern colours. Yes, he always keeps it.'

Andreas looked down and smiled into Ariana's eyes, and his thin brown face relaxed into a reassuring tranquillity. 'Come!' he said, drawing her up by the hands. 'It will be hours yet to daylight, we have time. They won't find you, Ariana. They'll never find you.'

In the morning light the Major looked out of his window, and saw the silvery coils of new barbed wire like a guardian serpent about the flagstaff. And above, afloat upon the restless wind, the expected flag, an enemy that could not be imprisoned or exiled or killed, and certainly could never be silenced. It would soon be down, of course. It could not be nailed to the staff, there had not been time, and silence had been essential. Tied, probably, before the ropes were cut away. It would soon be down; the only trouble was that it would go up again somewhere else. It always did. He was getting used to it.

He had spent several months of his life searching the little houses of these towns for explosives and arms, for subversive literature in the native tongue, for wanted men on the run; and as far as he could see the same processes must continue for ever. The only difference seemed to be that on every occasion the circumstances of the search became a little meaner and more humiliating. Now it was a little girl with a face stained by vegetable dye, who had made a fool of a homesick boy, and helped another boy to raise once again the ubiquitous flag. The Major felt an impatience to have the miserable business finished; but by daylight he no longer mistook for anger and hatred what was, after all, nothing but disgust and exasperation.

228

The grammar school opened at eight o'clock; at half past eight the Major presented himself there with a sergeant and two men.

It was a necessary act of restraint on his part to wait the additional half-hour, he found it important to prove to himself that what he felt was not the eagerness of the hunter, but only the determination of a man with a sense of duty. If he once began to disbelieve in his own sense of duty he might very well be sick with self-disgust when the moment came, and the terrified child was dragged forth from the back row of desks, shrinking and trying to hide her disfigured face behind a handkerchief. It seemed to him, when he thought of her as an individual girl, that all he had achieved in this war of attrition was to turn little schoolgirls of fifteen into viragos who ran towards danger instead of away from it, and hurled clawing cats into the faces of the enemy; which might be considered a remarkable achievement in its way, but had not been at all his intention.

He was punctilious in waiting in the entrance hall while the headmaster was fetched out to him, though he could no longer be sure whether this was out of consideration for the man's feelings, or from a desire to compel him to lead the authorities with ceremony to their capture. The moment might be salutary for the teacher as well as the pupil.

'I need hardly tell you why I'm here,' he said, when the headmaster came, his spectacles a little askew on his antique and aquiline nose, his short-sighted eyes blinking mildly at his visitors. 'No doubt you've already seen the flag over the Town Hall.'

'I see it's still there,' said the headmaster gently. 'I thought you would have had it down by now. But no, naturally you need not tell me why you are here.'

'We intend,' said the Major, 'to make an example this time. If you allow your children to move up into the front line, you must consider that it is you yourselves who inflict their punishments upon them. We would infinitely rather deal with you.'

'We would infinitely rather that you did,' agreed the headmaster. 'You must do what you feel to be your duty. But so must our children. Would you like to begin with the little ones? Forgive me, but your gambit leads me to believe that you are looking for someone more than usually embarrassing as an opponent.'

The Major would have liked to think of a cutting reply, but he had long accustomed himself to the realization that his position would not stand it. The situation had placed irony clean out of his reach.

'I am looking for a girl of about fifteen. There was also a boy, but I have reason to believe that he will not be so immediately recognizable. You may not be aware that we have recently adopted the use of a spray-gun loaded with one of the local vegetable dyes. The girl will be stained purple. This time I can promise you there will be no collective punishment – this time it will not be necessary.'

'Purple,' said the schoolmaster reflectively. 'A royal colour. Also the colour of mourning. A nice choice! And you think the boy escaped?'

'I think it hardly matters. Once we have our hands on the girl he will come forward of his own will.'

'I see you have not entirely wasted you time with us,' said the schoolmaster with a polite smile. 'Very well! You wish to inspect our senior forms? I have kept them assembled in the hall for you. Please!'

The Major strode across the polished lobby, the sergeant and his men keeping step behind him. The headmaster, advancing his hand to the knob of the hall door, levelled one sudden, glittering glance into the eyes of the invader, and it seemed for a startling instant that what he felt for him was no longer simple antagonism, but almost pity. Then he pushed the door wide, and stood back for his visitors to enter.

The Major marched over the threshold with the briskness of complete confidence, almost of triumph. Fifty-three young heads, with marvellous unanimity, were raised to confront him, the challenging light of fifty-three pairs of dark, wide, Byzantine eyes bristled at him like bayonets, and he checked in his stride and wrenched himself sidewise into stillness, as though he had indeed run his beribboned breast into a thicket of steel. He had come looking for a marked outcast. He beheld a regiment, a Pyrrhic phalanx of embattled children, all their delicate, olive faces spattered from forehead to chin with the resplendent purple of royalty and mourning.

I am a Seagull

When I was a child, I had an aunt by marriage who came
from the Hebrides, and after she was widowed she used to
come and stay with us sometimes, in our incongruous
suburban house in North London. I don't remember what
she looked like, or even the sound of her voice, but I know
that she brought something of the islands into the town
with her, besides her accent and her songs; a sort of secure
restlessness, a stormy peace.

It was she who first told me all the old stories about the
seal-wives, those mysterious creatures who came out of
the sea and sloughed their skins to become women, like
other women to all appearance, but more dangerous and
more unobtainable. Almost always they came for love of a
mortal man, or, at any rate, somehow let themselves subside
with deceptive tameness into a mortal marriage; but always,
in the end, it was the sea-half of their dual nature that won
them back. They made female excuses about being forced
to depart if their husbands struck them three times, and
then took advantage of anything, a touch, a stumble, to

pretend that they had suffered the three irremediable blows; but somehow it was always clear to me that these pretexts covered the revulsion of their own unassuageable longings. They returned to the sea because in the battle of desires the sea was the stronger.

Brought up on fairy stories of another kind, in which marriages existed only to continue happy, and unrecorded, ever after, I suffered seriously from the contemplation of these separations.

'But why,' I protested, 'is it always the sea that wins? If she loved the fisherman, how could she love the sea more?'

My aunt said simply, as though it admitted no argument, that the sea was stronger than the land, and the sea life than the land life.

'But that means it always has to be an unhappy ending,' I objected, my human sense of justice troubled, for I felt the sorrows of those fishermen more than all the pathetic contrivances of Hans Andersen.

She gave me – this I do remember – a surprised but tranquil look, and said mildly: 'Why should you think that ending unhappy, more than the other?'

I never found an answer to that; it was a kind of terrible window into the seal-woman's heart, and I spent long, solitary hours exploring new sensitivities within my mind, trying to determine whether she had the same right to happiness as her mortal husband, and whether it was right to try to keep her when she was destroyed with the scent and desire of the sea. Children sometimes become involved very deeply in problems like these, and

I was already an imaginative little boy.

But my aunt also lost her battle with the ocean, and went back to the Hebrides, and gradually these stories which had so terrified, ravished and perplexed me faded from my mind.

I grew up an inland man myself, from head to foot, and, what with school and Oxford, congealed into as satisfactory an ordinariness as any parents could wish; and by the time I was nineteen, and confronted, like all my generation, with an unwanted but accepted war, and the problem of what to do about it, my only eccentricities were writing poetry and struggling with an occasional play. I had a few promising contracts already, when the stage went into cold storage for a couple of years, and I into the RAF for seven. When I came out, my father was dead in an air raid, and my mother settled into a little house in a Midland town, where I joined her, in a curious mood of suspended will, to try to think what I was going to do next.

Did the war really teach me very much? I don't think so. Or rather, what it taught me became, as soon as it was over, sealed off into another compartment of my life and was of no more practical use to me. All I remember clearly from those days is the uneasy ecstasy of flight, and my painful dissatisfaction with the machinery of it, which permitted the experience of just so much of bliss, just enough to drive me mad with what was withheld. If you've ever dreamed of flying – it's quite a common experience, I'm told – you will know what I mean. To be free and light in the air, to turn and take the curl of the wind at will, without that odious intervention of the containing, the alien machine! That was what I longed for, and could not have. Sometimes I dream of it now and wake up trembling, with tears in my eyes. Because I could not have it when most I needed it. Because of Lucy.

I had a dwindling gratuity, a rusty gift for words, no job, and a blank wall in front of my senses at twenty-six. I went off with a decrepit little car, a poor substitute for the wings I wanted, to fritter away my leave in Cornwall, and came in October to a fishing village on the north coast, a wild, cliff-closed bay with an impossible harbour, in and out of which the diminutive fleet could inch their keels only in good weather and a southerly wind. One zigzag street rolled down by cobbled leaps into the bay. When the wind was high it drove the spray far above the roofs and the tide up to the edge of the square. Each side of the obstinate little lightning-flash cleft of human dwellings, the cliffs reared their wet, slate-black sides to a crumbling huddle of heath, and gorse, and tussocky grass, screaming with gulls.

I liked it there. I stayed at the only hotel, at the top of the jagged street, and I walked on the cliffs in the wildest weather October brought us. It was the nearest thing to flight I could find – dangerously near sometimes at the edge of the sheer, fluted slide of slate, looking down on the boiling bay and the streaming blue-black beach.

It was raining, too, in a wild downpour, the day I met Lucy; even the air had become lashing water, and as I went up the cliff-path there was above me an inverted cauldron of cloud, boiling, too, and casting up spinning, blown, crumpled debris of gulls. They screamed through the howl of the wind, like demons. Their voices seemed to me to hold the whole of desolation, but the whole of joy, too. I went up, flapping in my oilskins, to where the rocks, like broken teeth, jutted on the cliff's edge, the wind round them like a coiled ribbon, black, oily, streaming storm water.

There was someone there, on the extreme edge, arching a slender back to balance birdlike on the rim. Raincoats are sexless, but when this being heard or sensed me, and turned a sudden intent face to stare, I saw it was a girl.

The gulls were blowing round her like aimless fragments of paper on the wind, and the rain was salt with spray. She was wet as a seal, her short black hair streaming water, her eyes brilliant, her face sleek, everywhere the gloss and glaze of the water flowing down her, and polishing her with liquid grey light. She looked at me and laughed, straight into my face, because I must be as mad as she was, to be there in such weather. In all the gestures she made there, I never saw any of shielding herself, or shaking off water, or hiding even her eyes from the sting of the driving rain. She arched her head, her body, her face into it, and let wind and weather break upon her as if she felt only a caress, and exulted in it. And she put an instant hand upon my arm as I reached her, and leaned to watch the thunder and slash and hollow withdrawing cry of the waves beating in under the cliff.

'Listen!' she cried. 'Listen! Isn't it magnificent?'

I screamed obvious things at her, feeling that she ought to be indoors and dry and sane, though I might act like a lunatic if I chose. Only when the wind subsided a little could we hear each other's words without shrieking, and therefore our conversation there on the cliff was nothing but breathless laughter, and the exchange of glances. I loved her before ever I knew her name. She was beautiful like a slender, bright, ardent bird, muscular, and wild as the wind.

We came down into the town together at last, and when the walls sheltered us we could speak, and exchange names. It was too late then for us ever to be strangers again.

'You're not staying here?' I asked, half-surprised when she did not turn in at the inn door, for indeed she had not the look or the sound of a native of any place familiar to me.

'I live here,' she said, 'in the white cottage near the harbour. My name's Lucy Hillier.'

I asked if I might walk down there with her, and we went, water running from us all the way as if we were the revenants of drowned people, and we not caring, hardly knowing. As we went she looked at me and laughed, and her laughter seemed to ring from wall to wall of the empty street.

'You like the wind and the storm, too,' she said. 'Most people think I'm crazy because I love it.'

When we reached the cottage she asked me to come in, and I wouldn't, because I was chary of bringing all that water into her mother's house; but also because it gave me an opportunity to ask if we could meet again next day, instead. She said yes, and I knew she was glad, and all the way back to the hotel room where I shed my soaked clothes

238

I was in a kind of wary dream, conscious of the danger of waking, and the necessity for walking and even breathing with infinite delicacy, not to puncture the thin shell of sleep that kept such delight possible.

I saw her again next day, and the next, and now that the wind had dropped, and the sun came out over a placid sea, Lucy appeared to me more ordinary, more accessible, but not less wonderful nor less to be desired. On the seventh day I asked her to marry me, shaking with nervousness, because I was no great catch for any girl, and her happiness seemed to me so vulnerable that I was terrified of touching, much less taking, her. She drew herself against me in the sun-warmed grass on the cliff-top, and wound her arms round me, and said yes, she loved me, yes, she would marry me. And suddenly she said, against my cheek:

'Take me away to your inland town. Take me away from the sea!' Quite softly and thoughtfully, while the sea sparkled and basked innocently among the rocks three hundred feet below us.

'The very thing that frightened me most,' I said, startled, 'was that you wouldn't want to go. I've got the offer of a job in a school there, but you love the sea so much, and I was afraid—'

She put her hand over my lips, and said again: 'Yes, I want to go, I want you to take me away.' And when I asked her why, she said: 'I love you, and I don't want to have to share myself out between you and the sea. I want to be only with you.'

I promised her, gladly. Her saying she wanted it could have made me embrace a far worse fate than teaching

English in a school in a dim little town. And the sea never said anything then, only lay sleepily babbling to itself among the rock pools, and ignoring us, so it seemed no one had any complaint about our future, and no one wanted to interfere with us.

I went to see her mother, and break the news to her. There wasn't any father, Mrs Hillier was a widow. She was Cornish born and bred, a small, elderly, competent creature so unlike Lucy that my imagination could make no connection between them. Mr Hillier had been a well-to-do fisherman, with his own boats and this house, and Mrs Hillier was exactly the relict of such a man; and where did Lucy come in, if this was all? But it seemed that Lucy wasn't theirs, she was a foundling they'd taken in and reared because they had none of their own. At least that made her credible.

'You ought to know it,' said Mrs Hillier, 'though it's never made any difference with us, and I don't suppose it will with you. Hillier found her among his nets on the beach one morning, all wrapped up in a blanket. Just a young baby, she was. We took her in, though, of course, we had to tell the police, and the County Council people. But they never found out whose she was, or anything about her, so in time we adopted her legally. Some poor local girl's child, I expect. It happens everywhere. Though I never could see any resemblance to any of the folks round here, I must say.'

I didn't pay much attention, all I felt was a kind of satisfaction, because this story made things more comprehensible to me; and it was only a loving curiosity about everything connected with Lucy that prompted me to put even the questions she expected. About the answers I no longer cared at all, except to resolve to love Lucy more for her solitariness and strangeness, and be parents and brother to her as well as husband and lover. I was relieved, too, that Mrs Hillier was ready to let her go with so little fuss.

'I'm only sorry about taking her so far away from you,' I said apologetically. 'I know how fond of her you must be.'

She looked at me with a startling calm, and said: 'Well, to tell the truth, though I have cared for her like a daughter, I've never let her get inside me too much. Somehow it never seemed safe to be too fond of her.'

'I understand,' I said, really believing I did. 'She's so lovely that sooner or later she was bound to be taken away from you.' And I thought that Lucy's not being her own flesh and blood had made it easier for her to keep her heart armed against that inevitable time.

'That's right,' said Mrs Hillier. 'I always felt that sometime she'd go.'

A month later we were married. What is there to be told about a happy marriage? Nothing could have been less exciting, on the face of it, than the quiet, contented life we led at the small public school where I taught, about as far inland as you can get in this sea-haunted cluster of islands. We adored each other, and it was excitement enough to be together, always assured of each other, and always newly startled by our own happiness. She grew softer, plumper, all her sudden lines of face and body mellowed into a golden serenity that lasted three years.

I had begun to write again, and had one play running in London, one about to be produced, and one in the writing. I felt in my bones that the second one was headed for more than a success of esteem, and when it finally saw the light the results more than justified me. I had already decided to risk giving up my job, and give all my time to writing, even before we had word of the sudden death of Mrs Hillier; but that made the decision easier for us, because she had left us the cottage by the harbour. There we could not only save the rent, but live more cheaply in other ways, too. We never hesitated; it seems incredible, now, but there was nothing to make us hesitate, nothing. In three years we had grown into such a unity, such a fused and final security, that we could not even remember how it felt to walk precariously among the perils and terrors of love. We had forgotten that the sea had ever had anything to say to us.

It was like that, no tremor in the placidity of our happiness, for at least a month after we settled in the white cottage. The weather was calm, late summer, with the sun drowsing day after day over a lazy, pacific sea. I wrote and wrote, and we walked and gardened, and re-painted our little house, and were happy.

Late in September, the wind began to rise, and this sleepy cat of a sea got up and clawed the cliffs, and for seven days lashed itself into a temper, until the night of the storm. I was working and had hardly noticed the mounting gusts that pulled at the walls, or the crescendo of the surf raking the beach, until suddenly the papers were plucked from under my hands by a great swirl of wind that blew through the living room, and the ceiling light swung in a wild arc, and the coldness of the night struck me like a breaking wave. The invasion stung me instantly into terror, and still I don't know why. I jumped to my feet, the pages of the play spinning round me, my hair erect in the gale.

Lucy had opened the window wide. She was standing there leaning into the twilight, with the spray blowing over her, and her face lifted to the screaming wind; and when I plunged to her side she turned a glittering face upon me, and cried:

'Listen, darling! Listen to the sea!'

I hadn't seen until then how she had begun to change. She was already thinner, and her look and movements were bright and strange and urgent, full of a secret excitement that rose with the cries of the sea and the demoniac voices of the blown gulls, tumbling and drifting under the cliff. I pulled her away by the waist, and got the window closed, and held her clutched in my arms with the force of a fear I could not understand myself. Her black hair was wet, it clung to the delicate shape of her head in flat, glistening plumes. She called me silly, and said I was hurting her; and when I let go she went back to the window, and watched the darkening patterns of the spume and the rhythm of the waves breaking, with her cheek against the glass.

In the night I was afraid to sleep. I kept an arm across her shoulders, and tried to watch out the dark hours without dozing, but the clamour and crying had become a constant and drowsy thing to me, and lulled me like a pebbly river. She lay beside me hard and alert, full of a restless joy, and the beating of her heart was like the pulse of the sea, rhythmic, peremptory, irresistible. I heard her whispering in my ear, when my senses were reeling with sleep:

'Listen, darling! Listen how it's calling!'

I awoke suddenly from an uneasy doze, and she was gone from the bed. It was the wind and the rain beating in at the open window that awoke me, and the first bleak, drowned hint of pre-dawn was tossed in with it, and spilled wet and wild over my feet as I stumbled out of bed. The curtains were streaming inward soaked with spray, the window swung wide upon the black, chaotic, sea-crying night; and Lucy was not there. Not in the room, not in the house. I felt her absence, an instant and killing pain. I ran down the stairs, crying out for her, and there was no one to answer me. The walls rang in terror and desolation: 'Lucy, Lucy! Where are you?' but she never answered.

I tugged back the bolts of the door, and ran out into the howling dark and the rain, and the wind took my shouts, snatching them from me as I ran towards the sea. I heard from a long way off, high in the air, tossed from rock to rock: 'Lucy!' in my own voice. The gulls were beginning to cast themselves into the wind, with their reckless, demonish delight, with their self-abandoning resignation, possessed creatures in ecstasy. My feet slithered on the cobbles at the edge of the square, the pebbles of the beach began to wrench at my ankles. The cold of the spray soaked me and chilled me to the bone, and I found myself standing in the frothing rim on the incoming tide, barefoot, crying: 'Lucy!' into the boiling throat of the sea.

It seemed a long time that I was alone, and then to my cry the piteous scream of a gull replied, and I heard the convulsion of wings, and suddenly another cry, light and lost in the gale; and down the stony incline of the beach close to me Lucy sprang, and in the instant that I felt myself again completed by her coming, her arms were round me. It was as if she had alighted from the air. The very motion of her arms folding round me was like the folding of wings.

I snatched her up and carried her home, and all the way we were both weeping, and the wind flattened the very tears we shed into the salt coating of our cheeks. She never said a word, only clung to me, rigid, her cheek against mine. She was wet and cold and smooth as a fish, and she smelled of the sea – not the sea of harbours, but the outer sea, the depth and the greenness, the unrest and the calm. I carried her in, and stripped her drowned nightdress from her, and dried her, and laid her in the bed, and then dried myself and lay down beside her, because she clung to me so that I was afraid to separate myself from her arms, or let her for an instant out of mine. Until the true light came I held her like that, and she held me, until we grew warm together, and ceased to weep. When we were eased of the trembling, and lay quietly, I began to ask her: 'Darling, why did you leave me like that? Where did you go? Why did you frighten me so?'

But she only began to tremble and to cry again, and wound her arms round me so desperately that I was again afraid; and all she would say was: 'I love you, I love you!

Hold me, don't let me go!' So I stopped asking her questions, for fear I should kill her, because it seemed to me that she might break into pieces.

The smell of the sea had come in with her, it filled the room. Once, as she lay in my arms, I felt her stir and rise, and her hair against my cheek brushed cold and sleek, and as she struggled for an instant against my hold her arms were hard and strenuous as wings. Then she relaxed, embraced me, sighed and slept.

When it was almost light the wind died down a little, and I drew myself out of her arms, and dressed, and went down to make tea. Only when I found myself gazing at the drawn-back bolts of the front door did I remember that I myself had pulled them back when I ran out in search of her.

It is true that there was another door at the back; but that was still bolted. And yet the house was empty of her before ever I left it.

From that moment I was afraid. I watched her steadily, hedging her up from the very sound of the sea, until she grew silent with being watched so, and her eyes were veiled and, I sometimes thought, hostile. I could not bear it, it was not possible for us to live like that.

Without asking her, I had the cottage offered for sale; and until I could take her away from it I haunted her like an enemy, like an assassin, I who loved her more than my own life. When we had an offer for the property, and I had to break the project to her, I did it with my heart in my mouth, fearful of grief and pain; but she laid her cheek against my hand and sighed, and made no difficulties. I no longer knew whether she wished to go or to stay; I think she wanted only to have the decision made for her, and to hold her mind intact, since everywhere about her was danger.

We bought, in haste, a house in an inland town again, and moved there early in November. A river town it was, double-bridged and hilly and beautiful, and from our window we had a view over the silver ring of water, and the roofs, and the meadows beyond. It was very quiet there, and out of the sound of the sea she became normal and calm again, and softened almost into the Lucy of our first happy years together. She could change very quickly. During that placid and still winter she grew rosy and easy, and seeing her taut eagerness relax I was happy, and believed in my victory. I was careful not to reflect, never to wonder; to wonder is to invite the enemy in.

Then in March came the sudden iron frost, that clanged in our narrow streets like armour, and shut down upon the river a hand of stillness and silence. All the echoes were distorted under ominous slate-grey skies; day after day the ice grew thicker on the water, and the mornings whitened and rime stood an inch long on the leeward rims of leaves, and fell, tinkling like chandeliers, when the brushing of a sleeve passed by. And in the incredible stillness of the nights Lucy would rouse a little, lying listening beside me, and whisper sharply: 'Listen, darling!' On the breath of an excitement which seemed to me now to have no origin, to be at most a memory.

Round the west coast the storms were frantic; but we had an iron, a dread stillness. In the late evenings she opened our window upon the stars, shivering and intent.

'Listen!'

I asked her: 'What can you hear?' but when she turned to look at me it was with a look of veiled and aching love, and she said: 'Nothing! Did I speak? There's nothing to hear but the silence.'

But in the morning, when I went down into the town, I heard with my own ears the sound for which she had been waiting. All about the frozen river and the bridge there was a wheeling and crying of birds; at first I could hardly believe in it, so alien was it to our town. The storms had driven the sea birds inland, the open stretches of water were thronged with black-headed gulls, screaming with hunger and uneasiness. At the sight and the sound of them I was filled with the old, the unassuageable terror, and I forgot the errands on which I had gone out, and turned to rush back to Lucy. For I knew then that because we had fled the sea, the sea had reached out after us, sending its messengers to fetch her home.

Our house was on a curve of the hillside, just above a narrow alley walk; and always, when I came in sight of the windows, I would lift up my head towards the house to look for a sign of her.

Now I saw her at the upper window, and it was open, and she leaned out into the glittering day, for this was no longer an act nor an affection of the darkness. She was not looking down at me, but outward at the white river and the arching bridge, where the gulls complained; and a cloud of them had left the water and were threshing about the window, back and forth, hovering and tumbling, strident and vehement, their wings turning like blown leaves before her glimmering face. Her black hair glistened, her head turned with the brilliant, restless exultation of a bird wheeling, her shoulders arched towards the frosty air.

I cried out to her, but she did not seem to hear. I began to run, into the house and up the stairs, calling her still. The room was empty, the window swinging, the cloud of gulls winging away with wonderful, challenging cries towards the river, flashing and glittering in the wintry sun. On the carpet at my feet the little green ribbon from Lucy's hair lay forlornly, all I had of her to snatch back from flight and hug to my heart.

I shouted her name from the window, but she did not come back to me; and when in my despair I ran out of the house and down to the paved path which edged the water, one of the flying gulls came curling gently about my head, crying sadly. The chilly wind of her wings brushed my cheek, her sleek little black head gleamed for an instant in the white noon light; then she soared with a scream of joy after the drifting throng of her sisters, and mingled with them, and was lost to sight.

Carnival Night

You could tell as soon as this thing came round the corner off the estate, and the folks down there got their first look at it, that it was going to be the kingpin. You could hear the yell of joy the kids let out right up to the top of the street, where I was sitting on the wall of Bray's yard alongside Joe, with his bull terrier up between us.

That dog always had to be in whatever was going on, talk about inquisitive! He couldn't wait for the wagon to come up the street, he started to whine for it as soon as he heard the squealing and laughing down the bottom end. It was like playtime at the primary school. The women were going, 'Oooooohh!' and 'Eeeeeeh!' up the scale till it would have split your eardrums, like they do for the off-colour jokes at a seaside show, and the kids were shouting and screaming fit to bust.

Joe says, 'Sounds as if they've got a real good 'un this time.'

Everybody started craning to see before the lorry was anywhere near. Nobody was giving a glance to the Mothers'

251

Union's mock-up of The Archers, and it was a pity, really, because you could have cracked a few ribs on that lot. Nor to the English Rose dance troupe nipping it up in their little pink flatties and flapping their little pink nylon paws like mad. Nor to the Boys' Brigade band sharpening up their march tempo into a KSLI canter to get closer to the girls.

Paddy Ross had his old lorry out as usual, with the pirate ship that's been going the rounds of all the local carnivals for years, but that wasn't what was raising the riot; and the Miners' Arms customers had done a lovely job of a comic pit-head baths on the big NCB haulage wagon, but that wasn't the one either.

It was a smaller lorry coming up behind that was getting 'em. The noise ran alongside it all up the street, and noise was what we got first from the gadget itself, a lovely low-pitched whining purr like a happy tiger, but punctuated here and there by a few other noises too, a hissing and a crackling, a dotted peep, like a marker buoy on a shoal.

The first we actually saw of it, head on before it came alongside, you couldn't tell it was an ordinary lorry at all, they had it so well camouflaged. There was what you might call a cab, all right, but it looked like a sort of fancy cockpit, and all the bonnet was shelled in with aluminium plating or something made to look like it, nicely shaved off for streamlining; and the streamed plating came down so low it nearly touched the ground, hiding the wheels altogether.

When it came nearly abreast of us we could see a sort of comet-shaped body that curved off from the cockpit and tapered away to a finned tail, and a lot of odd valves and vents that went along its sides like scales, and a kind of gauge amidships that ran a thread of metallic green liquid up a graded tube like mercury in a thermometer. There was a thin antenna shaking like a live thing on top of the cab, and a plastic globe some way back, and a few other mysterious whatnots that you couldn't call anything in particular because there was nothing they really looked like except themselves. Oh, it was a masterpiece, no question.

There were two fellows in the cab, you could just see their heads and shoulders. They were got up something weird, with horned helmets, and blue plastic over their faces, and antennae on the horns of the helmets, too, and close-fitting black overalls, one-piecers got up to look like spacesuits.

Then there was a third lad who kept popping up in the globe behind them and doing things with little instruments there, and every time he touched something the oddest things happened. One time it would be a jet of steam that shot out of one of the valves, another time there'd be a bang like a gun going off, or a red light would come on at the tip of the tail-fin, or a shower of sparks would shoot out of the end of the antenna. You never knew what was going to happen next. He was doing his tricks nineteen to the dozen, and every time he let off another fizzer the women would yodel and the kids would shriek and dance up and down and near kill themselves laughing.

Joe's dog got an eyeful of this lark, and started to bark like mad, and fell off the wall; he always tended to propel himself backwards when he let fly, and when excited he was liable to forget he wasn't on the ground. He near bust something in his hurry to scramble up again before the thing got past.

But the best of all was the way those three blokes were playing it up, dead serious and businesslike with the machine, but pleased and excited at the reception the crowd was giving them. They'd look at their gauges and switches and valves with such loving care, and then when they had a minute to spare they'd lean out and grin and wave back at the kids, and carry on as pleased as Punch. And when the folks howled with delight at one of the bangs the young chap at the back would give 'em a stream of green sparks as an encore.

Laugh, I thought Joe would have done himself an injury, and the women were wiping the tears away. I tell you, that was the best tableau we ever had at our carnival and we've had some champions in our time.

'Who on earth cooked up that contraption?' Joe says when he got his breath back.

'Dunno,' I said, 'but whoever it is, they're not competing, there's no name or number on it, or anything.'

'Competing?' says Joe. 'They wouldn't spoil a thing like that by sticking a comic name on it, man; they're artists, that's what they are. What's a prize to men of that calibre? They know their worth.'

And he lets out a yell as a blue flash shot out of one of the vents, and after a minute struck speechless with laughing he says, 'It'll be the REME lads from the ordnance depot, I bet you. Who else has the means and the know-how to concoct a whizzer like that? Those boys'll do anything and go anywhere for laughs. Shut up!' he says to the bull terrier, who was getting shriller than the women. 'I can't hear the bangers for your blating.'

We slid off the wall as soon as it was past, and joined on with the rest of the folks following the procession out to the carnival fields. We could hear the fair organ going before we were past the crossroads. The contraption ambled along gaily, spitting and flashing and shooting away like a royal salute and a firework display all in one, and the three merry men were getting gayer and gayer, and showing off their Royal Electrical and Mechanical Engineering skill like nobody's business; and by that time they had so many kids trotting after them they looked like a new sort of Pied Piper into the bargain.

Well, when the procession reached the field, and all the tableaux and the groups and the jazz bands and the dance troupes were drawn up for the judges, I saw Councillor Biggs, who's chairman of the carnival committee, conferring with the judges and grinning to himself, and shaking his head over the contraption as if he still couldn't believe it. Then he comes over to the lads who'd brought it. They were out on the grass by that time, stretching their legs; one was maybe fortyish, short and brown and bandy, and the other two were big lads with cropped fair hair and healthy grins on them.

You couldn't see 'em for kids from the waist down. The little 'uns wanted to see what the helmets were like, with all that fancy stuff on them. One of the fellows obligingly took his off and put it on one of the nippers, and then he somehow made one little spark hop out of the left antenna, and the kid nearly took off for outer space on the spot, he was so overcome with excitement. They were talking, too, but some lovely gibberish they made up as they went along; the kids' jaws were hanging and their eyebrows were in their hair, they were so fascinated.

Oh, they were a treat, those chaps! You couldn't fault 'em on a single detail, and you couldn't catch 'em out. When they put on a show it really was a show, down to the last button.

Well then, old Biggs goes up to 'em and he says, 'Boys, you know you really should have entered that interstellar flitoscope of yours in one of the main classes, you'd have walked off with the first prize easy.'

They all three looked at him, grinning but mystified, and the oldest one comes out with a lovely line in gibberish, very polite and friendly, sure-you-mean-it-kindly-what-ever-it-is-but-no-savvy, you know. His smile was an open book in any language you care to name.

I thought old Biggs would have split his ribs, laughing. He bangs the nearest young fellow on the back, and the plastic stuff he was wearing makes a sort of musical noise like twanging an elastic.

'You're a masterpiece, lads, that's what you are,' says Biggs, wheezing away like a grampus. 'You kill me! I tell you what I'm going to do, I'm going to award you a special prize off my own bat. I like a bit of enterprise, and I'm all for thoroughness. Here, boys, you spend that round the fair, and enjoy yourselves.'

And blow me, he outs with a five-pound note and plonks

it into the older chap's hand, and staggers away mopping his eyes and still quaking.

I watched to see how they'd deal with this one, and I wasn't the only one watching, but they weren't foxed, not for a minute. They all three stood turning the note in their hands and looking at it back and front, as curious as monkeys, as though they'd never seen one before. So some of us thought we'd give as good entertainment as we were getting, and we moved in and made signs to them to come along with us into the fun fair.

We took them gently up to old Gertie in the paybox of the dodgems, and got her to change the note for them, and then we took them round the sideshows, having a bash at this and a ride on that all the afternoon.

I've never had so much fun at a fair since I was a kid, and all the sideshows were real space fiction to me. I did things I haven't done for years, just to see those boys acting up as though they were riding on the Mont Blanc for the first time, and taking their first crack at coconuts. They should have been on the stage, and that's a fact. You ought to have seen their innocent wonder at the rum things that went on in the Noah's Ark, and their excitement and delight when they once got the hang of all this lovely nonsense. Once they had it there was no holding them.

They didn't miss a thing on that field, not even the candyfloss; and to my knowledge they went on the dodgems five times, and on the caterpillar three times. But even when they were bashed across the floor backwards by young Bill Brady, who drives on the dodgems like he does on the road, they didn't forget themselves and yell in English, not they. I hung around with them all day and they never put a foot wrong. Everybody had a go at them, it got to be a game trying to catch them out, but nothing doing. You'd have had to get up early in the morning to get a rise out of those three types, I'm telling you.

Any other carnival night I should have gone home pretty early and called it a day, but this one was a day and a half.

Three or four of us took them along at opening time to the Black Boar, solemn as judges, and set up the drinks and got some cheese sandwiches out of Jenny. Would you believe it, those boys still kept it up, letting on they were tasting beer for the first time, on top of everything else. For beginners, they took to it like ducks to water. You should have seen their eyes sparkle when they poured down that first pint of draught.

And darts – what were those? They'd never set eyes on a board in their lives, but they didn't half pick it up quick. One hour and three beers after they started, the little bandy fellow was playing Sam Braddick round the clock so fast and accurate you'd have thought that was how he spent all his evenings.

It must have been well turned nine o'clock when one of the young ones suddenly pulls out a little gadget from his overall pocket, a thing like a light-meter or something of that kind, and looks at it, and nudges his pals, and in his deadpan way says, 'Eh, look at the time!' or words to that effect. And the older one makes motions to us, polite-like, excuse us for a few minutes, and they go into a huddle.

Then one of the boys puts his helmet on, and touches

up a button or two, and the antennae start to quiver and spark. With one finger he touches out the sparks, while the other two watch him and chatter at him, laughing and making suggestions, and looking as happy as sandboys.

It all reminded me so much of three lads on the spree writing a postcard home that I leaned up against the bar and made believe to be translating as the sparks crackled.

'Having a wonderful time. This is a smashing place. Wish you were here. Back for tea, seven light years from now.'

We were all trying to get into the act by that time. What with the free flow of beer and the general gaiety, I was about ready for anything.

Then off came the helmet again, and they were back at the bar like ferrets after a rabbit. The older one makes expansive gestures round the whole lot of us, and pulls out all he had left of the five-pound note old Biggs gave him. It wasn't much by then, not half enough to set 'em up all round, which was plainly what he intended. He soon learnt that one.

'Sorry lad,' said Jenny, smiling at him proper motherly, and giggling because she still thought he was a card, 'but it won't run to it. One, two, three, maybe four, see? But not the lot. Can't do it.'

He looked back at her hopefully, and never moved a muscle to let on that he understood a word. His face was brown as chestnuts, this chap, and now I came to look at him, his ears were a funny shape, narrow and pointed.

'Sorry,' said Jenny, shaking her head vigorously. 'Not enough – get it? Too little!'

He got it. He slipped a hand back in his pocket, and pulled out a coin and slapped it on the bar. Only it wasn't a coin, or if it was it was a foreign one. It looked like an old campaign medal or something like that.

George came along behind the bar and picked it up, and he looked at the three types all looking back at him with their trusting well-intentioned smiles, and he was fair shaking with laughing. You couldn't help it, they were marvellous. After the beer they'd put away it was a miracle they could still keep control of their faces like that.

'You boys are a cure,' he says, his chins all wobbling like a three-tier jelly. 'Set 'em up all round, Jenny, they're on the house. I'll keep this as a souvenir, mate – something to remember you by. And by gum, I shall remember you, too.'

So we drank to the next time, because by then this time was getting along to its last hour. It was a good hour, though, and we didn't leave until the Black Boar closed at eleven. They had an extension, being carnival night.

I went back to the field with the lads to see 'em off. If they were only going back to the ordnance depot it wasn't so far, but I just wanted to see 'em start up, and make sure they were capable of getting home safely. Me, that was half-seas-over myself! But I meant well. I liked those three, they were the real whole-hogging kind.

We went down the road all four abreast with our arms round one another, singing two separate songs, me in plain English, them in Venusian or carnivalese or whatever you like to call it. The young 'uns had a coconut each, and the little 'un had a golliwog he'd won at the fair, shooting clay pipes, and they were all as happy as piglings in clover, and so was I.

The fair had closed down by the time we got there, the lights were gradually going out, and all the decorated lorries had gone, except their space special. It was dead quiet, nobody stirring but us. They climbed into their contraption, and waved to me and grinned as they started her up. And I waved back until they were out of sight. And that was the end of the best carnival we ever had.

Except that about a week later I ran into Councillor Biggs in the market, and he grabs me by the arm and takes me on one side, looking very serious.

'Tom,' he says, 'about that spaceship, or whatever it was – that thing that made the big hit at the carnival. You were with those three lads most of the evening, weren't you?'

'I was that,' I said, 'it was the best night out I've had for years.'

'And they never let slip where they were from?' he says.

'No,' I said, 'but we weren't much bothered. Why? What's on your mind?'

'Just this,' he says. 'I was talking to that REME major two days ago at the school open day, and I said to him, "That was a great show your boys gave us at the carnival." "Not ours, old boy," he says, "none of ours were out that day, I should have known if they'd been planning a do like that. No, that was those GPO engineers from the weather station at Bondheath, I thought you'd have guessed." Well, just to be sure this time, I phoned the station. All they said was, "Not us, lad, or we'd have charged you for the juice. Try the RAF cadets, it sounds like them." And I tried 'em, but it wasn't them.

'Tom,' he says, breathing heavily in my ear, *'it wasn't anybody*. And, Tom, I've just been talking to George Morgan. He showed me that coin the little fellow turned out of his pocket. It's metal, but it's no metal I've ever seen.' And he hauls off and looks at me very solemn indeed.

'Did you see 'em off? Did you see which way they went?'

'Sure I saw it,' I said. 'For Pete's sake, there's only one way to go from the field, isn't there? They just got in and started her up and went. You think I was still in sight when they got to the crossroads?'

'No, I suppose not,' he said, very uneasy. 'But I wish I knew who'd been pulling our legs, all the same.'

'If you ask me,' I said soothingly, 'that's the sort of elaborate joke the science students from the Tech must have had a hand in. I shouldn't look any farther if I was you.'

And he went off more than half-convinced. I hope! Anyhow, I've heard no more about it, so I take it he's given up worrying.

I didn't actually tell him any lies. It just came over me, remembering what I remembered, how different it can be dealing with ordinary folks like us at the Black Boar, and getting mixed up with authority, even as high as the Borough Council. Say you're markedly different and you drop in on our local carnival – you come with goodwill, goodwill is what you'll meet. But once let the authorities get wind how very different you are, and all they'll think of doing is pointing a gun at you. Better if they don't get wind of it, that's what I thought. Just in case those three boys ever want to pop in again for a quiet game and a pint.

So that's why I only told him half a tale. They got in and started her up and went.

Well, so they did. Vertically. That little ship took her nose off the ground and snuffed the air towards the moon, and took off like a bird. A pretty awkward bird at first, say an elderly swan; she just about got over the hedge, and she lurched a bit just for a minute, what with all that draught beer. But then she got her head towards home, and straightened out into speed and vanished like a silver flash in the direction of Orion . . .

I'd like to see those boys again, but in a way I hope they never do come back; our reputation's safer that way. Right now there must be one place at least in the galaxy where they think well of Earth; it would be a pity if they ever got to know us better.

The Ultimate Romeo and Juliet

All we wanted was a world.

A world to take the place of the one we'd been busy making untenable for generations before we realized how far the process had gone, and that it couldn't be reversed. A world with a breathable atmosphere, with a climate we could adapt to, if we couldn't adapt it to ourselves, with water and vegetation, and preferably fauna not too far removed from what we knew on earth. Just an ordinary world.

We'd even have settled for a smaller one than the old, if necessary. The mutants were becoming a pretty large minority by then and, though more acceptable in appearance than the earlier ones, they were mostly infertile, and there was no point in evacuating them.

But ordinary worlds were few and far between, it seemed, in any of the galaxies we had the means of reaching, or else we and the world we'd wrecked weren't so ordinary as we'd thought, and the norm was something quite different, and not for us. Because three years after the search began, we still hadn't found what they'd sent us out to find.

We were the third research ship employed on the great probe, the third team tied night and day by watches to those several tons of instruments and equipment that were to locate and document our future planet for us. The one we had would last our lifetime, but children were being born every day, not all of them the shape you'd choose for your children. We hadn't blown up the world, oh, no, reason and moderation had prevailed. Only too late. They'd even given up attributing the distortions to drugs by now, because only a comparatively few of the mothers had treatment records that showed the use of new drugs. Nobody had expected a harvest, so long after such a gradual and unwary sowing, but it had come, and whether we liked it or not we had to reap it. A doom is a doom. So there we were in space, looking for a world. Like the old one, only clean.

We were probing the remotest outliers of Galaxy Parthenis I. They named it for its outline as seen from Earth, tall and slender, with projecting helmet and spear like the Athena of the Parthenon; and we were fighting shy of both projections, because the physicists' theory was that these jutting lights, brilliant blue, indicated the presence of anti-matter that was being annihilated. The galaxy was a moderately powerful radio-transmitter. I can't remember its exact observed output; nothing like the enormous kilo-wattage of Cygnus-A, but more than enough to warn us off. But the fringes of the galaxy, out of range of this violent energy, promised better. Especially

Parthenope, remote at Athena's sandalled foot. Quiet, she was, and peaceful to look at, with very little radioactivity and no signs of conflict. So we were dropping in gently to orbit, and training all our instruments on the hopeful planet that might prove a possible host for our descendants.

Thank God I'm not a physicist! What I knew about matter and anti-matter in collision was limited to the things one does at school with cloud-chambers and scintillation-counters, and the trajectory plates we used to study, showing the tracks of anti-protons exploding in stars of fragments after impact with protons. Matter into energy, and energy into matter again. To me it was always a magical interchange. I never wondered at its being danger-ous. Magic is dangerous.

No, my job was plain plant biology. Vegetation is stuff you can see, photograph, classify, smell, taste. You can see it with the naked eye from miles up, the unmistakable pattern of woodland and grassland and marshland and upland meadow, the colours and shapes of land. In the nightwatches that Gennadi and I kept together, as the junior members of the team, we used to sit and watch the iris-blue belt of Parthenope's zone revolving rosily into its dawn, and map the silvery strands that were rivers and the clear grey eyes of seas, and the dark, lustrous growth of forests like the furry pelts of sleeping beasts. From miles up it looked like home. Why don't we, I said every night, get on down there and settle in? This planet had everything.

There was also movement there, we could trace it with our long-distance probes, and it seemed to be animal, and pastoral at that, because it followed a daily pattern. And that meant that Parthenope had the last asset and the first drawback of a world destined for colonization. Man. Parthenopeian man, at any rate, the intelligence that compiled the pattern that moved the beasts. It was almost inevitable that where all the advantages were, there should the dominant and possessor be, also. After a few days of recording and shifting we found plenty of other indications of his presence, too: canals, fields, buildings, aircraft.

So we spoke to him from space. We had experts on board who prided themselves that between them they could break any language compiled from any of the sounds producible by the larynx of any known primate, and provide translations in the main tongue of all the known speaking groups, terrestrial or otherwise. They set to work and produced translations into some fifty basic languages of the speech our chief political officer wrote for them, and we started putting it out twenty-four hours a day, aimed at Parthenope. How we came in peace and goodwill, bringing greetings from our own planet, how we desired better knowledge of the inhabitants, and intended, with their permission, to effect a landing in order to make their acquaintance. We told them over and over that they had nothing to fear from us, that we meant them nothing but good.

'This is like an echo of ourselves overtaking us,' said Gennadi, listening to it on nightwatch. 'Have you read much history, Francis? Don't be alarmed, we want nothing from you but your world!'

But he was a Slav and a poet, what could you expect? We had about ten Slavs on board in our multi-racial, multilingual team, and at least three poets, but the Commodore was American, and his deputy good, solid Pan-African, so we could afford to carry our dreamers for ballast, like a conscience.

'We've got the next generation to save,' I said.

'So have they,' he said.

'And whatever their population may be, it doesn't seem to be pushing them. We're not trying to oust them, we'll be quite satisfied to share.'

'We always were satisfied to share what was somebody else's,' he said. 'At least for the first few years.'

He was twenty-five, and single, and good-looking, and didn't have any troubles except for a girl in Communications who kept putting herself hopefully in his way; but you'd have thought he'd come down through time along with the Wandering Jew, with a rucksack of doom on his shoulder. He still had the black hair and eyes, and the fiery bones and the tremendous energy of the Georgians; not even world government and five generations of well-mixed marriages could breed that look and that temperament out of them. Some of the less dominant strains had given up the struggle by then, but the strong ones persisted. The English hadn't changed much, either; I knew it every time I looked in the glass. Even my space helmet, before we finally discarded them in craft, used to have a sort of bowler hat look about it.

'I wonder,' I said, 'if they'll answer us? If their world has all the favourable conditions ours used to have, why shouldn't they have progressed as far as we have?'

'And since it still has the favourable conditions,' said

Gennadi, tuning down his videoscreen to the finest definition, and watching the unbelievable colourings of the Parthenopeian dawn begin, 'why shouldn't we conclude that they may have progressed a good deal farther? And why should we suppose they want, any more than they need, our peculiar genius grafted on to their nice, clean world?'

A physicist who is also a poet is liable to have complex vision. When he's Russian by birth into the bargain, the added complication of a political and philosophic bent is inescapable. But he was a nice fellow to work with; and he was almost always right. He was right that time too. Parthenope didn't want us.

It happened towards dawn. All our receivers began to crackle as though someone somewhere was feeling his way into their use, gently and easily and confidently, but handling something of a type not encountered before. And then the voice came, full and emphatic, pitched in a low baritone register, repeating the same short message over and over. They had understood us.

The trouble was, we couldn't understand them. Our experts sweated over those almost continuous, singing sounds for three days, and couldn't begin to break the pattern. The voice slowed down to half-speed at the third lengthy transmission, but they still couldn't get it. And some of us said, go in anyway, but the Commodore wouldn't risk it. If they'd understood and answered us, between the two sides there must be a way of working out some kind of two-way communication.

Soon after that the voice stopped, but the transmission was taken over by a very slight, throbbing vibration on a deep note. It was hardly audible, it wasn't language as we understood it; but in a few minutes we felt it transfer itself to the inside of our heads, and go reverberating through our minds. The Parthenopeians had gone farther than we had in one way, at least. They could transmit mental concepts, prohibitions, impulses, influences. And what they were telling us was to stay out; what they were saying to us was: No, no, no, you mustn't come!

'So that's how they're going to react! Draft a second and fuller message,' said the Commodore, 'and tell them exactly why we're here. Explain our need and ask for their help. Then we shall see if they still refuse to let us land.'

And we did that, and translated and transmitted it. But the emphatic, unintelligible answer still ticked back to us, and when it again failed to get any acknowledgement the receivers turned on us the same mental battery of absolute rejection. Parthenope wouldn't have us at any price.

'The natives are unfriendly,' said Captain Abukaba, and looked haunted for a moment, as though a racial memory had caught up with him. 'But we have a sacred duty to our own people, we must not let them be turned away so easily. I say we should go in and land. Then we can negotiate with them man to man.'

'Wait!' said the Commodore. 'Give our lingual experts more time, they may break into the language yet. This is probably only a misunderstanding.'

So we went on orbiting. And that night on watch the receivers were silent; only in our instrument room Gennadi sat with his transmitter switched on, and his screen tuned down upon the dark blue planet, and began to talk to

Parthenope as sometimes he talked to himself.

'I am one man,' he said, among many other nonsenses, casting his voice and his smile as a fisherman casts a fly. 'I am not a soldier, I am not a politician, I am not an enemy of anything that lives. I am a scientist, and curious, and lonely, and you reject me and my curiosity if you reject us. In this ship we have one-man research hulls, how if I should take one and come? How could I be a threat, alone? What would you do if I came?'

I think he had never expected anything, but how can I tell? The blue of the screen was convulsed with a great tremor, and the silent receiver sent out a violent impulse of: No, no, no!

Gennadi said softly: 'I am becoming sensitive to this language of the mind. If you had concepts for all those things that move me, and I had any grasp of the concepts you live by, we might talk to each other like this, silently. But how can you convey to me images which don't exist in my world by any name? You warn me off – very well! Am I necessarily to put the worst construction on that, as if you were my own kin? Answer me this: if I went away now, back to my diseased world, would you wish me and mine a fair deliverance by some other means? Do you wish me well?'

A sudden quivering warmth of assent answered him. I felt it as clearly as the: No.

He said in a gentle voice: 'Parthenope!' From then on everything in him began to change, and on the fringe of the change I could sit and watch, but I could neither join in nor draw him back to me.

'He said: 'Parthenope, speak to me. Say: I wish you well!'

The receiver sighed, the cloudy screen lost colour, like a troubled pool. In the unknown, singing tongue a voice repeated something faintly; and the voice was a woman's voice, soft, warm and low.

'There is no language anywhere in any world,' Gennadi said, 'that has no concept for: I wish you well! If the men had no need of it, the women would not be able to live without it.' And after a moment of silence he said: 'Let me look at you. I know you can, if you will.'

She came into the screen; cloudily, brokenly, but she came. Have you ever wondered how they would look, the inhabitants of a planet enjoying conditions much like our own, even to the single moon? Why should it be the blankest of all surprises, the most stunning of all shocks, that they should turn out to look like us?

I saw her only by glimpses that night, I never saw her clearly, the image was always fluid, like a reflection in water. But I believe that he saw her from the first more clearly than I, and by the end like one defined in fixed and perfect light. She had a face like a human woman's face, but smaller and of a more delicate pallor. I saw a cloud of dark hair in motion round her as though in water, and two great eyes alarmed and bright. I don't know how much she had of beauty, I only know beauty came into the room with her impress, and that the harder I stared the more her image shook, but the distillation of loveliness was never shaken.

I said: 'So they look like us!'

'No,' said Gennadi, 'like our mirror-image. They are us reversed. They are what we could have been if we had always chosen the right turning.'

He sat looking into the screen, and he said: 'You are beautiful.' And after a moment: 'Do you still say to me that I may not come to you?'

No, the air shuddered, you can't come, you mustn't come! And the face that did not try to speak to him in sounds warned him away with parted lips and fixed eyes.

'But I can't go, now, either. I have seen you now. This is the only world I want.'

The screen swirled, and sent her features sparkling away like drops of water, and all the room was convulsed with: No, no, no! Gradually the turmoil settled again, and her eyes came back first, wide, intent and wary. I knew by the look in them, and the way they brightened at the deepening of his smile, that she saw him clearly, and was as lost as he.

'If you wish me well, and this is the only world in which I can ever be happy, why do you send me away?'

The impressions came from her in pulsations that seemed to carry waves of colour with them through the cabin. I didn't even know if I was interpreting her rightly, but he, I am sure, no longer had any doubts. What she had to say was being said to him, not to me, and he was quick and sensitive to meet her every thought, and who am I to say that the contribution of his willingness, no, his rapture, had no scientific validity?

'It is because I wish you well that I want you to go.'

'Should I, then, be coming to harm if I came to you?'

'Yes.'

'What is harm?' he said. 'What is good? Is there a worse harm than to turn away from the only thing you want?'

The questions I heard, the answers no one heard; but he, I think, understood. But I know that to this there was no answer. Only a kind of pause for thought and wonder and self-questioning, as though she lowered her eyes to look more closely at what he showed her. And then she looked up at him again with so naked a radiance that the lines of her face paled away all to light.

And she was gone. The deep blue of the world below was paling to iris in the screen, the first saffron of dawn showed upon the arched horizon. She was gone, and he was stiff and silent and wide-eyed over his instruments and looked up at me blindly when I touched him, as if he had stared into the sun.

He said nothing to me then, and nothing to anyone afterwards, about the encounter. And I said nothing, either. The affair was wholly his, not mine.

He called her again the next night, and she came.

I might not have been there. All night they talked together, and at first there were words on his side, but soon the very words stopped. As she conveyed her will and her mind to him, so he began to speak to her without the need of language. Only sometimes the warm waves of passion and sympathy formed sentences even for me, but whether I was imagining them or whether they were truth I couldn't tell.

It seemed to me that he said: 'I will not go away. I will never go away from you.'

'You must go. I am afraid for you. You must go.'

'To be afraid is to submit to deformity. Now I want to be whole. Without that there's nothing, no future, no love. And I love you.'

'I love you.'

'And I will not go.'

'No! Don't go.'

'I am coming to you.'

'I am coming to you.'

The mirror-image encompassed even their silent utterances now, and the dialogue had become unison.

He came off watch with me like a man still dreaming. We lay on our bunks in the forward cabin, and he said to me: 'Francis, you know, don't you, what happens when two mutually destructive particles collide?'

Half asleep, I said I did. They were destroyed on impact.

'But new particles are generated. Don't forget that. And supposing these mutually destructive particles had consciousness to feel with, hearts to love with, minds to speculate with, souls to adventure with, and came together of their own will and purpose? What then?'

'Then you'd have left physics for metaphysics.'

'Where is the boundary?' he said. 'I know of none. Where is the conflict between God and science, when every mystery resolved only uncovers a hundred new mysteries, and every demonstration of energy still leaves us meditating will and intent bigger than the energy? I see no conflict.'

Nobody but the Russians and the Indians still orientated themselves by the concept of God. Once I used to think it was because they were natural mystics, but now I'm not sure it isn't because they're natural scientists.

'God is inseparable from the science. You might say,' said Gennadi deliberately, 'that God's most inspired creation is science, and the ultimate achievement of science will be the discovery of God.'

'If you like,' I said. 'But your two animated particles would still be blasted out of existence when they collided, whether it was God or science or both accelerating them.'

'But something new would be born, Francis, never forget that,' he said, smiling up at the ceiling. 'Something new would be born.'

And that was the day he went to Professor von Schlucht and the Commodore, and volunteered to go down alone and make contact personally with the Parthenopeians.

I knew nothing about it until afterwards. I slept through the day, and got up a few hours before my watch to hear all about it from the junior who was coming on duty with me in Gennadi's place. It seemed he'd argued the whole proposition out for them in detail, and made complete sense of it. One man landing alone could hardly be construed as a threat. If he succeeded in opening negotiations so that the ship could land, then we'd have accomplished the first stage of our mission. And at worst he could make useful observations which might enable us to make a more effective contact later, after we'd had more time to work on our tapes of the language. It was essential that the envoy should be a capable physicist, and surely expedient that he should not be either of the two seniors. I knew him, he could argue his way to anything he wanted. And they'd jumped at his offer, and he was on his way before I was even awake. In the Number One hull, a silver shell just big enough to contain him and his micro-equipment.

I was afraid, and I didn't yet know why. I went down to the cabin alone, and turned on the radio and the screen, and probed after him. And he came in almost immediately, as if he'd been calling me. Maybe he had. He wasn't so far from us yet.

'Gennadi – what are you up to? Why didn't you tell me?'

'You might have tried to stop me,' he said. 'Only you had any reason to try. Only you knew. I'm going to my girl, Francis. This is the only way I could get them to send me out. I'm going to her, and she's coming to meet me, up here, clear of her world.'

'You're supposed to be landing,' I said. 'What is this? What are you trying to do?'

'Listen, Francis! Go to the Commodore for me, go now. Tell him to get the ship away from here, as far and fast as he can. Tell them they can never colonize Parthenope, no use hoping. Don't wait for me. I'm not coming back.'

'Not coming back? And why is there no hope? Why can't we colonize it?'

'Because matter and anti-matter can't live together. That's why they've been warning us away. We thought when we found almost no radioactivity that it must be because there was no anti-matter present. But we were wrong. There's no conflict *because there's no matter*. The whole of Parthenope is composed of anti-matter! Tell them! And tell them to get away from here.'

'But *you*!' I howled at him. 'If this is true, for God's

sake, what do you think you're doing? *Anti-matter!* If you even touch her hand.'

'I know!' he said, and he smiled. 'Goodbye, Francis!'

His face flickered out.

I went scrambling and leaping up the companionway and into the control-room, I shouted at them what he'd said, what he'd done. I should have known, I should have guessed before, when the two soundless voices melted from counterpoint into unison, when he talked of mutually destructive particles, and of the mirror-image of man that was at once his twin and antithesis. I should have known when he spoke of adding will and purpose to the collision of opposites, so that annihilation might become as it were union, and the generation that resulted might launch upon creation new particles of matter, the first fruits of reconciliation. I should have known when the woman said no, and no, and no, while all the time her eyes were saying yes.

We rushed to the screens, we called and called him. The Commodore ordered him back to the ship, but he never made any answer again, and he never looked back. What more was there we could do? We set course outward at speed, and withdrew into space, and still we hung over the screen and watched the thin silvery fish recede from us.

'He'll never touch ground,' said the Professor, wringing his hands over the dials. 'He'll burn up as he enters the atmosphere.'

'She's coming to meet him. He said so. Coming to meet him, clear of her world. They know, they both know. They don't want to be saved.'

'They'll both die. There's no other possibility.'

Gennadi would have said: What is death? Gennadi would have said: But something new will be born, never forget that. Something new will be born.

We watched the iris-blue curve of Parthenope's zone, where a scintillating point of silver had soared and hung in air. She was coming as she had promised. They drew towards each other in two great arcs, flawlessly, and then his hull touched the atmosphere and sheared into it like a glowing knife, leaving a trail of fiery light behind. They were good hulls, triple-proofed and made to survive high speeds. He lived to meet her, though the outer shell of his craft was molten fire by then. Parthenis I had a new star.

What could we do but hold our breath and watch, as they came together? They had slowed to touch, and in the instant that the two light-shells kissed there was a blinding flash that turned all the limpid dark to day. The sound came late; it was in silence that the shell of metal glowed from orange to white, and disintegrated from round him. In the heart of the unbearable brightness we saw the two small ships drip into liquid, and the golden drops consume away in the heat before they even had form. We saw them embrace, those two terrible lovers, a fused shape of shadow in the heart of the aurora, a man and a woman locked in each other's arms, Gennadi and Parthenope matched and mated for the first and last and only time.

They were the core of a new sun, and then they were light itself, and a cry, and the following thunderclap was like a fanfare for their incredible marriage.

One instant, and then we saw them no more, we could

not look, the brightness burned our eyes, we hid our faces and clung to our controls, and ran and ran from the cataclysm, out of the galaxy, scorched and limping, back towards our own maimed world. But long hours afterwards, when we dared to look back, there was a lamp still blazing in the place where they had vanished, and outward from its deep, red heart, eddying away on their own inscrutable courses, spark after glittering spark went curving and flying, outward into orbit, outward into space, the firstborn of the children of light.

A selection of bestsellers from Headline

OXFORD EXIT	Veronica Stallwood	£5.99	☐
THE BROTHERS OF GWYNEDD	Ellis Peters	£5.99	☐
DEATH AT THE TABLE	Janet Laurence	£5.99	☐
KINDRED GAMES	Janet Dawson	£5.99	☐
ALLEY KAT BLUES	Karen Kijewski	£5.99	☐
RAINBOW'S END	Martha Grimes	£5.99	☐
A TAPESTRY OF MURDERS	P C Doherty	£5.99	☐
BRAVO FOR THE BRIDE	Elizabeth Eyre	£5.99	☐
FLOWERS FOR HIS FUNERAL	Ann Granger	£5.99	☐
THE MUSHROOM MAN	Stuart Pawson	£5.99	☐
THE HOLY INNOCENTS	Kate Sedley	£5.99	☐
GOODBYE, NANNY GRAY	Staynes & Storey	£4.99	☐
SINS OF THE WOLF	Anne Perry	£5.99	☐
WRITTEN IN BLOOD	Caroline Graham	£5.99	☐

All Headline books are available at your local bookshop or newsagent, or can be ordered direct from the publisher. Just tick the titles you want and fill in the form below. Prices and availability subject to change without notice.

Headline Book Publishing, Cash Sales Department, Bookpoint, 39 Milton Park, Abingdon, OXON, OX14 4TD, UK. If you have a credit card you may order by telephone – 01235 400400.

Please enclose a cheque or postal order made payable to Bookpoint Ltd to the value of the cover price and allow the following for postage and packing:

UK & BFPO: £1.00 for the first book, 50p for the second book and 30p for each additional book ordered up to a maximum charge of £3.00.

OVERSEAS & EIRE: £2.00 for the first book, £1.00 for the second book and 50p for each additional book.

Name ....

Address ....

....

....

If you would prefer to pay by credit card, please complete:
Please debit my Visa/Access/Diner's Card/American Express (delete as applicable) card no:

Signature .... Expiry Date ....